AMANDA

GW00702733

Geoffrey Leet

*To my friend Jo.
From her friend

Geoffrey*

ARTHUR H. STOCKWELL LTD.
Torrs Park   Ilfracombe   Devon
Established 1898
www.ahstockwell.co.uk

*British Library Cataloguing-in-Publication Data.
A catalogue record for this book is available
from the British Library.*

*This is an entirely fictional story,
and no conscious attempt has been made
to accurately record or recreate
any real-life events.*

By the same author:
*From Bulls to Balls
From Furrows to Fairways*

ISBN 0 7223 3478-8
*Printed in Great Britain by
Arthur H. Stockwell Ltd.
Torrs Park   Ilfracombe
Devon*

AMANDA

I first caught sight of this 'child' at a party in London and I was told that she was the prettiest girl in our somewhat selective society and that she said that she was eighteen years of age. Personally, looking at her over the rim of a nice glass of champagne, I wondered as to whether she had actually reached that age; she somehow looked a bit younger. Whether it was the sudden alertness in her very beautiful eyes when confronted with an obviously infatuated young man, I don't know, but from my point of view, it didn't really matter, I was nudging fifty and whether I wanted to or not, she would not be interested in an old buffer like me.

I was lucky in that I led a comfortable life. I had a London mews small house and also a cottage in the country. Although on the other hand I missed my wife who had died some two years earlier, and I just could not go on living in the somewhat vast house that we had bought together when I retired from farming, years previously, so I sold it, and as I had quite a number of friends in London, I retired there for the autumn of my life.

I soon found that as an unattached fairly well-off single male, my company was welcome at any party in my immediate neighbourhood and what was more, I also, much to my surprise soon noticed that I was wanted in more ways than one by a number of attached and unattached ladies in my immediate area of London. Why they wanted me, not only as an escort but also in bed, gave me many moments of wonder. For after all, as I have said, I had reached the age of fifty. I was not, on the other hand fat and out of condition. I was in the region of 6 feet and 12 stone to go with it, and not, as I was told by various female friends, all that bad looking.

So life went on. Parties most nights. I gave some myself in my little mews house and the poor little building creaked with over thirty

3

people enjoying themselves way through the midnight hours. But in every party that I was invited to, there was the proud and very beautiful Amanda, surrounded by young eager males, but as soon as I entered the room and was greeted by my host or hostess, I could not avoid the stare that came from this girl, or child to me; for she focused her whole personality straight onto me, and in some ways it was just slightly embarrassing.

It got slightly worse at a dance a few weeks later for my hostess insisted that we have an 'excuse me' quickstep. I was more than happy with the girl who had grabbed me and we chatted away whilst whirling round the floor. I enjoyed dancing as long as it was not pop, and so it would appear did my partner, but just as I was getting somewhere with this nice young thing, I had a thud on my shoulder; not a tap, but quite a blow and a voice said "Excuse me" with such a firmness that I expected my dancing partner to fall flat on the floor. She did on the other hand look somewhat startled when she saw who it was that was hijacking her partner; me. She left me without a word and I turned round and there was Amanda looking very determined, and before I could even say, "Good evening", I was grasped round the waist. One of her legs seemed to force both of mine apart and she sort of slid into my chest; bosom and all. I am not often at a loss for words but this girl certainly left me somewhat tongue-tied, and in fact I nearly tripped and was told firmly to concentrate, which I tried to do but it was difficult for she seemed to worm her young body into the parts that I always thought were somewhat private. So looking down on this young thing I firmly disentangled myself and led her, for a change, instead of her manipulating me, round the floor. I must admit that the first thing I thought about was that from the dancing point of view I could never remember anyone who did the job so well. We chatted about this and that. I was not excused by anyone else and I had the feeling that Amanda was not above glaring at any female who even looked like taking me away from her.

After the dance was over she took me firmly by the hand to a table in an alcove with two chairs; told me what she wanted to drink; told me not to be long as she wanted to talk to me. So I went and collected a couple of drinks and came back to this somewhat stalwart young female, wondering as to why she had chosen me of all people, old enough to be her father, maybe her grandfather, to spend time talking, instead of enjoying herself with the countless

4

young men who pursued her wherever she went.

Her first remark after she had taken a sip from her glass, was straight and to the point. "How old are you, John?"

Wondering vaguely as to how she knew my name and also what was the point behind the question, I replied somewhat flippantly that "I am much too old for you, *young* Amanda." I purposely accentuated the 'young'. But she persisted and so I told her that I was bordering on being fifty. So what? What was it to do with her anyway?

"Quite a lot" says this girl, for she went on to say that she found me interesting to talk to, to dance with, and would like to know me a lot better because she was bored stiff with the young men who threw themselves at her feet and was not even inclined to help them get up!

"So how old are you might I ask?" said I with a smile?

"Have a guess" remarked this extraordinary female.

I thought about this for a moment whilst she regarded me with those so beautiful eyes, which kept me from even glancing at her figure. "Nineteen" I said firmly, "and you ought to know better, leading on an old man like me to even contemplate a liaison with a child such as you."

"Not a bad guess" says she. "Add a year and you would be spot on, and in just one year I can do what I want. I don't have to ask anyone what I can or cannot do; I can just suit myself."

"And what *do* you want to do with your life?" I asked.

I want to find a suitable mate; live a life in the country, assist my father and be happy with the man that I choose and of course raise a family, but he, this future man of mine, has got to know something about farming in quite a big way."

All this forthright talk stopped my vague thoughts in their tracks. I had been a farmer, and one or two other things besides. Did this girl know about my past life and if she did, how on earth did she find out and what was more, surely she was not contemplating me in this role of hers? And also, although I had never thought about another marriage, *if* the impossible did actually happen, I wanted a mate who had not been used as a plaything by countless males, and anyway the age gap made the whole idea quite impossible. Although on the other hand, just looking at this young thing made me sort of tingle! So I assumed a bored sort of expression and told her my life story. Australia as a cowboy, the war as a captain, marriage, then

Chile with 10,000 acres at my horse's feet and then Kent with 350 acres, which in later years I converted into a golf course. "So what?" said I.

"A golf course!" said Amanda. Now that is interesting. Could you 'do' another one and run a few acres besides?"

"Amanda," I said, somewhat firmly, "you are being an ass, a young ass at that. Beautiful I grant you in more ways than one, *but* I repeat what I said a few moments ago, I am nearing fifty and I stopped farming some while ago. I admit that I built a golf course but what on earth makes you even contemplate me building another one, and for what reason anyway?"

There was quite a pause after my outburst, with Amanda looking at me directly in the eye which I must admit I found just a little bit confusing and even worse when she said in a strong but young voice, "*Me.*"

"What have you got that I don't know about that concerns me in the slightest as to whether I get embroiled in giving up what I have got here in London; which consist of a nice small house, a fair income and a lot of friends for what? Going somewhere and getting down to building another golf course which, unlike the last, would not belong to me. And when it was finished, which would take at least a year, what am I then supposed to do? Run the place for someone else? Not a hope in hell! Come on Amanda, tell me, what is this all about, and why for God's sake are you even slightly interested in a man in the autumn of his life; old enough to be at least your father, or maybe your grandfather?"

"It is quite simple," says this fascinating female. "I want to settle down and raise a family if possible. I want an older man who has gone through life and come out of it reasonably whole. This man must have a knowledge of farming in a big way; be able to 'do' practical farming; be comfortable to live with and be able to get on with my father — *and I am looking in your direction!*"

I was quite silent through all this monologue. I was to quote a phrase, 'speechless' or maybe 'spellbound'. I know not which, but looking back on all this, sitting in a reasonably quiet table surrounded by dancing couples, I seemed to see what she was getting at. I thought, 'We have only just met and here is this "infant" proposing marriage or something similar to a complete stranger!' "Amanda, you must be tight as a tick. What are you talking about? This night has gone on long enough. I think we ought to think about bed." As soon as I had said that, I felt a fool because she might just take that remark the wrong way, and of course she did, for her next remark was even more startling.

She said, "Which one, your house or mine?"

I am not often left speechless but this was certainly one that I would remember. For here was I, bordering on fifty-plus years of age and this child of twenty was asking that she should share my bed! "My dear girl," I said in as firm a voice that I could muster at that moment, "*if,* and it is a big *if,* I was contemplating another marriage I would certainly not choose a lady who has the reputation of sleeping with every Tom, Dick and Harry in town."

Amanda again looked me straight in the eye and stated quite firmly that she was a virgin and if necessary she could prove it.

"How?" said I equally firmly.

"By being examined by a surgeon of your choice," said she.

Again this girl staggered me, I had never dreamt that the tales that I had heard about her were a figment of the tellers' imaginations and also their wishful thinking.

"Alright" I said, "I have a surgeon friend as a matter of interest, and if you are serious about all this, then by all means, let us get you examined and I will pay the bill."

"No you won't" says Amanda more than firmly. "After all it is my body that is being looked at."

"Right," said I, "it will be my house and it will be your choice as to whether we share a bed and the possible consequence. *Or* you have your own room and of course your own bed."

"The latter," said Amanda at once.

"Alright fair enough but can you answer a few questions before we advance this quixotic notion of yours any further. You want me to give up my present mode of living, which I enjoy? You want me to manage some land that your father owns and if there is room available build another golf course? And what about such mundane subjects as to salary? And how many acres does this father of yours own, and who is running it at the moment? *And* just as a matter of interest *if* we do get married then where do we live, in a tent?"

I ended up my tirade feeling just slightly annoyed in that here I was, a fairly tall, quite strong male and I felt that I was being manoeuvred by this quite small female, and as my thoughts wandered on I saw a sight at the next table which gave my male pride a feeling that I would stop being bullied by this girl. There was a

7

couple doing what is called 'fist lamming' which consists of putting your elbow on the table and the opposition does the same, and you grasp hands and endeavour to push the opposing hand and elbow to the surface of the table. I have done a lot of this and generally came up the winner, but there is a knack and I wondered if Amanda knew it. So I pointed out the scene to her and asked her as if she would like to try her luck?

"Of course" said she, "just my thing."

So we got in position, locked hands and at the word 'go', we started. She was strong, no doubt about it, and as I forced her arm back onto the table there came a look of almost wonderment into those two beautiful eyes.

"Do you know, John, you are the first male that has ever done this to me. I can now look at you with just a different light, for I have done this trick with countless of my would be suitors and not a one came anyway near you." She then got up and although I didn't protest, she kissed me on the mouth with a very lingering kiss.

"Let's go" I said.

"OK" said she, "but I must organise myself" and at this she pulled out of her evening bag one of these quite new mobile phones, prodded a few keys, and then when someone answered the other end, said "John, is that you? I want you to do one or two things for me. I am at (and she gave this address) to wake Mary up and get her to pack a few night things in a case. Get yourself a taxi and bring it to where I am now, and take my car back home, but be here within twenty minutes" and then she hung up!

"Who might John be, and did he sound happy at being woken up at 02.00?" looking at my watch. "And then what about Mary? You seem to have disturbed a whole household, so explain."

Amanda thought for a moment and then answered quite directly that "John is my butler/chauffeur/handyman, call him what you will and Mary is my maid."

"Well you bewitching piece of the feminine gender, I must make one thing quite clear, I do *not* have a butler etc., neither do I have a maid and if you are still willing to share my humble abode, then let us get organised; wait for your John, and then home to a decent bed."

So in due course of time John arrived, and the next thing gave me food for thought, for when he confronted Amanda with her overnight case, I had the distinct feeling that he said "Your

8

Ladyship". I was probably mistaken and I forgot all about it, for driving home to my little mews house with Amanda by my side, I must admit that I felt more than happy.

I unlocked the door for her, led her upstairs to my minute sitting room, and took her not so light suitcase through to what was to be her bedroom and turned and asked as to whether she would like a nightcap, to which she answered that a small amount of port might assist the problem of sleep. So we sat both nursing a modicum of port, and Amanda admired my portraits, and asked as to who the painter was. To which I answered "Me."

"You are surprising me tonight," says this girl. "Not only can you farm, build a golf course, and make a profit, but you can also paint! Who is that gorgeous lady over the fireplace?"

"That was my wife," I said, "killed by a drunken motorist some years back."

"Do I compare?" says Amanda.

"In some ways you do. You are without a doubt very pretty, but she on the other hand was more than beautiful. I have no idea as to whether you can run a house, do the laundry, knit when necessary, keep a reasonable size garden in an immaculate fashion, raise two children on your own, help me when necessary on the farm and a host more things that go to make a happy marriage. Does that answer your question as to whether you compare?"

I noticed as the list of things that I was spelling out, Amanda's face grew just a trifle long and her answer when at last it came was dodgy to a degree, and she implied that she was sure that she *could* do all those things that I had mentioned, but she always had staff which made a difference and she thought that her washing was sent out, as was her father's.

This raised another point in my mind whilst we were getting down the port as to what her father actually did for a living?

"Oh he has independent means" says Amanda.

"And then," said I gathering strength, "who runs the farm at the moment and how long has he held the position, and for that matter *what is* his position? Manager? Factor? And has he any idea that if all this goes through his lifestyle might suffer somewhat? For I do not suffer fools, honest ones or otherwise, all that gladly."

"The present manager is my second cousin and I think that he is a crook of the first water," says Amanda with a toss of her silken hair.

9

I longed to ask a whole heap more questions but it was late, so rose, helped Amanda to her feet, planted a good-night kiss on her cheek, to which she replied with both of her arms round my neck and her open mouth on mine. I disentangled myself, not without some difficulty, patted her stern gently and hoped that she would find the bed to her liking, ushered her through to her bedroom and firmly shut the door.

I washed and got into bed but sleep would not come and thoughts flitted through my head. Was I being a fool giving up my present quite pleasant mode of life with all my friends around me, to marry this almost complete stranger who promised the earth including a vast salary, a nice house and a free hand in running this farm of her father's? I could never get out of Amanda as to how many acres the place consisted. And then what happens if I *do* find out that the present manager is a crook? If you know your business which I pride myself I do, it wouldn't take all that long.

I finally nodded off and woke about 08.00 with the distinct feeling that my bed was not now entirely mine, and there was an arm thrown across my shoulder in a nonchalant fashion and also there were a couple of hard points pressing into my back, and whoever was there? It could only be one person and she was as naked as the day that she was born. I moved very cautiously and turned over without upsetting the sleeping body, and there was Amanda with her hair spread out over the pillows and sleeping without a care in the world. I pondered as to whether to wake the girl or not, thinking about what I have just written, I think it is the first time that I have alluded to her in my private thoughts as a girl, instead of a child. Looking at this young body I was sorely tempted just to finger a nipple, but I had given my word that I would be good till we were married and then 'devil take the hindmost'. So I nudged her with my toe and she woke, and those glorious eyes viewed me with almost an expression of surprise as she was suddenly aware that here she was naked in the bed of a man.

Suddenly she said something that really made my day, "You know, darling John, that I have *never* been in this situation before, but in the middle of the night I just thought that I ought to get the feeling of a man, my man beside me, so I crept in and didn't wake you. And let me tell you right now, it was nice. You didn't fart, as I always thought that men did. You didn't snore, again I thought all men snored, and you kept your word that we would not enjoy (I hope)

10

ourselves till the knot was well and truly tied." So raising herself just slightly so that both breasts were hanging free so to speak, she said that today was Wednesday and tomorrow was her twenty-first birthday and she was free to marry. "What about it? I have been in touch with the registrar's office and they can fit us in at 11.00 hrs tomorrow. OK?"

"No Amanda," I said without a lot of thought. "I should at least have had the chance to ask your father for his daughter's hand. He and I have never met, and he might hate the sight of me."

"He won't" said Amanda. "I have described you to him, your background and all the rest, and he abides with my judgement. So?"

"Oh very well" I said, "but be it on your head. I have the feeling that you just might well be in for a slight shock."

"Why?" says Amanda.

"Well for a start you seem to be surrounded by hordes of servants, which I am not used to, and I would expect you to be just an ordinary farmer's wife, nothing more nothing less; can you cope?"

"Of course I can. Let's just snuggle and go to sleep and think of what we shall do today because it is my birthday and I am twenty-one and am allowed by law to do what I want."

"You really are an idiot," I said. "Why didn't you tell me, for I would have liked to have given you a present?"

"What would you have given me?" asked Amanda, who by now was showing a bit more bosom than I cared to view, seeing that I had given my word not to touch her. "Well" said she, "how about an engagement ring? And whilst you are buying that I might as well be fitted out with a wedding ring as well!"

"You really are a most extraordinary female," I said. "Here we are in bed; you stark naked and you talk about marriage. You have offered me a job at a very decent salary. You have said that we ought to get married, which with the deepest respect, is not your line, it is mine, I should ask you, and whilst I am at it, I should mention that I love you. Now you did all that at that dance where we met more or less for the first time, although we have 'viewed' each other from a distance for at least a year. It was you who suggested, almost ordered me to marry you with not a vestige of love on your side, and here you are in my bed talking about *our* future. I repeat, you must be feeling disorientated. Your turn."

"No," says Amanda with her voice smothered with a sheet over her face. "I *do* want to marry you. I think that I can make you fall in love with me and I with you, and I would like to get married *today*."

"Today!" I exclaimed. "Amanda, I have no wedding gear to waltz up an aisle. It hasn't been used for years and the moths have probably got at it."

"You won't need it" says Amanda pulling a sheet aside and looking me straight in the eye. The wedding will be at a registrar's office at 14.00 hrs today. It is all arranged."

"You are as daft as a coot, Amanda. Supposing I said that I had no intention of marrying you and also, have you thought that the possible groom has to ask the father of the proposed wife to be? I haven't even met your father. He might loathe the sight of me and then where will we be, married, no job and not a lot of money!"

Amanda sighed, pulled back the covers, sat up, her pert breasts all alert and in line and told me that she had in fact talked to her father about me, and he had relied on her good judgement and what was more was looking forward to meeting me. So she had made a date and time with the registrars and didn't I think that it was time that we both got up, had a bath and I had a shave and go out and buy a ring or two?

I sat up in bed, the first time in my life that I had been in that position with a gorgeous female next to me and had not done something about it, and thought what had I to lose? She was beautiful and she certainly had an organising head on those pretty shoulders of hers. So without further ado, I turned to the girl, avoiding glancing at those gorgeous bosoms, looked her straight in the eye and asked her to marry me, and for good measure implied that I was rather fond of her.

To all this, without further ado, she said "Yes, I will." She tousled my hair with her fingers and leapt out of bed and into the bathroom.

So I got out my electric razor, an implement that I dislike but time seemed to be of the essence. I went and sorted out some clothes and the right sort of tie, and hammered on the door of our only bathroom so that I could get a bath. I thought that I might as well see how she cooked, for when she came out I told her what was in the fridge and that I would be ready for my breakfast in twenty minutes.

So when we were seated down at the table just like any other married couple, bar for the fact that the deed had not as yet been done, I started asking questions, I asked as to how many acres her father possessed?

To which she replied, "I don't know the exact amount, but it is pretty large."

"And who is running it at the moment? Your father?"

"No" says Amanda. "It is my second cousin who has run the place for a number of years, and personally I think that he is doing my father out of a lot of money. I want you to find out where things are going wrong."

"How many cows are you milking at the moment?" I asked.

To which she replied "About 100."

"Sheep?"

"Yes" says Amanda. "But I don't know how many, but I think about 500."

"Pigs?" I ask.

"Yes about forty breeding sows."

"And what about corn? How many acres of corn is harvested?"

"Don't know," says Amanda. "But quite a lot."

"And what income does your father get out of all this?" I ask.

"Nothing" says Amanda. "He has in fact made a loss for years. But the trouble is that the man concerned is a relation of ours and Father will not do anything about the matter, although I am sure that he suspects that something is wrong. That is why I want you, my future husband, to take over full charge of the place and discover what is going wrong."

"OK" I said. "So let us sort out this morning. We have to go and buy a ring or two. We have to have lunch somewhere. I want my two children to be there, and I also want my son Richard to be my best man, so I must do some phoning forthwith. You sort out where we want to eat, which must be somewhere near the registrar's office, and tell me within thirty seconds *where* so that I can tell the children. When I say children, my daughter is twenty and my son is nineteen, they might have a slight surprise awaiting them."

All this was done within half an hour, and a very well-cooked breakfast was awaiting me after I had bathed, shaved, done some phoning and had dressed in something suitable for a registrar's office.

During breakfast we waltzed through the easy crossword in the *Telegraph,* and I noted with some trepidation that Amanda, after having done most of the easy one, was well away with the hard one; something that my brain had always refused to even look at.

Then a swift wash-up, and into the car and away to Regent Street where we looked into one, if not half a dozen shops, till Amanda found what she was wanting as an engagement ring. I was glad to see that the cost was reasonable, and then to the wedding ring which we found in the same place and then, all in a dash, onto the pub to find my two children wondering as to what it was all about.

"Let's find a table" I said.

"I have one, Dad," says my son and they were both looking at Amanda in amazement.

I let them look for a moment and then thought that I might as well throw the 'bomb'. "Amanda and I are getting married this afternoon, in, looking at my watch, one hour and a half, and Richard I want you as best man, and you Jenny to look after my future wife and for that matter, your stepmother."

Amanda then, bless her heart, rose swiftly, got both the kids together, threw her arms round them both and exclaimed in quite a loud voice that she was extremely happy and would look after their father to the best of her ability.

My two children returned to their seat, and both looked at me in astonishment that I could 'capture' such a young very beautiful girl, and then the questions came thick and fast. Most of which I fended off, for I really had little idea of my pending future and finally, what were they to call their future stepmother?

"Amanda of course," says Amanda.

Then we got down to the question of what to eat. I ordered a bottle of champagne, in fact by the end of the meal there were two empty bottles and everyone was more than happy, and so the time arrived and we, tottering just slightly, walked the few yards to the registrar's office, I having remembered to give the wedding ring to my best man, and then the ceremony started.

There was a stunned silence when I was asked as to whether I would take *Lady* Amanda Hastings as my lawful wedded wife, and I can remember turning my head slightly to see if this girl was really the one that I was about to marry. Amanda caught the look and those beautiful eyes of hers twinkled. My children were standing like statues not knowing what on earth their father was doing. But in the end I said 'I will', and that more or less was that.

I said a reluctant farewell to my two children, for I had the vague idea that Amanda wanted to explain a few things, so back to my little mews house.

"Firstly," says Amanda, "it is very important that we get down to our new house as soon as possible and sort a few things out with my father."

"Just a minute," I said. "I did not know that we had a house, and has your father the faintest idea as to what is going on? For instance, does he know that you and I got married this morning?"

"Yes," says Amanda, "I have kept him up to date with this," and out came that mobile phone. "And what is more," continued Amanda, "he has arranged a small party for us this evening, and you will want your dinner jacket and all the trimmings. In fact if you could start packing right now, it would help. And darling husband, I do apologise for all this, but in a few hours' time you will understand the importance of what I have done, and I promise in future to do what *you* want and never to order you about as I have done in the last hour or so."

So I packed, or to put it more correctly Amanda did most of it, and we lugged the lot down to my car and shoved it into the boot.

"Now" says Amanda, "on to my place for my things and then off we go to what I think, I hope you will find quite an interesting life."

As I drove, my mind was in a whirl. Firstly I had a new very beautiful wife, who for some reason or other had a title. So that was my first question to my 'child bride' sitting by my side and just occasionally looking up at my somewhat intent face. "Why Amanda, have you a title? If you have one, not that I know much about these things, but that means that your father has a title as well."

"Right" says my wife.

"Well what is the title?" I said somewhat impatiently. A knight, lord or what?"

"Go up a bit" says my wife. "Oh I might as well tell you, he is the Duke of Sussex."

I nearly shot into the nearest ditch. I had not the faintest notion of any of this and she hadn't told me. Although thinking back whilst I got my car back under control, I did hear her addressed as 'Her Ladyship' just the once, but thought nothing of it.

"And what is more" continued Amanda in a somewhat quiet voice, "he has been very ill over the past six months and is only this moment recovering, so he has not been able to manage the affairs of the estate. They are in a mess, a big mess and we want you to sort the mess out."

I digested this snippet of information with some difficulty. "What about your mother, Amanda?" I asked.

She died giving birth to me all those years ago, so Father is going to welcome you with open arms."

15

"But how do you know?" I asked. "The poor man has never seen me; he doesn't know me."

"Oh yes you two have met a long time ago, and it was you who told me of your life in France during the war. Do you remember telling me how on the retreat to Dunkirk with you, as a dispatch rider, before you got commissioned, picking up a wounded second lieutenant. You took him to a hospital, and you never asked his name. That my darling husband, was my father, and when I told him on the phone weeks ago that I thought that I was at last falling in love with someone sensible, and told him something about you, my father exclaimed, *'Marry him at once.* He probably saved my life'."

"Good Heavens!" I exclaimed. "What a small world. What do I call your father when we meet?"

"As long as you don't call him 'Your Grace' you will be OK. Let him tell you, but I have the feeling that you two will get on like a house on fire, for you are very alike."

I tried to digest all this sudden information, even trying to turn my mind back to Dunkirk and all that; seeing this figure lying on the ground, waving an arm, with a spreading pool of blood around him, and a smashed-up car behind him, I stopped, put the bike on its stand and lifted this chap off the ground. With a bit of a struggle, I fitted him on the pillion of the bike, asking him as to whether he would mind if I took his tie off so as to make a tourniquet for his leg. I took him to the one hospital in Dunkirk which was left standing and handed him over, but quite forgot to ask his name, but I remember I did not forget to salute the chap as I went off.

"Slow down" says Amanda, "We are nearly there. Turn right and through those gates."

Off we set through a lovely park with ancient trees swaying in the light breeze, till we came to an imposing mansion and stopped at the front door which was opened by some servant or other. Through the door came a slight figure with a limp and I recognised him in a flash, it was the same man that I had been able to help all those years ago.

Amanda flew into her father's arms whilst I stood somewhat nervously wondering as to what would happen next.

It was made so easy and very happy for the duke approached me with hand outstretched and said "Good afternoon John. Welcome to my home. Come along in and by the way I am Peter to my friends and you are one as from now, so no arguments."

The servant who held open the door for us, said "Good afternoon Lady Amanda, and to you Sir John, may I also welcome you."

I had the feeling that I ought to have a look around to see who this chap was talking to, for I was just a plain 'mister', but Peter was beckoning, so in I went into a vast sort of study with the walls lined with books and a table to seat at least twenty in the middle, and down we sat. Peter was about to say something but I somewhat rudely interrupted and asked as to whether I could say a word or two?

"Of course" said my host.

"Firstly Peter, somewhat late in the day, and you might say that the horse has bolted, but *if* there had been time I had every intention of asking your permission to marry your daughter. And then secondly, your butler at the door called me 'Sir John', which I am not. Could you tell him when you have a moment about his mistake?"

"Right John," says Peter. "Let me deal with the first question. I had already given my approval to your wedding, for my daughter told me all about you and what was more told me about certain adventures that happened to you on the retreat to Dunkirk. If you cast your mind back, you will I think remember that Amanda referred to the question of the wounded second lieutenant that you kindly picked up, carted to the hospital, after saving my life by applying a tourniquet to my left leg, using my tie. Do you remember her asking you once again to describe what had happened, even down to you saluting me as you continued your journey while I was on a stretcher — remember?"

"Yes," I said "I do. And now what about this 'Sir' business at your front door?"

"Well" said Peter, "let me explain that for the moment in minor detail. You see when I discovered that Amanda was in love with you, and I also discovered that it was you who had saved this particular duke's life all those years ago, it was the least that I could do when at a private dinner at the Palace, to tell the Queen this story. She said 'If he marries your daughter then I shall knight him, for it is not every day that one of my nicest dukes is saved from an unpleasant death.' So Sir John Teele and of course Lady Amanda Teele, I personally think you make an excellent couple. And now John, if I might say a few words on this auspicious occasion? The reason why this marriage has been slightly rushed is somewhat complicated and I will try and explain as shortly as I am able. My last manager died some two years ago and I had a distant cousin who somehow or other heard of this and what was more heard that I was advertising for another manager. He applied for the job and as I knew the family very well, and Michael (that is his name) had all the right qualifications, I offered him the job. I then got ill and spent most of the better part of a year in hospital. When allowed out I was still very weak and was not able to look after the estate as I had done in the past. It soon became apparent that Michael was a crook of the first water. He was selling my stock all over the various markets in Sussex and the resulting cash was going into his pocket. Also the estate was getting slack; fences were falling down; the milk cheque was almost nil although we were still milking, as far as I could tell some seventy cows; the sheep looked terrible and the pigs seemed to be dying. What was I to do? I had no wish to accuse this cousin for it would have been a bitter blow to his parents, but I had to do something, and then you, John, appeared on the scene and I started to get ideas. Firstly I had prior knowledge that something big was going to happen here on the estate in five days' time, but I had no idea as to what it was. So I am afraid that I encouraged my little daughter that if she was happy with the thought of marrying you, and equally you were more than keen on her, then for goodness sake get on with it for I wanted you, John here by my side as soon as possible. To this end I have divided up the estate between you two with effect from today. You Amanda will have the western part, and you John will have the eastern part which also includes all the stock. And you John have four days to discover this plot and stop it, and whilst you are at it, sack Michael. Now before you two start to say that I cannot do this, let me say quite firmly that I can and what is more I have. It is all sealed and signed, but in all matters pertaining to this somewhat large deal, there are certain safeguards from my point of view. The first one is that you two have to stay happily married for the rest of your lives, and also you have to pay me a rent. Here are two envelopes, and in each you will find the deed drawn up and witnessed. In your envelope, John, you will find a small memento of yesteryear in the shape of my still blood-stained tie, which you might like to keep for old times sake. Now shall we have a drink and then you can ask what you want."

There was a complete silence in the room for a few seconds till Amanda broke it by coming round and kissing her father, and then for good measure, her husband. What about the house, Father, is it the one I asked you about last week?"

"Yes dear it is," says Peter, "and what is more I have taken the liberty of employing some servants to look after you. Their wages are paid for, so again no arguments. And you John, I can see that you are itching to open your mouth for all this must seem somewhat of a mirage to you. You have found a wife; found a new father-in-law; have some 5,000 acres in your name plus quite a bit of stock, so my boy, it's all yours have a go."

"Peter, I must admit that I do feel somewhat overpowered with all this, and I shall have some words with that lady over there," pointing at Amanda. "But first things first, you say that your stock is disappearing but that no monies are coming in your direction. So firstly who are the main auctioneers in this part of the world and have you got any letter headings, for the names of the directors are always printed on them, and over the years I have got to know a number of them."

Peter withdrew some papers from one of the many files on the table and showed me the main and biggest firm first. Glancing down the directors' names, I saw quite a number who I knew personally and one in particular that I used to play golf with on a regular basis.

"Can I use your phone, Peter?" I asked. So I dialled the number concerned and asked to speak to my friend, and asked him as to whether his firm had any dealings with stock from the Duke of Sussex's estate. The answer came back without any hesitation that more or less every month they sold some stock, and the resulting cheques were sent on the duke's authority to this man Michael. And what is more in a few days' time the duke was selling all his milking herd. There was a pause and then he told me the date. Now Richard, what I am now going to say might sound a bit odd, to say the least, but I am with the Duke of Sussex at the moment and he is about to tell you to cancel that sale. He will confirm that in writing and the letter will be with you tomorrow morning." At that I handed the phone over to Peter and he confirmed what I had said. Peter handed the phone back to me and I suggested to Richard that it might be worth his while if he paid a visit to the duke at some convenient time and matters would then be explained.

I must admit that whilst all this was going on, my brain was in somewhat of a whirl, because I just wondered as to whether I had been hoodwinked into firstly a marriage, because without the marriage I would not really be available to Amanda's father to help him out of the mess that this man Michael had produced. But going back over the last few hectic days; the declaration of love from my young wife and her obvious eagerness to wed me; was it all real or had she acted a well-known love scene well enough to fool a man of my somewhat mature age? There was only one way to find out, and that was to consummate the marriage. I was certain that I would know whether she was acting out a love scene or not, and 'let's face it,' I told myself, 'I am certain that I adore her. So let us get on with it and find out.' So I turned to my new father-in-law who was engaged in a long conversation with his daughter, mainly about the house and the servants, and said, "Right Peter, just in case you have forgotten, we two are on the start of our honeymoon, and whilst all the staggering information that I have just learned is all most interesting, we intend, my young wife and I, to get on with our life for the next twenty-four hours at least. Then I shall start getting this estate back in some sort of order. But," I continued, "there is one thing that you could do for me, and that is to write a letter to this Michael, telling him that you have transferred the estate into our names, and that no doubt I shall get in touch with him in due course. But in the meantime to do nothing with regards to the management of the place till I have seen him, or words to that effect."

"OK" says Peter, "that I will do with some pleasure."

So I turned to my waiting wife, gave her a hug and said that we ought to go and view our new abode. "Let's go." I said goodbye to Peter and told him that I would see him at tea time tomorrow, and off we went.

Into the car, and as I was driving I asked my new young wife the way, and she snuggled up to me and said "First left." I couldn't resist asking as to whether she knew our future abode or not, and she replied that she had known it for years and that I would like it, and she was more than happy and thanked me for the way that I had accepted my somewhat new and unexpected life and hoped that I would be as happy as she knew that she would be.

After a while a quite large house came into view. A nice garden surrounded it, and as I drew up to the front door an obvious manservant appeared plus a woman. He opened the door to my wife and said "Welcome, Lady Amanda and to you Sir John. May you be both be very happy in your new abode and I trust that my wife and I will be able to assist in any way." He then introduced his wife, a nice-looking girl who said that she hoped that we would both like her cooking, and what time would we require our evening meal?

I looked at my wife, for this was our wedding night and felt that she ought to have a say in the timing of this and that, but Amanda replied that as usual we would like it at 8 p.m., but *not* please, a vast amount, because we had had quite a day and enough was enough.

So they left us to wander round our new abode, and I must admit that my mind was whirling around. The mere thought of having to worry about food and all that, was left in the far distance, for I had a challenge and I liked challenges. I had owned years ago, my first wife and I, 10,000 acres in Chile after the war, so this 10,000 didn't worry me all that much. The thought of Michael gave me food for thought, but more important was that I must meet my staff tomorrow, and as honeymoons go, this was going to be somewhat shortened.

All this time we had been wandering around this quite delightful house; a study for me with book shelves waiting to be filled, even a computer tucked away into a corner. Then the dining room, palatial to a degree with at least sitting room for twelve people in reasonable comfort. The drawing room, because that was the right description, I had been used to calling it a sitting room, but this was somewhat different and had a certain flair to it; so a drawing room it was. Then there was a conservatory which bordered onto the garden and would be handy for a small drinks' party; a downstairs loo and shower. We didn't dare go into the kitchen quarters for we felt that those two had enough of us for the evening, but here I was wrong because, Ambrose, (the manservant) knocked on the door and asked us what we would like to drink. I looked at my watch, it was drink time, dead on 18.00; I warmed to young Ambrose.

We both had our usual whisky, me with a squirt of ginger wine in it, and we sat and the conversation flowed in no mean way. "What plans have you got?" asked Amanda.

So I told her that I planned a meeting with the whole staff at 12.00 tomorrow, and that I intended to view this Michael sometime and see what he was made of. At 06.00 the following day he would be told to appear with me and milk some seventy cows because the cowman deserved a day off, which so far he didn't know about, but I would tell him tomorrow and then I would find out Michael's worth from the milking point of view.

Amanda was silent for a while and I looked at her sitting more or less next door to me, and I could see thoughts dashing across her lovely face. Suddenly I felt a bit of a heel, for after all this was supposed to be our honeymoon and here was I dashing off hither and thither tomorrow and leaving my new quite adorable wife to sort out the day, or most of it without her new husband. So I leaned across the gap, kissed her neck and suggested that we view upstairs, for we had seen most if not all of our new abode with the exception of the kitchen quarters, and also where Ambrose and his wife lived; were they comfortable and all that?

So up the wide stairs we went, Amanda still silent but holding my hand which was something, for I had the feeling that she was worried and it didn't take much reasoning on my side to guess what she was worried about. She was a virgin and a doctor had proved it, and she knew that I was quite an old hand at this sex business; what with one marriage behind me and loads of girlfriends in London, maybe she felt that I might not be satisfied with what I found this night! Anyway we wandered around a lot of bedrooms till we came obviously to the bridal suite; vast double bed and furnishings quite out of this world. We explored it all still hand in hand, till we had come to a halt and I thought that I had better do something. So I put my hands around her slim waist and pulled her into my body. As I did it, she looked up with such a trusting look and said in a small voice that she hoped that I would not be disappointed with this our wedding night, but could we wait till bedtime? I kissed her gently and said that if she loved me as much as I loved her, then her worries might be small ones. She giggled at this and said that I had better wait till nine months were gone and then see how things went. So down we went again, rang the bell and had another drink and wandered out into the garden with drink in hand. We had fifteen minutes till dinner and Amanda came straight to one of the points that had been worrying her which was she hoped that I didn't think that she had rushed me into a wedding just to please her father and get rid of this wretched Michael. But it all seemed to fit, for as far as she was concerned this was the happiest moment of her life and she hoped that she would make me happy as well.

Out came Ambrose, on the dot of 8 p.m., and in we went to a gorgeous meal, washed down with some super red wine, which reminded me that I must investigate the cellar and see what my new father-in-law had provided in the drink line. We dawdled over a port for me and some peculiar beverage for Amanda, and once again we went out onto the terrace, hand in hand and just wandered.

From my point of view I was so overcome with happiness, that conversation flowed and I talked about things that we might do together; about this new job of mine; how nice her father had been to a new son-in-law, but I noticed that Amanda had become silent and I just wondered as to whether she was worried about our first night together. Would she be able to make me happy or would there be a ghastly flop for after all she knew nothing of this marriage business whereas I knew rather a lot? Finally it was she who broke her long silence by asking me as to whether I minded if she went up first and had a bath and she would see me in half an hour. She looked at her watch and I did the same.

So off she went and I departed to our nice study to be asked by Ambrose as to whether I would like a nightcap, to which I replied that I had had enough. I thanked him for a lovely dinner and told him that I would not want him any more that night and would see him for breakfast at 08.00. I had the idea that his eyes widened just a bit at the time that I wanted breakfast, for I presume that his last employers, whoever they might have been had their breakfast at a more civilised hour, such as 09.00 or even later. But there it was, I had a busy day in front of me and my thoughts were torn between tomorrow and what I must do, and tonight and what I hoped to do, to make two people more than happy.

So the half an hour was more or less up and I wandered up to our super bedroom wondering what I should find. I must have made a noise coming up the stairs for there she was, my Amanda, waiting by the door with her arms outstretched and they fastened round my neck. What clothes she had on, opened down the middle and there she was, two pert little breasts with taut nipples, a flat belly with that triangle of black hair showing up, and she murmured in my ear. "Now my lovely husband, make me as happy as I hope to make you." So without any further ado, I lifted her up and took her to our vast double bed; stripped off my clothes and there we were clinging to each other, and I knew then and there that this was really the real thing. There was no make belief on her part, she lived and breathed just for me and so I took her gently through those parted legs and in a moment she sighed and I knew that I hadn't hurt her and she had had her first orgasm; one of many, I might say that night. But all nice and lovely things must have an ending, and around midnight, she crept into my arms and fell asleep and in a while so did I.

I woke at my usual hour of around about 6 a.m.; crept silently out of bed; found some farm clothes and left a note to my child bride, saying where I would be and that I should be back in a short while. But honeymoon or not I wanted to see what movement there was on this quite large farm. What time did they start milking? There was a foreman as far as I knew and also of course this elusive manager, one Michael, but didn't expect to see him around at this hour. There was a brace of tractor drivers according to Peter, a shepherd and an odd-jobman, but all I could find was a large bunch of cows waiting impatiently at the gate bordering on the milking parlour, but I might have been the only one on the place.

About 6.30, the sound of gumboots and two men arrived at the gate. They looked at me in some wonderment, and one came along and asked as to whether he could be of some assistance. His offer I declined but explained who I was, and for better or worse gave them my new title and asked their names and what time did they usually start milking?

There was a bit of a pause and the first one who had spoken to me exclaimed that usually it was six o'clock but they were late and he apologised. He let a number of cows into the milking parlour, started up the pump and without a pause put on the first of the four cups.

At this, I said "Oi," or words to that effect and asked the man as to whether he hadn't forgotten something. He looked puzzled and when I went to the next cow and put my hand down onto a filthy udder and deliberately showed him a handful of 'muck', he looked somewhat abashed.

"Oh you mean wash the bags, Sir."

"Of course" I said, "every cow *must* have a clean and spotless udder before you put the cups on. And also," for I thought that I might point out one or two other obvious facts, "how much milk did this cow give yesterday?" Looking round for the usual milk register, I asked where it was, and I was told that they didn't have one and never knew that it was necessary. So I explained as to a child that a cow gave a certain amount of milk free of charge so to speak from the grass that she ate, but if she gave more than say two gallons then she must be fed at the rate of 4 lbs of nuts per gallon.

"You know something about cows, then Guv?" said the head cowman, so I explained as gently as possible my farming history.

Just then as I was finishing my somewhat lengthy monologue, another man came in and I was introduced to the foreman who 'knuckled' his cap and looked a bit shaken when I told him firstly that the cows were about half an hour late in milking; there was no bucket; they never washed a bag and there was no milk register. Would he sort that out *now* please, and come and tell me up at the house when he had sorted things out.

By this time it was bordering on 07.00 and my conscience pricked me for I had left my new young beautiful wife lying supine in bed, and if she woke and found that her new husband had already forsaken her, it did not bode well for the start of a somewhat hasty honeymoon. So without further ado, I went home, crept upstairs, waved to Ambrose who was also up and about and who regarded me with just the faintest of surprise looks in that I was not tucked up in bed with my new wife. I opened our bedroom door very gently and found to my great relief that all was well. She was still asleep, so I tore off my now somewhat smelly clothes and shoved them into an empty drawer and crept into bed as naked as the day I was born, for I couldn't find my pyjamas.

I lay for a while, thinking of the coming day and also considering as to how best to deal with this Michael fellow, and also I wanted to have a meeting with all the staff but did not want Michael present; how to manage that one?

As if on a signal, my young wife woke and viewing me awake, threw her arms round my neck and willy-nilly I did my bounden duty to the pleasure of both of us. We lay and chatted about the coming day and I told her what I thought I must do but didn't mention that I had been up with the lark. She said that whatever I did, she would like to come along, did I mind? "Of course not" I replied, "your presence will be more than welcome." I told her of some of the things that I planned to do, and the first was of course the meeting with all the staff. I felt that I did *not* want Michael present and that I intended to start a profit-sharing scheme with the cows, pigs, sheep, and the corn. At this Amanda hugged me and said that she thought that was the idea of the century, and did I know how it would work? I replied that I would get the accountants on the job, but I thought that with new management new ideas might be welcome, and she agreed wholeheartedly.

By this time we both thought that the day should be inspected. Amanda went and had a bath and I had a shower just behind her bath. As the water trickled over me Amanda started to talk, firstly in a somewhat hesitant way but as she went on, her voice got stronger. The gist of what she was saying was that she had the idea I thought I had been 'talked' into this marriage all because her father was in trouble, and she thought that I could extract him from the mess into which 'dear' Michael had placed him. She paused and I light-heartedly threw my flannel at her and it landed on those two taught nipples, to which I added that was a good shot!

So I said my piece in that there was a time when I *did* have thoughts on the subject, but that last night had altered my vague ideas for no woman could have behaved as she had done unless she was head over heels in love with her husband, and for better or worse I thought she was and just for the record, the whole idea was reciprocated. "Now what about some breakfast? I will ring down to Ambrose. What do you want to eat after all the exercise that you have taken over the last eight hours?"

So I talked to Ambrose, not forgetting that we had already met as I was coming in, and ordered two bacon and eggs and all the trimmings such as toast, etc., plus a decent sample of home-brewed coffee.

I retrieved my farm clothes and put them on, and down we went to be greeted by both of them; what a nice couple we had been given.

As we finished, the phone went and there was Peter on the other end who said that he had seen a strange figure round about the cow shed from his bedroom window. I hastily changed the subject and bless him he understood that I didn't want my early-morning ramblings to be broadcast. I did say that we were in the best of health and more than happy and then told him of the immediate plans that I had for the day, and suggested that he gets hold of Michael and send him on a long journey to get something or other for him which was important, to which I had the required answer.

So once Michael was out of the way, together we went to find the foreman and told him that I wanted all the staff in the barn at 11.30 sharp. We then wandered, my new wife and I, firstly to the milking parlour. I was glad to see that the place was having even then a clean up; the walls that had been covered with muck were being cleaned, and generally the place looked a lot better than when I had seen it a few hours earlier. Then on to the piggery where according to the somewhat vague figures that Peter had given me, there should have been twenty sows. I found the pigman having a smoke and a coffee, half asleep on some bales of straw and asked him as to how many sows he had or thought that he had?

"Well Guv," said he, "we used to have about thirty sows and their litters, but every now and then a van appears and a sow and her litter are taken away and I ask the manager, to which he replies that the duke had ordered it, so who was I to argue?"

"Get the place cleaned up; muck out and fresh straw in; separate each litter into a separate pen and remind me in the near future that *each* sow and each piglet has to have an ear mark. See you at 11.30."

We still had some spare time, so thought that we might have a look at the sheep for lambing time had passed and I wanted to see what the new lambs looked like. In those days, it was usual for the whole flock to be brought into a yard or pen and fed in a trough. This was being done but the numbers of ewes no way matched the figures that I had been given, and as for the lambs, I had never seen such a poor display. After searching for the shepherd I had the usual tale that lambs, when they were old enough, had been carted off in various means and this was all that he had left. As the whole flock was filthy, I suggested to this so-called shepherd that a little 'dagging' might come in handy and would he start forthwith.

"Dagging Guv, what might that be?" said this so-called shepherd.

"Cleaning up their backsides," said I. "This flock is a disgrace. See you at 11.30."

I could see the foreman trailing behind us in the distance and each time he stopped, first at the piggery and then at the sheep, I could see him shaking his head. But now it was time when I wanted to meet the whole of the staff, so we headed towards the barn to find quite a chatting crowd assembled, for the wives had come as well. There were the two cowmen, two shepherds, two pigmen, and then two tractor drivers whom I had not as yet met and an odd-job chap who mended this and that, which made nine on the payroll.

So in we went, my wife and I, and I had been given a small platform on which I was to do my stuff. So I started by saying, "Gentlemen, good morning, my name is Sir John Teele and this is my wife Lady Amanda Teele. Between us we own the whole of the estate and hence forward you are working for us as against your previous employer, the Duke of Sussex." I then gave them my previous farming experience, mentioning as to the fact that I had worked 300 acres on my own for some three years; giving the number of cows milked; the milk round of 1,000 pints per day for six days per week; the number of ewes that I possessed and not forgetting the pigs, and for good measure I showed them with not a little pride two ploughing cups that I had won all those years ago. "But gentlemen I feel certain that your expertise in your chosen role is equal or better than mine. I wandered on in this manner but then brought in the question of a percentage of the profits each department made in a financial year, and said that I intended to bring this into being right away. I could feel the sudden interest in all concerned, so thought that I ought to give them some sort of guidelines and started with the cows. I made it plain that each department would have certain costs levelled at it, and looking at the two cowmen who I had seen that very morning, "You for instance are getting on an average some two gallons of milk free per day. After that you feed concentrates, *but* who supplies the first two gallons?" And here I looked at the two tractor drivers, "They do and their costs have to be met into the bargain such as ploughing, concentrates, seed and all the rest but part of their percentage in profits comes from the cow department." I went on to sheep and their lambs; the wool cheque; the sale of surplus stock. But again the sheep have to eat and again grass is their mainstay, and again the tractor drivers are responsible. I noticed that the two tractor drivers were starting to look as if they were the top of the bunch and would earn a far greater percent of the profits than any other department, so thought that I had better cut them down to size and mentioned that their fuel bill amounted to quite a bit, especially when they forgot to turn off their engines. There was silence but quite near at hand was the rhythmic sound of a diesel tractor which somebody had forgotten to turn off. One of the two tractor drivers looked a bit shamefaced. Came the turn of the pigs and again I went into detail of their costs, and finally wound the whole thing up by mentioning such items as land tax, tithes and the expense of fencing, water, drainage, light and power. "So gentlemen do not expect some vast sum to come your way every year, but I expect you to earn something from your own efforts. If you don't then something in your particular department is wrong and will have to be put right. For if you don't make a profit, then neither do I, and that will never do! Just in case your foreman feels that he has been left out of all this money making, I can assure him that he will have a 'nibble' out of each department. For it is he who will see to it that you are working to possibly new principles than in the past, and these are of course, my own. So Gentlemen have you any questions to ask me? For now is the time, but I hasten to add that leaving my title quite aside, let me assure you that I am a working farmer and in the main will be working alongside you a lot of the time." There were a few questions, not a lot and not all that important to mention but I felt that they were astonished that they were going to get a percentage of the profits, an idea that they had never dreamt about, and I think that they were eager to discuss the whole meeting together once we had got out of the way.

So back to our nice house, the usual G&T for both of us. In fact Ambrose must have seen us coming because we hardly had time to sit before two brimming ice-cold glasses were in front of us, and we were asked as to what time we would like lunch. Amanda, first getting my nod, said that we always had our midday meal at 13.00 hrs, unless there was some emergency.

Then there was a ring on the front door and Peter, my very nice father-in-law was ushered in and said that he thought that he might also cadge a drink off his new neighbours, and were things working out for me?

So I told him about the cow department, when Amanda said that she must go and spend a penny, and asked him to keep that episode between us two; the pigs which were in a parlous condition, joined by the sheep and finally the two tractor drivers; one of which had been ploughing with a four-furrow plough with two points missing, which didn't improve the plough. I also told him about my new idea of profit-sharing and I must admit that Peter was astonished that I had thought this one up, and thought that it was an excellent idea, but what about Michael?

"Well Peter," I said. "Firstly, tomorrow is the day when something *big* is supposed to be happening, so have given both cowmen the day off and told Michael that I wanted him to help me milk the herd, and I will then see what he is made of. Also I had the idea that *something* might happen which will give me a clue as to what this *big* thing is all about. I had sent a letter by hand to Michael informing him as to what was going on, and telling him that he and I were going to milk the herd starting at 06.00 tomorrow. "Peter, you will stay to lunch, won't you?" I said and Amanda backed me up and implored her dad to do just that. Finally Peter after enquiring as to whether we really had enough for five, counting in Ambrose and Helen, his wife, rang for Ambrose and told him to lay another place

29

for lunch. Then we all dived into what was fast becoming a fascinating future life for both Amanda and I.

Peter knew a lot more about farming than I had thought at the start, but lacked practical experience which of course I had, and I suggested that one of the things lacking was egg production, and thought that a battery of about 1,000 birds would fit well into the empty barn in which we had held our first meeting with the staff. The other item from the point of manpower which was missing, was a man who could weld, carpenter and do general odd jobs around the estate, and here I would provide one. I said this because I could see that Peter was about to say that *he* would be responsible for that cost, but I felt that he had done enough; so that was also agreed.

After lunch I went down to my future office and started rummaging around the somewhat untidy room. I was looking for account books and details concerning the various different departments on the estate, but they were nowhere to be found. I did find quite a nice computer which was locked solid and knowing quite a bit about these machines, soon found out the reason why it had seized up, and what I found was more than interesting, in so far that dear Michael had been idiot enough to write down on this machine more or less all the illicit deals that he had done over the past couple of years. Lastly on that point it showed that five lorries would be arriving at the cow parlour tomorrow morning to take away *all* the cows to be sold at auction. I got the printer to work, had the lot typed out and put the result in my pocket. Then just for the fun of it, and feeling just a wee bit bitchy towards this bastard who had rooked my new father-in-law out of thousands whilst he was ill, I rang up the auctioneers to whom I had previously cancelled the lorries, and asked that just *one* should be sent without telling the driver anything bar that he must report to Michael as to why he had come.

The day passed; a phone call from Michael, making his number so to speak and asking as to whether I *really* wanted him that early in the morning, to which I said that I did and was looking forward to meeting him.

I went out and bought myself a second-hand Honda motorcycle as I wanted to be able to tour the boundaries quickly and see what was wanted, and Amanda insisted that she ride pillion and off we went; she holding a map of the place and telling me which way to go. It was lucky we did, for we found part of the boundary fence down and a number of our neighbour's cattle stealing our grass. So we persuaded them to go back to their proper quarters and then back home quickly to detail someone to go out and mend the fence. This little exercise again proved that we were lacking in types who could do this job, for the tractor drivers hadn't a clue as to how to strain wire or for that matter how to use a hammer and a staple, and as to shoving in a post, that was quite beyond them. So I with my new knighthood firmly attached, took a tractor and trailer out with the necessary equipment and showed an astonished pair of tractor drivers how to do such a simple farming job. Two barb and one plain wire was what I was taught all those years ago when I was a jackeroo in Australia, although I must admit I did have thoughts about that, in that it would have been better to have put up mesh. Just in case we ever had sheep out in those far-flung pastures.

But we would deal with that matter when it arrived, at the moment I had tomorrow to think about. Dear Michael, who imagined himself with yet another fool of a rich knight who knew nothing about running an estate, was in for just a slight surprise. Feeling somewhat wicked I went into the milking parlour in the middle of the afternoon milking and made sure that they knew that they were both having the morning off and they could start work tomorrow with the afternoon milking. The nasty thoughts came into my mind. I wondered as to what Michael knew about milking a cow; he must know something. Could he for instance milk by hand. Most of us started that way all those years ago, where you would have a three-legged stool, your cap turned back to front and your head dug into the flank of the cow, sometimes with a rope round both hind feet because although most cows never kicked a human, there were some who enjoyed that little exercise. Then machines came into the act, and milking parlours were built. I seem to remember the first of these where you were able to milk two cows at once; what bliss! Then came four cows and in this case here we milked eight at a time.

But of course what one did with the end product, i.e. the milk, was quite another matter. You had your milk from the cow travelling along a pipe, and the milk then fell into a container which had a tap, and the milk flowed over a cooler and finally through either two or four milk churns down on the ground. That was fine as long as you remembered that milk churns hold ten gallons and no more. So you had to come along and change the full churns to empty ones, then when the Milk Board's lorry arrived you had your churns perched on a ledge which was the level of the floor of the lorry, and the driver gave you a chitty for what he had taken away. This was the present system here.

That system was fine bar for one or two slight snags, firstly the afternoon's milking had to be kept in a cold room for the night, taken out and added to the morning's quota. Me I favoured the tanker business, where all your milk flowed into a vast cooled container and the tanker man when he came in the morning, merely stuck a large hose into your tank and sucked the lot into his and of course gave you a record of what he had taken. But in all these systems you had to have some sort of sieve through which all the milk had to pass, and that sieve was in a container and again there was a tap at the bottom of this container. So I thought that I might just test Michael's knowledge of this set up, for he had been in charge of it for some two years or more, so I turned *off* the tap and wondered as to whether he would spot it. Although the part I was really looking forward to was the advent of just one lorry and the message that the driver was going to give to Michael, and I was going to make damn sure that I was within hearing distance of the message.

So the day passed as all days do. The night was bliss and we were both almost ashamed to agree that we were just starting to think that we had both made an excellent choice.

Sleep came. I woke at about 05.00 and crept out of bed, into my farming clothes and silently left the house, having remembered to leave a note for my wife as to what I was up to, although we had discussed all of my plans, bar for the tap set up. I thought if I told her that, she might think my mind was somewhat twisted, which in this case I think it was, for I was determined to show this wretched man as to what an utter bastard he was.

I pottered round the place for a bit for I had plenty of time. I thought that it might be an idea to enclose the whole of the farmyard with some decent fencing and keep a reasonably good guard dog on duty during the night, but thought that I had better ask Peter about that one first.

05.50 came and not a sign of Michael as yet. The cows were all at the gate and complaining loudly that they wanted to be milked, and just as important they were looking forward to their nuts. 06.00 came and still nobody but at 06.15 along came a slouching figure; a slow walk, nothing urgent so I kept out of sight and Michael came to the door of the parlour. As he was about to open up I came into view and firstly having said a somewhat curt "Good morning." I asked him what time his watch had, at which the long unshaven face looked down at his wrist with just the faintest look of annoyance on his face and told me that it was 06.15.

So I barked, an original bark that I had learned on a parade ground, and this shook the man for he muttered a "Sorry. Must have over slept." So in we went and I explained that I wanted to see him milk the herd, and hearing that Michael exclaimed, "What, all on my own!"

To that I agreed and added that I had done it for some three years and with this set up it was simple. "So off you go" I said.

What a shambles, firstly he didn't know where to turn the motor on; the light switch baffled him; he forgot a bucket to clean a bag, plus of course the cloth, and he never even glanced at where his milk was going to end up, so my tap stayed firmly shut. He let the cows into the yard and by this time they were more than impatient, and Michael did not move quick enough for he was pushed aside. But I thought that I must do something to stop this chaos for otherwise instead of eight cows coming in to be milked, the whole seventy might try to get in. So when eight got in, I shut the door firmly with Michael on the other side!

"Well," said I, "what next?" To which he looked blank. "Where is the cow register? Where is the bucket for cleaning the bags, not forgetting the cloth? And some of the chains are still hooked up from yesterday's afternoon milking. Undo them man and for God's sake get a move on."

So with almost a frightened look on his face, he let the first eight in. He tied them in after I reminded him, and went and found a bucket and the cloth, and then paused; panic struck for there was utter silence in the parlour where there should have been the busy hum of the electric motor.

So I stopped him rushing around like a lunatic, looked him straight in the eye and asked him point blank as to whether he had ever milked this lot, or even helped to milk the herd in the time that he had been manager here?

He dithered a bit and started to say "Well I."

"*What*" I roared. "Answer just a plain question with a plain answer."

C

"No I never have been to any milking. I didn't think that it was part of my duties," said he.

"I wonder what your duties actually were!" I replied. So I took him round this strange building; showed him the various switches and pointed out where the milk should end up. *And what is that?* I asked pointing to my closed tap.

"Oh I see" said a now somewhat meek and mild Michael, "the milk comes out of that pipe."

"Bloody well get on with the job or we shall be late for the lorry."

"What lorry?" says Michael, his voice rising in panic as he suddenly remembered what was supposed to be happening this very morning.

As fate would have it, just at that moment, there came a tap at the door and a man peered in and said, "All ready Guv, but I don't know what has happened to the other three lorries, but shall I start to load?"

Michael's face was a picture. I wished that I had a camera and the chance to take that look, it was as near panic that I had ever seen. "Everything is cancelled" said Michael in a choking voice.

So I thought that I might make the matter plainer and asked the man what this was all about, knowing full well the answer. He told me quite straight that the duke was getting rid of all his cows and they were going to market this morning to be sold. "The estate has changed hands and that exercise is cancelled. Good morning. We will talk about this later at 10.00 hrs in what used to be your office, but *now* just watch what I am doing and copy me exactly, and then you might learn something." So I took on the first four cows, told Michael to get another bucket and cloth and proceeded to wash a bag or two, and watched him try and do the same. It was obvious that he had never in all his life been asked to do such a menial task, and what was more the cows seemed to twig as well for a placid-looking cow aimed a sharp hoof in his direction which distracted him for quite a while, and I had finished my first four when he got to his second. I had to teach him about *stripping,* for you don't just shove the 'cups' on to the cow, you have to make certain that she has given her 'all' when the milk stops flowing, and this of course you do by hand, a task which Michael loathed.

Onto my second lot of four and I thought that I might remind Michael about the churns, to which he replied, "What churns?"

So once again I had to take this so-called manager by the arm and show him four nearly full churns and ask what he was going to do about them? He looked blank, so I told him about such items as labels for the churns and what went on the labels; in this particular case, *my name*, and again he looked blank, so I told him just once more who I was.

And so the morning ended, or nearly so because as we got the last churn out on the ramp, up came the lorry and Michael and I loaded them up with the thanks of the driver. Then I asked Michael as to what came next before he had his breakfast? Again he looked quite blank, and it was obvious that he had never done this job before let alone superintend what went on *after* the milking, which was to take a couple of bales of hay out on a tractor and trailer and spread lumps of the quite nice-smelling hay round that particular field.

I must admit that I felt just a bit guilty, because if Michael was going to do this job then he had to back a trailer through a gate to get at the bales of hay, and I would have bet £100 that he would not be able to do that particular exercise. And of course he couldn't even hitch the tractor onto the trailer, which I then showed him as to how it was done. Anyway he hoisted a couple of bales onto the trailer, and found that he couldn't even get into first gear. So I lost my temper and told him to shove off and that I would see him at 10.00 on the dot in *my* office.

I fed the cows, parked the tractor and trailer and went back home to find that breakfast was waiting, and so I had to explain to my hungry wife as to what had gone wrong this morning. I also told her that I had been able quite easily to 'hack' into Michael's computer and had all the evidence required for a prosecution. I took this out of my pocket, so we talked about it, my young wife and I, and we agreed that he must go and the sooner the better, but should we show the evidence to her father, the duke or not? Amanda had her say and thought that we ought, so I rang Peter up and asked as to whether he had the room for a coffee for we had a bit of news for him. He was with us within five minutes; in his dressing gown of all things. So I told him of this morning and what a ghastly mess his manager had made of things, and even more important showed him the contents from the computer in what was Michael's office. At a rough guess we reckoned that Michael had got away with over £20,000 in the last two years.

"So Peter, what do you want to do?" I asked, for go he must and soon.

"What about a week or prosecution, John?" said he. "I leave it to you. You have done marvels in the brief time that you have been here, but keep me informed."

Peter stayed for a while chatting with his daughter and I made preparations for this meeting at 10.00 hrs for this would be the crux; he had to go and without fuss.

09.45 I was in my office, everything neat and tidy and at 10.00 on the dot the door opened and in came Michael to which I said, whilst still sitting, "Oh I am sorry I didn't hear you knock." At which Michael started to find a chair and I asked him what he was looking for?

To which he replied, "A chair."

"When I want you to sit," said I in my most military style, "I will indicate a place, and just in case you are thinking of smoking," for I had the idea that he was about to drag out a packet of cigarettes, "I do *not* like the smell of cigarettes. Take that chair and explain this." I thrust in front of him the typed contents of all the thieving that had been going on during the last couple of years. "Well," said I, "I want some sort of explanation right now, and whilst you are thinking about it, the jail sentence for a crime such as this would be about ten years. What thoughts have you on that particular subject?" He was quite silent. I had the vague idea that he was about to cry on my desk, so I thought that I had better give him a break. "Speak man, right now. And whilst you are thinking of an explanation which might be impossible, also consider the frightful mess that you made of the milking this morning. How dare you take on a job such as managing a 10,000-acre estate when you hadn't the faintest notion of more or less anything from a practical point of view, or maybe from any point whatsoever."

Michael was still silent with his head cradled on his two hands and I could see that he was shaking. Then he did something which explained a lot, for he withdrew from his side pocket a small much-used pouch. In the pouch was a silver spoon and he dipped the spoon into the powder and swallowed the lot, and one could see the change come over him in seconds. So it was drugs; what kind I have no idea, but that was his problem. He had to have money to buy the wretched stuff, thus all the pilfering. He looked up, met my somewhat steely eye and quite simply asked the question which I was about to make myself. "How long have I got to get out? And please, please don't tell my parents about this." He pointed at his pocket and that pouch. "Are you going to prosecute or not?"

"If, Michael you are out of your house within seven days and the duke agrees, then there will be no prosecution; is that clear? And what is more I want that house of yours spotless from top to bottom, and I shall come along and inspect it on the day you are due to leave. Is that clear? I shall want a signed declaration that you have been responsible for the total amount that you have stolen over the time that you have been here, and I have prepared that for your signature *now*." I am a great believer in hitting when the enemy is feeling somewhat downtrodden, and Michael was a sorry sight. "So sign and I will get a witness for your signature. I pressed the bell on my desk without the faintest knowledge as to who would answer the summons for I was in the estate office, but a figure emerged and without further ado, for he seemed to know who I was, I said "I want you to witness this signature, which Michael has signed" and this man appended his signature below and that was that.

Michael then left. He did hesitate at the door and mumbled an apology, but we were dealing with a figure of over £25,000 which this wretched man had pinched off my new father-in-law and I had little sympathy for him.

I rang the bell again and once more this man appeared. I made my own introduction and asked him as to where he fitted in to this business. To which he replied that amongst his many activities, he was mainly the Duke of Sussex's secretary.

I then went to find Peter, only to find him arguing the toss with rose pruning and told him the facts of the last half an hour. To which he heaved a sigh of relief that the deed was done and any explanations to his quite near relatives, i.e. Michael's parents, would be in the hands of Michael himself.

"Now what about a drink?" said Peter. To which I replied that would be nice but as I had not seen my new wife for at least an hour, could she come and join us? So Amanda appeared on a bicycle which I didn't know she owned and we all sat, the three of us, and started to discuss the present state of our combined enterprises. I thought that we ought to have a stable for at least four horses, maybe more, for I liked to ride, so did Amanda, and the thought of giving lessons to all and sundry seemed to have some sense to it. Then there was the question of chickens. Peter had about a dozen for his own use, but with regards to the estate as a whole, there wasn't a bird in sight. So we talked about how to bring this new enterprise into being; either battery hens or free-range. Personally I liked the idea of free-range, less costly for a start but more labour intensive, and of course every fox in the immediate neighbourhood would have a feast, and the cost of the fencing might be considerable, so we came round to battery hens. Peter kindly said that we ought to spread the cost of the battery itself between the three of us, which was nice of him.

Lunchtime arrived and we went home and prepared for the afternoon's work. We got down to ways and means; how many acres of cereal; what had the crop rotation consisted of, if of course dear Michael had thought about it. So I rang up the foreman at his house and asked him to meet us two in the estate office after he had finished his lunch.

We told the foreman that Michael was leaving and gave him the approximate date when this would take place. To which the foreman whose name was Dick, heaved an audible sigh of relief, and it was so noticeable that I felt that I had to ask him why that vast sigh?

So the tale came out that Michael had been quite useless from the start, and also Dick suspected him of stealing left, right and centre, and now he felt that we could manage the place in a proper manner as it should have been.

I asked Dick to write down a brief summary as to what had happened over the last couple of years; crop rotation; amount of milk sent away and had there ever been a cow register and if so where was it? Plus the lamb count and what had happened to the pig population? "What about staff," I asked, "Have you enough, do you think and what suggestions have you with regards to next year's cereal crop, for planning now is of great importance?" Also for good measure I told Dick that I should be looking for a man who could do all sorts of odd jobs round the place from welding to mending, this and that, woodwork and in fact anything that needed doing from the repair point of view, and had we got a spare empty house?

"Well Sir," said Dick somewhat hesitatingly, "there will be Michael's house when he goes, whenever that might be, or there is another smaller cottage which has been empty for some time; depends really as to whether your odd-jobman has a family or not."

Then the talk became widespread, for I asked Dick about the question of work contracts and were all the estate houses let on a 'tied to work' principal? To which I was told that they were and that the system worked well, although in the past the duke had had some trouble with one or two of his men whose contract had been terminated, but they refused to move.

"I can sort that one out," I said and told Dick of what I used to do with a new man, in that he deposited with me the sum of £200 when he first came which I would invest, pay him a dividend, and he would get the money back if and when he left his tied cottage without any problems occurring.

"Now that's a new one on me," says Dick, "Did it work, Sir?" he asked.

I told him that it did and what was more was quite a popular idea, especially with the wives who knew if the worst came to the worst, they always had this nest egg to fall back on. "And now Dick, what about the cereal harvest of last year? How many acres? In your report, name the fields, if of course they have a name, and whilst you are at it, have you a map of the place showing each field? I then told him about the boundary fence that I had found down a couple of days ago. "Who inspects the layout of the place? This exercise should be done every day by someone; who? And from one thing to another, clocking in time, do you have a machine, for want of a better word, and if so where is it? Also does each man have a time sheet showing what he has been doing all the day, where and why and all that?" Again poor Dick was mystified because nothing like this had been done before. He thought that it was an excellent idea, but nobody had thought about it, till I came onto the scene. "You, Dick, want a foreman's office, for what we have been talking about needs *your* thoughts on the subjects concerned. Your ideas and a lot more, for you have been here for some seven years. Any ideas as to where this office might be?" So Dick said that he would have a think on those lines and he thanked me profusely for the mere thought of an office, for he had wanted one for years, but dear Michael said that it wasn't necessary! "So Dick, just concentrate on cereals for a start, battery hens next, manpower and any ideas that you have thought about but haven't voiced. Let me have the lot, and while I am thinking about it, here is a so-called toy for you in the shape of a mobile phone, for I have one and it could be handy; who knows!" I then showed him how the thing worked. "I would suggest that unless anything untoward happens, that we meet here in my office every day at 11.30 to discuss matters pertaining to the running of this place. My wife will be here as well for she has half of the place as her own and I have the other part together with the stock. Before you go, Dick, I want to find plastic discs for at least 100 cattle and some 300 sheep plus 200 pigs." I then told him about what I used to do all those years ago, so as to find out which line of stock did better than the others. "And for that exercise you *must* have identification which is all important."

And so we departed to our various homesteads and I was glad to hear that Amanda agreed with me that we could have done a lot worse than Dick. He had suffered under Michael and trusted that he would prosper under my wife and I. Of course in the discussion that we three had just left, there were bound to be items that we had forgotten, and one such item was of course the question as to what woods we had on the estate. For woods and pigs go well together, as I remember in my past when I only had some ten acres of woods, but I fenced them in and during the summer season, this quite small wood satisfied the appetite of some twenty-five sows and their various litters. Each family was housed in a wooden sort of hut which I could tow about the farm by a tractor. Each hut had a trough and I could go round and feed the lot in quite a short space of time. Water had been laid on and I wanted to carry out the same sort of exercise on our new combined 10,000 acres.

But as we sat having our usual midday lunchtime G&T, the talk as usual came round to how best to run this place. Manpower worried me. I could not see how two tractor drivers could cope with the amount of corn that we expected to grow next year, and then there were such items as combines. We hadn't seen one or maybe they had more than one, dryers and all that.

"Let's make a list out" said my thoughtful young wife. "I will write in this old notebook and you throw thoughts at me. Tomorrow we will throw the lot at poor Dick."

"Yes" I said, "but there must be an inventory somewhere. Find that and half our troubles are over. Maybe your father knows where it might be? Give him a ring," I said to Amanda, which she did.

But Peter had no idea as to the whereabouts of this inventory. "There was one," he said, "but since Michael arrived, that and a lot of other things appear to have vanished."

Michael had two more days before he was due to leave, so I rang him up at his house. By the sound of him he was tight, but I asked him anyway as to whether he knew where this inventory was? To which he slurred that he had no idea and hung up. That attitude didn't help much and again I made a note not only in my head but also in Amanda's notebook that she was compiling. If the worst came to the worst, we would have to get in an auctioneer or somebody similar and have a fresh inventory made.

The notebook by the time that we had finished lunch was filling up rapidly, and tomorrow's meeting with Dick, the foreman, might give him a bit of a headache, for we wanted firstly, a conducted tour of the whole place and this meant all the machinery; the logbooks of each vehicle, although I bet there wasn't one on the place; oil changes and all the rest. Thinking of all this, the sooner we found ourselves a man, who could look after and organise the place, let alone mend this and that, the better.

I had a portable Dictaphone and we decided, Amanda and I, that before we did anything, I must put a fresh tape into it because I intended to speak our thoughts into it that afternoon, because writing down everything was going to be a bit of a chore, to say the least.

Firstly we put an advert in the local press, saying that there was a job vacant for a man who could look after the machinery on 10,000 acres, and that there was a tied house thrown in and gave our house phone number.

I was astonished how Amanda grasped the ideas that I threw at her, for after all she had never done this sort of job before. She had never to my knowledge even driven a tractor, but here she was busily writing down most of our thoughts on the somewhat daunting task that we had taken on, and she asked now and then really good thoughts as I rambled on, and they were all down-to-earth and sensible. And what was more, we seemed to get on so well. I could at times see her eyes light up when she looked at me, and there was no doubt about it, I appeared to be just the person that she had been looking for. Also she was obviously more than grateful at the way that I had taken this vast load off her father's back, for although Peter was a lot better, he was by no means a fit man as yet.

We finished our lunch, the day was fine, so thought that we would take a view of our sheep which were scattered round in various fields. The best and quickest way seemed to take our motorbike with Amanda on the pillion, plus of course the faithful note and my recorder. First to find Dick and ask him where the sheep were situated, which we did and got instructions as to the best route to take and off we went.

We found part of the flock and a sorry sight some of the animals looked. Their backsides were covered with manure; a lot of them limped which meant that their feet needed a good trimming and very few of the ewes had ear tags. Their lambs needed their tails docking and again their backsides needed a clean up. At a rough count there didn't seem to be half the number of lambs that there should have been. I found myself thinking of our last estate manager for some reason or other, and found that Amanda was having the same train of thought after I had told her that there should have been a lot more lambs in view. The tups were still in with the main flock and they should have been separated a while ago, otherwise we were going to have lambing at all times of the autumn instead of the spring. We noted all that down both by voice and in a sort of shorthand notes and set off to find the shepherd.

It was unfortunate for him, for his couple of dogs who were lying outside a small hut, gave tongue as soon as they saw our motorcycle and we found the man concerned fast asleep inside the hut. I was just a bit brusque with this chap. There was a lot of work to be done in his department and it was only about 4 p.m., and he didn't finish till 5 p.m. I found a bit of paper and wrote down what was needed to be done with his flock and then suddenly thought that he hadn't a clue as to who I was, so I hastened to tell him the latest news concerning Michael who was due to leave his house in two days' time. I was then treated with a large amount of politeness and so of course was Amanda. I asked his name, which we found was Clive. I also asked the name of his house and where it was situated, and to his astonishment, I asked him as to whether he liked his situation here; and had he any problems with his house, and for good measure, was he married? He told us the name of his wife and that he had two daughters. Clive then said that his wife had trouble with the cooking stove and had asked Michael to have it mended, for of course it belonged to the estate, but nothing had been done. I told him that something would be done and as soon as I could arrange it. "*But* Clive, you have an hour before you go back to a no doubt well-earned supper, so just look at these notes." I reminded him that the next time I inspected his flock, I wanted to see some improvements. Before we departed, Clive explained about the lack of lambs, in that Michael had arranged a sale with a neighbouring farmer who had taken about 100 lambs a month or two ago.

Onto the bike again and this time armed with a rough map of the place, we toured the boundary and inspected the fencing. I was glad to see that the fence we mended the other day was still in good fettle, and the neighbour's cows were looking with keen eyes at the lush grass that we had as against their somewhat sparse 'keep'.

Back across the fields with Amanda clinging on tight. I asked her as to whether she minded if we called into my new office for a few moments, so that we could enter up the day's thoughts in the somewhat large diary that I always kept? Amanda had never seen this vast 'tome' and asked as to whether she could have a look at it? "By all means" I said, "help yourself."

"I want to look at your entry for our wedding day" says Amanda with a twinkle in her eye. "Then I shall know at first-hand what you really thought of that day of ours." She read it for a while and then said, just slightly to my consternation, that she liked my style and what was more, agreed with my somewhat basic male comments as to our wedding night. "I felt the same," says Amanda!

As we came out of the office, a tractor came up and the driver put it in its shed; got out of the cab and came across to us; touched his cap to Amanda and then asked me as to whether I was his new boss. To which I said that I was and what was his name?

"Pierre," said he with just the faintest trace of a foreign accent.

So having a guess, I asked him whether he was in fact French?

To which he said that he was, and that he liked working over here much better than his home country. "You get a house thrown in for free which never happens at home, and your machinery is far better than what the French have." He then asked as to why we never used the track-laying tractor, and I asked him the make. He replied that it was called a Ford County. I asked him as to whether he had ever used one, to which he said that he hadn't but would like to try.

So told that, time permitting I would teach him, for I used to own one. "Is there a plough to go with it?" I asked Pierre.

"Yes" said he, "with six furrows; cover a lot of ground with that," he added.

So off he went to his house and I told him that I would try and get this County working tomorrow. "That," said I to Amanda, "is yet one more thing for the diary, but I feel certain that we will then want more labour; something else for Dick in the morning at 11.30."

Then home to find a message on our answer phone from Peter asking us over for drinks and a small dinner party to follow. "Say about 19.00 hrs, and you will need a tie," added Peter.

"I hope that Helen hasn't started cooking our dinner," says

Amanda and made for the kitchen, which was empty. So she rang them up on the house phone and told Ambrose that we would be out that evening and hoped that his wife had not made anything special. Ambrose said that she was thinking of it but had not started anything.

So a bath was indicated for we were both somewhat sweaty. Amanda beat me to the bath, so I had the shower, which suited me for I could wash my hair at the same time. I heaved myself into a suit; chose my old regimental tie, and got Ambrose to shine up my shoes, whilst Amanda dried herself and put on an evening dress.

"I wish that my father had given us a bit more notice," says Amanda, "and also how big this thing is going to be, for maybe I should put on a long sort of ball gown."

I said that she looked fine and down we went hand in hand to be asked by the faithful Ambrose as to whether we would like our usual, to which we both agreed that the mere idea would make our day. I asked Ambrose when he brought the drinks in as to whether his house had faults that should be attended to, for I was making a list. "If there is anything, then let's hear about it, so whatever is wrong, can be put right."

"Well Sir," said Ambrose, "the plumbing is on the whole worn out. There is not a tap that doesn't need a new washer; the toilet leaks somewhere, and the shower doesn't work at all. Otherwise and with you and your wife now in charge as against the last somewhat," and here Ambrose coughed just a little bit and apologised for what he was longing to say, "ghastly thief of a man, we are more than happy, and I and my wife trust that the feeling is reciprocated." I hastened to say that it was.

We finished our pre-dinner drink (or so we thought), climbed into the faithful vehicle and off we went the half mile or so to my father-in-law's somewhat vast house. There we were greeted by at least fifty guests all waiting to view what Amanda had at last found to make an honest woman of her; for, and I learnt this a lot later, a lot of her immediate friends thought that she was playing fast and loose with half the males in London, which of course she wasn't.

Then Peter, dear father-in-law, he turned out to be, had to make a speech, firstly as to how we had met and how I had saved his life.

"Rubbish" I said in as loud a voice as I dared.

The speech, and it was just that, seemed to go on for ages, telling the assembled throng how lucky his daughter had been in finding little me, with all the in-built knowledge that I had acquired over the years in not only farming but also in the making or building of a golf course, which he hoped in time I would do the same on this estate.

This all ended in time and there were cries of "Speech. Speech." To my consternation, I found them all looking at me, so I also had to make a speech, about which I was ill prepared. I grabbed my young wife round the waist and up I got on to this 'rostrum' and said my bit. I then nudged Amanda to do the same, she rebelled till I said in a loud voice that surely wasn't it only the other day that she had promised to 'love and *obey*'. If looks could strike me down, I got a few from my young wife, but she did very well in her speech, in fact she kept on saying how clever she had been in choosing such a nice man. I had to nudge her to stop her repeating herself.

We then all trooped in to a sumptuous meal.

I should hazard a guess that there wasn't a single person present who hadn't got some title or other, and I was without a doubt the junior to them all. I found myself sitting between two nice girls who pointed out their respective husbands, both of whom were lords. There was also a lone duchess whose husband got ill at the last moment and couldn't make it. At the end of the meal, and there must have been at least five or six courses, I felt just a bit bloated and at a signal from someone, all the ladies got up and left us males to our port, and for those who smoked, their cigars.

Peter got up and proposed some toast or other, and to my horror suggested that I tell the assembled gathering how exactly he and I met. I sent him a friendly 'glare' across this vast table, but he merely grinned and said that it was not often that he had had the pleasure of eating at the same table with a man who had saved his life, "Over to you John."

So I lumbered to my somewhat unsteady feet and told the tale once again as to how I was fleeing on my trusty motorcycle towards Dunkirk and hopefully home, when I saw this arm waving from the roadside. "I found our present host and now my father-in-law of a few days, lying on his side with blood pouring out from a somewhat tattered limb. So observing that the recumbent figure was an officer and I was a mere gunner, I asked permission to take his tie off so that I could make a tourniquet, to which the figure gracelessly permitted, and I heaved his leg out of the tree, undid his trousers, found the wound, and tied the tie above it. I found a bit of wood, and tightened my somewhat strange bit of surgery till the blood ceased to flow. Then came the tricky bit, for my future father-in-law couldn't walk, so I heaved him up and staggered off to my motorcycle and sat him on the pillion, which by the way was merely metal bars. Again after asking his permission, I removed his hat and placed that between his bottom and the hard metal of the pillion and told him to put his arms round my waist and hold tight. Off we went to Dunkirk where I found a hospital and dumped my patient at the door into the arms of a medical orderly. We exchanged names, he was Sussex and I was Teele, and he thanked me profusely for what I had been able to do for him. I saluted him, which was the proper thing to do, and off I went. Here I might as well finish the tale, for this you, Peter, don't know about. I joined you for a short space of time in *your* hospital, although you didn't know it. The reason was as follows — when I arrived at Dunkirk, I was told to dump my poor old motorcycle into the nearest dock, and then keep my fingers crossed that I would eventually get away to Blighty. I joined countless thousands of men doing exactly the same thing, just waiting and trying to dodge the bombs that were being flung at us with monotonous regularity every half an hour on the dot. Some of us, which included me, got fed up with this and by various foul means and with the great help of REME fished out at least a dozen motorcycles from out of the docks, and when the Stukas were not operating, we had races over the sands. This is where I also got carted off to *your* hospital, Peter, for we had misjudged the time and we were bombed in the middle of a race and I got ejected into a bomb hole, which was unpleasant to a degree. You had a *leg* and I had a scalp wound, nothing serious but I was left on a stretcher for quite a while till I got somewhat bored with life and staggered up. I found an ambulance going towards Dunkirk and cadged a lift with some six other wounded types. The driver was French and had no stomach for this war, for in the middle of Dunkirk, he stopped the vehicle, and hopped out, never to be seen again. So someone asked as to whether there was a driver on board to which Teele, silly idiot said that he could drive always providing that someone would lift up and hold on to my bandage so that I could see where I was going, and off we set heading for the docks and that somewhat mythical place, Blighty. We finally got to a boat that had a mass of wounded lying on the decks and in a while off we set. So Peter," looking across the table at him, "that is something that you didn't know about." So ended my particular assistance to the evening.

After we had finished our port, off we went to join the ladies and we danced what remained of the night away. I found great pleasure in seizing my new wife from the arms of some male who no doubt fancied her, as I did in more ways than one. Finally at about 02.30 we called a halt and off we set for our various homes.

I found that I had made a lot of new friends, all of which I met again and again at various parties as the years rolled by.

There was one, a Viscount Freddy Bartholomew who was the only real working farmer, like myself in that nice 'gaggle' of new friends that I made that evening. I found myself somewhat stale as regards to present-day farming and he was a great help. He brought me up to date with things, and I was able to teach him how to plough with a crawler; an art that he had tried but had never got it quite right to his satisfaction.

The days and the weeks rolled on and slowly and I hope surely, helped no end with our daily meetings with our foreman, Dick, we started to get the place more or less shipshape.

It was the day after the party that I was due to see dear Michael out of his premises, and as usual with this man, things went a trifle wrong. He was supposed to be out of his tied house by 11.00 hrs that particular morning, and I arrived to find two somewhat large vehicles waiting patiently for his front door to open, so that the crew of the lorries could get the vans loaded. The time was 10.30, so I thundered at the knocker on the door, kept my finger firmly on the bell and finally a sleepy Michael arrived in his dressing gown and viewed me as to something that the cat had caught during the night and wanted to hide in the kitchen. So I 'thundered' at this wretched man that he had some thirty-five minutes to get himself the hell out of the house as otherwise I would personally throw him out. He viewed my 6 feet 2 inches with 12 stone to go with it and hurried away, trying to shut the front door as he went, but I had anticipated this ploy and had my foot wedged in the gap, so the door remained open. I beckoned to the removal crew, and what was a bit fortunate, in that Peter had been able to keep an inventory as to what furniture he owned, I showed them what was to remain and what was to go.

Michael arrived in the middle of all this turmoil and tried to get several bits of very nice costly furniture belonging to my father-in-law, out of the front door whilst my back was momentarily turned. But luck was on my side, I spotted this last bit of thieving before it was too late. His trunks came down last and I insisted on opening both of them, much to Michael's fury, for he had tried to pinch numerous silver items hidden under various clothes and I with great care threw a lot of his clothes onto the steps outside, just in case there was anything left which belonged elsewhere. At this we nearly came to blows, which I personally would have welcomed. I had the feeling that Michael realised that he had at last met his match, for he got his car out of the garage, and his parting shot was that he would be sending the bill for these two lorries, either to me or the duke, to which I replied quite simply, "*Get lost*." And off he went.

The last thing I heard with regards to Michael was a letter from another farmer asking me for a reference concerning Michael. I rang the farmer concerned and told him the story, for which he thanked me and that was that.

I retired thankfully to my own home, loving wife and the thoughts as to what we were going to do that afternoon. Thanks to Michael we had missed our usual morning chat with Dick, our foreman but Amanda had gone on her own and they had talked about deer, for this was one of the things that she wanted to start. Venison was at that time a rarity in the shops or the supermarkets, so that went down on the ever growing list of things that we were going to grow. We had to decide where on Amanda's acreage would be the best place. I suggested that she involve her deer in a mixture of woodland and grassland.

I should add that by this time we both shared a girl secretary who wrote letters for us, kept the books and did all this on a part-time basis from 09.00 to 13.00 Monday to Friday.

One of the many things that we needed was a reasonably large-scale map of the estate. I asked Peter if he had one but like a lot of other items it had vanished, so I got hold of the local Rural District Council and asked them whether they could provide one. They said that they could and asked what sort of scale did I want? I told them the bigger the better and that was one thing settled. Within a week they sent it and together we plastered the walls of our estate office, assisted by Geraldene, our new office girl. She was proving more than useful, because it meant that I could get out onto the land and do some work, instead of sitting on my behind for half the day, because there was quite a lot of work to do. What with writing letters; filing the copies; keeping the ledger up to date, we soon found that we had to have more or less two of everything, because costs were generally halved between Amanda's acreage and mine, although we agreed more or less from the start that we would also have a joint account for such items as our house costs. For a start, the simplest thing was to have a direct debit from our own individual accounts paid monthly, which would sort out such things as the phone bill, the gas, the electricity and general repairs.

On the day that Michael left we asked Peter over for a drink that evening, to tell him of the events pertaining to Michael's departure that morning. He was delighted that we had been able to stop the dear man from pinching a lot of furniture that never belonged to him in the first place.

We talked and talked, the three of us till Peter said, "Any ideas about the river?"

To which I apologised but said that we didn't know that he had a river. Amanda interjected by saying that it was her fault, she knew all about the river, but in the rush of getting wed and all that, had forgotten to mention it to her quite nice husband. So I was then told that between us we owned some 700 yards of both banks of this stretch of water and my mind immediately jumped to the future golf course that I intended to build on the place. This of course started a long conversation as to which of us would own the course, but decided that it was early days and it would be better to get the place running first from the farming point of view, but always with golf in the background. And so the day ended as they generally do. Dinner was served on the dot of 8 p.m. and our conversation as usual concentrated on what we were going to do where, when, and how. So to bed, holding hands as we always did. Our sex life after the first somewhat hectic first few weeks calmed down, but we enjoyed each other's bodies once or sometimes twice a week and we were blissfully happy.

I forgot which of us suggested that we have a farm shop at the gates of the estate, but few if any farms in our area went in for this sort of thing. I thought that it had possibilities for both of us, although there was always the cost of hiring someone to run the place, but it was worth thinking about, and at our next midday meeting I told Geraldene to put it down on the agenda.

Dick was all for it, for on a previous farm on which he worked, the farmer concerned had done just that and it was very popular in the immediate neighbourhood and the profits took a lot of the load off running the farm. So when I saw Syd, I told him of this plan and

D

asked him to let us know as to what he would want to build a shop roughly 30 ft by 15 ft, and to let me know when he thought that he had all the necessary materials.

By now we had been on our new home for some three months and although we had done a lot of planning, we felt that we had to get down to work to make the place worthy of being called a well-run double estate. The office, with its walls covered with maps of the place, was studied and lines were drawn so as to show what we would grow here and there. It soon came apparent that although we would halve the costs and of course the profits, it would be a lot easier if we forgot the amalgamation and treat the whole place as one.

So firstly we had separate meetings with Clive concerning his sheep. How many ewes did he think that he could handle on his own? Then Guy and his pigs and so on and so forth, so that in the end we collectively knew what stock we wanted, although the numbers had to be checked for this estate had to pay and pay well for if you remember we, that is Amanda and I had to pay her father a fairly decent sum each year.

Then came the question of cereals because we both, Amanda and I, thought the same. We should grow as much home-grown meal as possible, which meant bringing the two tractor drivers into the act and asking them as to how many acres did they think between them they could manage; not forgetting that I wanted a 'working finger in the pie', and I could cope with a certain number of acres on my own.

About this time I thought that it would be wise if I asked the National Farmers' Union for some assistance in sending some expert along to take a look at our figures, for although I had managed my own farm for years and made a profit out of it, that was all past and today was quite another matter. So a man did come along and was more than helpful. He admitted that his knowledge with regards to Amanda's future deer was somewhat scanty, and he promised to send another expert along to guide us on that particular path. He also was a bit surprised that I wanted and in fact insisted that I would take part in the work on the estate. I knew how many acres I could do on my own each day, and he admitted that he had never ploughed a yard, but his theory was first-class and that is what we both wanted so as to make a proper start. For instance he thought that two tractor drivers for the amount of corn that we expected to grow was just not practical; we needed at least two more. Then we started on combines; what machines did we have, and were they baggers or tankers and what about dryers, and what was on the estate to cope with the amount of corn that should be grown?

By this time Peter and I were getting to know each other and he seemed to like what he saw in me. It was quite obvious to anyone that his only daughter doted on me and I on her, and he asked me one day as to whether he could come into the fold, so to speak and help with the running of what had been his estate, handed down from generation to generation. He told me privately one day when Amanda was out that he had been told off by close relatives for having more or less given away the Sussex Estate.

I thought about this whilst we were both toying with a gin and tonic, and I replied that as long as he bought his own equipment, about which I would teach him as to how to handle it, then I would employ him for a sum per hour for the work that he might do on the combined estates. To my surprise, he agreed, so I had another tractor driver without the hassle of having to buy another tractor.

When I told Amanda about this, I had the feeling that she thought her father was being just slightly conned by his new son-in-law, but as I pointed out he could do work for her when he felt like it as well as for me, which calmed her down!

We woke up one morning and suddenly realised, both of us at the same second, that we had been married for six months and further more we had been in this house for the same time and that the combined estates were just starting to prosper. For instance we were milking just on 100 cows, some of them I admit were on their first lactation and not giving much more that three gallons, but they would improve. The sheep had soared ahead, and we now had almost double to what we had when we started. The pigs were also on the increase; we had commandeered a wood between us and we had some twenty pig huts scattered round the place, all fenced in nicely and the litters were putting on pounds per week when we weighed them.

Our pigman Guy, nice chap bar for the fact that he was always fighting with his wife, so much so that one day she came along to Amanda and asked her advice as to what she should do to stop this battering that she was getting more or less every day. Amanda, wise girl told the wife, whose name I always forget, to come and see me, which she did. So I learnt the whole story from this girl, and it was merely the question of cooking of all things. She would appear to cook things that Guy didn't like, thus the rows. So I got Guy into the office one day and told him what was happening to his marriage and possibly his job, and asked him to write down what he loathed most in the culinary world. This he did, and then after a decent interval, I went and saw the wife and showed her the list. Don't cook any of that for your husband and then you should find that things have calmed down. At which she almost wept with thankfulness for what we had both done for their marriage, and in fact peace did reign from that moment onwards in the pig department.

Guy was intrigued with this idea of mine as to how to cull out an unwanted family who were the worst of the bunch, merely by weighing each litter each week, and see out of all the litters we possessed which was the best from the weight point of view.

Amanda's deer were quite another matter, for although they looked a fine lot, they were always leaping out of what we both thought was a reasonable height for a fence, which in this case was six feet. But neighbours would ring up and ask as to whether we had lost a deer, always with a slight giggle at the end of the remark, giving one the thought that they, our neighbours, didn't really think we knew what we were doing in the farming world. So with quite a bit of cost, we increased the height to nine feet and that stopped the rot. The herd or flock, am never quite certain as to what one should call a 'mob' of deer, stayed in their quarters which consisted of a fifteen-acre wood and another fifty acres of grassland.

The hen battery, which we inserted into an old barn which was not really doing anything, was booming and here we were lucky enough to find a nice woman from the village who had a stalwart son, so we employed both of them. I had to teach the son the use of a tractor, for the amount of FYM that 1,000 hens produced per day was enormous, and we did in the start have slight problems as what to do with it all, for it came to about 3 cwt per day. Finally I purchased a second-hand manure spreader which took more or less a week's supply of this smelly material, and spread it over the field with the worst manurial value according to my monthly soil samples, that I checked each month and would get the result marked up on the map in the office.

We discussed all this whilst still lying in bed which made us late for breakfast, but as it was a Sunday, Ambrose didn't complain; not that he ever did.

That Sunday was a day to be remembered by both of us, for we had got into the habit of not doing much on a Sunday, but this one we thought that we really ought to start doing something about our garden. It was quite large and had been beautiful at one stage in its life, till we came on the scene. In the start we really didn't have the time to mess about in a veg patch, or a flowerbed, let alone a lawn. We also had about a dozen apple trees which badly needed a good pruning, so I took this job on and Amanda got herself busy round each tree, on a kneeler taking out weeds from the small bed which surrounded each tree. We chatted away as usual, me up a ladder and being careful not to drop anything on my wife's head, and suddenly there was a cry of pain from down below. I shot down the ladder to find Amanda spread out on the lawn clutching her stomach. I rushed over to our tool shed, got out the cleanest barrow that we had and gently levered the poor girl into it and wheeled her the 100 yards or so to the house. I got her out and into a comfortable armchair and dashed off to find a small glass of brandy. Back to our sitting room and gave her the glass and then started asking questions, such as "Do you want the doctor?"

"No" says my young wife. "I have the vague idea that you, my darling husband are to blame for this pain!"

"What are you talking about?" I asked and then a thought struck me, and I looked at my young wife and asked quite firmly as to when she had had the 'curse' last.

"Clever boy" says Amanda. "You hit the nail right on the head, and if all is well you will in due course be a father once again and I shall be a mother for the first time. I am thrilled," says my young wife. "Come here at once and let me give you a hug."

This I did with a lot of pleasure and a load of relief, for although Amanda knew my age, I had sometimes wondered with the age gap between us as to whether she had ever considered that I might just be a wee bit too old to father yet another child, but it appeared that all was well in that direction. But after the kissing had calmed down, I put on a stern voice and said "Now no more physical work, Amanda, just take it easy and rest. I will keep you posted with regards to your part of the farm, so don't worry, just keep fit. So shall we go and tell your father this wonderful news right now?"

This we did and drove up to the old house to find Peter toiling away in his garden, with two of his own gardeners doing just the same thing a few yards away, and they were chatting away, all three of them with no thought in their collective heads that one of them was a duke of the realm. Anyway Peter looked at us as we got out of the car and Amanda waved and pointed at the door. The signal got through and Peter came along, kissed his daughter and asked as to what if anything was the problem.

"Nothing" says his daughter calmly. "Merely to advise you of the fact that in a while you are due to be a grandfather."

"Good Lord" says Peter, doing mental arithmetic. "So it wasn't anything to do with my old Purdy after all. May I offer you both not only a decent bottle of champagne right now, but my love and blessing to the three of you."

So we polished off one bottle and Peter opened another. We were about to demolish that as well when I suddenly thought about all this alcohol washing round our future child, and thought that he or she would turn out to be a drunk. So I whipped the glass, which was half empty anyway, from Amanda's clutching hand and said sternly "You have had enough. Think of your offspring!" At which the party ended and we said farewell to Peter and left for our lunch at home.

The conversation at lunch was pure sex and nothing else, for Amanda said that she liked her bit of fun either before we went to sleep or in the morning, before we were properly awake. I told her that the absence of sex was just as unpleasant for me as it was for her, and we didn't want to damage the infant, did we? "But" said I, "There will be no harm done providing that you go and see our local doctor, who is a nice chap, for we met the other day at Peter's house, and he should give you the once over just to make certain that everything is OK. Then when you are getting dressed, I will put the question to him about our 'romps in the bed' and see what he says. OK?"

"All right," says Amanda, "but it is a waste of time, although I must admit that I also like the man having known him almost from my childhood days. I will ring him up and fix a date. But I promise you I will not do any manual work, that would be daft."

After lunch I had to go to the office for a while. Whilst fiddling about with accounts for both of us and putting some letters down on our Dictaphone for Geraldene, there was a knock on the door and Clive our shepherd came in and asked as to whether he could have a word?

"Of course, take a seat. What is the problem?"

"Well Sir," said Clive, "I think that we are losing sheep. I do a rough count more or less every day, and two days ago I did an exact tally and we were twelve sheep missing. I have looked everywhere but not a trace of them, and this morning there is another dozen gone. What is more I am pretty certain there are tyre tracks into the field. Would you come and see Sir?"

"Of course" I said, "I'll take my bike and you have a tractor."

After Clive had told me the field, I set off and waited a bit for Clive to come along and he then took me to where he had seen the car tracks. He was quite right, there were tyre tracks of a heavy vehicle and the wire had been cut and then mended again in a professional manner.

"Right Clive, many thanks and leave it to me for the moment. I will keep you posted."

I went and saw Peter first and told him the news, also told him what I was going to do that very night, in that I was going to keep watch with my shotgun and a .222. Just for company I was going to ask our foreman as to whether he wouldn't mind acting as my rear guard. Peter thought that it was a good idea and warned me to be careful.

I then went home and told Amanda, who at once said that she would come too. "No bloody fear you won't. Be sensible, you are with child. I shall not come to any harm, and if you are really worried I will take the spare mobile phone and keep you posted. I shall have company in the shape of Dick, plus my own 12-bore and that .222 rifle that you know I have."

So with a lot of reluctance I was allowed to make my own plans. I rang up Dick who said he would be willing and we made arrangements to meet at 22.00 hrs that very night. I explained to Dick what I thought had happened, and that this truck had entered the field about some thirty yards from where we would be hidden, and I intended to let these chaps go a certain way but no further. I then intended to blast their windscreen. "Whilst Dick, I want you to aim for their tyres if of course you are able to see them."

So we met, Dick and I, and I handed over the .222 and explained how the thing worked. I told him how to adjust the telescopic sight for we would be some thirty-five yards from our possible target, and finished with the fact that it had a safety catch and the rifle would not work if it was *on*.

And so we waited, with a nice hedge between us and where I thought that these types would try again. The sheep were all grazing and content, and suddenly in the darkness one could hear the muted exhaust of a vehicle without the vestige of any light coming our way. It halted within nice 12-bore distance and three men appeared. One heard the snip of wire cutters going through our fence and then to my surprise, two sheep dogs were let loose and I wondered as to whether they would smell Dick and I, but they didn't and off they went to gather up the sheep. The three men were well out of harm's way and I whispered to Dick to fire after my second shot. I aimed at the windscreen of the truck and let fly.

Immediately Dick did the same and exclaimed, "Got the bastard!" by which I hoped he meant a tyre.

I had time to reload and aimed another blast at what was left of the windscreen. Then I thought that it might be the time to retrace our tracks, so we left with the hope that the gap in the fence would not be noticed by any of our sheep, and we would mend it first thing in the morning. Walking back through the gloom of the night, Dick suddenly exclaimed that those three men were probably the same types who used to steal your sheep via Michael all those months ago. We heard the truck back onto its return journey, and I was determined to find out from some friendly police that I had got to know over the last six months, as to who had a burst tyre and also a somewhat broken windscreen. I had remembered to get in touch with Amanda on the way back and she was glad that it was all over, it wasn't but what we had done this night should ensure peace for quite a while. And so I crept into my bed with my wife snuggling up close to me, which I was glad about for I was somewhat chilly.

The next day I made it my business to contact my friendly policeman with some flimsy excuse, and in course of conversation asked him as to whether he knew of a lorry in the district that had a broken windscreen and for good measure, a burst rear tyre, the latter the result of good shooting on Dick's part. He asked why and I thought that it would not do any harm if I told him about my previous missing twelve ewes.

"Funny that you should ask that, Sir," he said "for I was on duty at the cattle market the other day, and I remember twelve ewes being shoved into a pen. The reason for remembering this was that the three men who did the 'pushing' had a row and they were shouting at each other. I had to go and stop the racket and one was saying that *it* must be divided up three ways."

"Any idea as to who bought the sheep?" I asked.

"Sorry Sir, I don't, but the auctioneer would know."

So I thanked him and went to the office of the auctioneers and asked them. They told me that it was a farmer some twenty miles away, and what was more the sheep were taken to this farm in the same vehicle that brought them to the market in the first place.

"Do you by any chance take a note of the ear marks, if any, on the stock that you sell?"

"But of course, Sir. Always have done. Let me have a look in the books for that day. Ah yes, here we are," and he gave me the ear marks concerned.

"Now do you by any chance have a register of animal registration marks handy?" I asked.

"Of course, Sir. Hang on for a moment and I will look it up." So I sat and waited and back he came, this nice lad, and said that the sheep had been sold on behalf of Sir John Teele, whose registration the animals bore. "May I ask Sir, the point of all this?" he asked.

"Simple my lad. I am the owner of the sheep concerned and I did *not* give my permission. In brief they were stolen," and I gave him the date the theft occurred.

"Oh Lord" came from this lad. "But we didn't know as to who the sheep belonged to."

"No" I replied, "but I bet you know the name or names of the people who asked you to sell them, and for that matter as to who you sent the sales cheque to and their address."

"Yes Sir, I do and again if you would wait a moment, I will get it for you," which he did.

I thanked him for his help and off I returned to my friendly copper and told him the tale.

"Right Sir, leave this to us for the moment. You may have to attend court, and what happens to the innocent farmer who bought your sheep in the first place, I have no idea, but no doubt that will all be sorted out in due course. I hope that you get your animals back in good shape."

So I returned to my hearth and home only to find that there was an irate merchant in my office being rude to our nice Geraldene about the prices we were charging in our farm shop which Syd had erected in the last month or more. The shop which started on its first day with just one sale of 52p, for what I have forgotten. I then went the rounds of all the supermarkets in our immediate area, made a note of the price for each edible produce, and took quite a large percentage off that, and found that we still made a quite handsome profit by growing our own cabbages, carrots, potatoes and a host of other items. So large were the queues that we had to import another helper to cope with the demand. Our labour force was growing by the week.

More or less on the due date, with Amanda waking up in the middle of the night with just a slight shriek, our first son was born, and having assisted on hundreds of births from cows to sheep to goats and even rabbits, I became the midwife and withdrew quite easily really our son from the place in which he had lived for the last nine months. I weighed him with due care and sang out to Amanda that he was just one ounce short of nine pounds. "Good girl, now just take it easy, I will do the washing, not forgetting the 'cord' and then you can have him all wrapped up in various garments that we have kept for this event." So that was that, we awoke three in a bed instead of two and found that our son took to the nipple like a ewe on to new grass.

Amanda who had looked somewhat strained over the last week or two was a changed girl. She was for want of a better word, 'radiant' and she chattered ten to the dozen, but every moment would cast an eye on her progeny to see that he was OK. Every evening she enquired after the 5,000 acres; how was it doing and what was going on on her patch?

I told her that in the last fortnight she had increased her deer by four fawns and all was well.

"What about the hens in the battery? How are they doing and what number of eggs are we getting per day?" And so on and so forth. I couldn't keep the girl quiet.

"Now what more do you want to know?" I asked. "You seem to have forgotten the shop!!"

"Yes I have for at least a fortnight" replied my young wife. "Have you opened it yet and how is that woman doing that we hired?"

"Not woman" I said, "but women. She couldn't cope on her own with the queues that formed once the prices that we charged got to be known round the neighbourhood. I will find out her name when I have a moment, but things have been busy one way and another, what with the thought of rabbits, goats, the potato harvest, where we had some twenty women picking and sorting and we clamped the lot. I mustn't forget your bull calves that are being reared on one of your fields, and remind me to tell you about such mundane things like sprouts and carrots, all of which I have been busy with whilst you my darling girl have been busy at providing me with a son. Which reminds me, what *are* we going to call the child? What other names for instance has your father? We could do worse than have one of them!"

"Now John my darling husband, will you please take the weight off your feet find a drink. I *think* that it is time that I had one as well, for I feel certain that a wee dram won't hurt my milk supply, and bring me up to date with everything that you have done in the last three weeks."

"Well" I said, "the end of the sheep stealing business was a bit fraught, for I found out who the three men were who actually did the stealing. They got sent to jail, but the trouble started when I found out who had bought the animals, for he was a perfectly sound and honest farmer, living not all that far from here and he objected strongly to *giving* the animals back to me for nothing. So that was a bit of a problem till we jointly found out that the three jailed men who started the whole thing were the people responsible, and it was they who in the end had to pay back the monies concerned. Then I found out that our cowmen, for don't forget that we are now milking nearly 100 head, had no idea as to how to rear bull calves with the assistance of an aged cow who didn't want to participate. So I had to teach them some old-fashioned methods which generally work."

"What are these old-fashioned methods?" asked Amanda.

"Well you collect the urine from the cow concerned who is reluctant to take on a suckler calf, and when you have about half a bucket full, you pour it over the calf concerned. You don't have to use the lot, just a sprinkle from nose to tail, and the cow takes a sniff, has the feeling that this really is her calf and that is all. Our two cowmen were astonished at the simplicity of this exercise. So now between us we have some thirty-two bull calves being mothered by a suitable number of foster parents and that department is doing fine."

"What else have you been doing?" asked my wife.

"Well" I said there was the somewhat explosive business about all the workers' contracts, because of course as we employ them and not your father, new contracts had to be worked out and of course signed. There was a certain amount of unrest with some of the men, because firstly I started with a time clock, i.e. every one had to sign in via the clock when they started work, and also for good measure I introduced work sheets because it is important how long a job takes. I was not fussy about a minute here or there, but I wanted to know for instance how long it took to plough a certain field. In the end they saw the point of this, but the big issue was that as most of them lived in tied houses I wanted some form of guarantee that *if* one of them left our employ, then he had to leave the house concerned within a certain length of time. I asked each of them to deposit the sum of £200 with us and we would pay each family a decent percentage, way over the current market price. This caused a bit of uproar till the first pay out came in their weekly pay packet and they all suddenly noticed that we had paid them more than their usual salary, or so they thought till I explained that the extra was their yearly dividend off their £200 divided by fifty-two weeks which would continue as long as they obey the letter of their individual contract." I told Amanda that her deer herd was increasing by the day and now she had seven fawns and I had spoken to firstly a butcher and then a supermarket manager as to whether they were interested in buying venison.

"They both said that they were, so what are we to do about that particular situation? From my point of view I am not 'up' with deer, what to cull and so on, so I suggest that when you are better, you take that problem under your wing and teach me something about the matter. The butcher also, to my surprise asked as to whether we had any rabbits for sale, to which I said that we hadn't but would give it a thought with my partner, which means you, my dear girl. By the sound of it, and the prices being asked in the butchers, they might just be a paying proposition, but I have not the time to go out with a gun and shoot the odd rabbit. *If* we do anything in that line they would have to be hand reared in hutches, and that might just mean more labour, but who knows maybe one of the present staff given a percentage of the profit might take on the job. Any thoughts on the subject?"

"Let me have some time to digest all that you have done whilst I have been increasing the Teele family," said Amanda. "What else is hidden away in that active mind of yours?"

"*Milk*" said I. "Here we are milking about 100 head, and more or less giving the end product away to the Milk Board. We ought to start thinking of selling most if not all to housewives, a job that I have done before long ago and it pays! So why not advertise in the local papers that *if* the housewife cares to come and collect her very fresh milk, then the price per pint would be XXX, but if she wanted the same fresh product delivered then the price would be YYYY. What do you think? And whilst you are thinking, the end product, i.e. the milk and maybe cheese and even butter and cream if we ever get clever enough to make it, would be sold in the farm shop which would increase sales no end. And on the subject of what I did before I had the pleasure of meeting you, I have often wondered as to how you found me because you must have had some sort of information as to where I lived, what I looked like and even more important what I had done during my life. Because it was that which gave you some ideas with regards to your father and how you thought that he was being done by that wretched man Michael, and you wanted someone who could not only marry you but also take Michael's place. Quite a tall order if I may say so, because just supposing you had found me but at the end of the day we loathed each other, what would you have done?"

There was a long pause after this little outburst from my side of the room, but finally Amanda after looking at me somewhat searchingly, said that she had hoped that I would never ask because she felt just somewhat guilty about the whole thing. "But I will tell you how it all happened, if you really want to know. It all started about a couple of years ago, when Dad got ill and I used to visit him at the hospital more or less every day. He started to tell me things about Michael and what he thought Michael was up to, and he remarked one day that although I was the apple of his eye, he sometimes wished that I had been a male and then I could have looked after the estate. I then said without really thinking about what I was saying, that I must find a nice farmer and get him to the altar. My father then told me about this man Teele saving his life at Dunkirk. 'Now he was a farmer,' says Dad. 'Nice chap too on the brief moment we had time to chat, before he had to dash off on his bike to catch up with his regiment.' 'Where did he live?' I asked. 'I have not the slightest notion' says my father, 'but I have the idea that it was south of the Thames, why I don't know. Why are you asking?' 'Well' I said 'I might just try and find him and thank him anyway for saving my father's life.' 'Don't be daft,' says Dad, 'and anyway what would be the point?' 'Nothing really' I said 'but I have the time to spare, and it might be interesting,' and that was that for the moment." Amanda continued with her story and I found it fascinating, for she was so very fond of her father and was determined to get the estate run properly and not continue to let Michael get away with murder which he seemed to be doing.

So Amanda went to Somerset House and found that there were some seventy-six Teeles in this country. She made it her business to get in touch with each one, bar for the one who happened to be in jail, but she did find out his age and he would not have fitted the bill anyway. Most of them were on the phone, and although some objected being asked somewhat personal questions about their life, she did in the end come down to the last six. By now she was getting a bit desperate but took a lot of time and money for that matter to enquire from foreign countries; the USA for one, and they had a lot of Teeles, but nobody fitted, firstly the age-group and also, and this I found quite amusing for Peter, Amanda's father had indicated that the man who had saved his life was a 'Gent' or at least he and I spoke the same sort of language, so whoever Amanda spoke to on the phone the voice on the other end had to have the right accent, which narrowed the hunt down just a bit.

Then at last she actually came to me and she caught me at a bad moment. I was furious about something, I have forgotten what but I do remember picking up the phone and more or less yelling into it, something like, "Don't you know what the bloody time is? I have had a bad day and I am dog tired, so what do you want?"

"I am sorry to disturb you," says this very charming voice. I promise that I don't want to sell you anything."

To which I interjected with "Thank God."

"But could you tell me as to whether you were in the Army during the last war?" I replied that I was, and then the voice said "Excuse me being personal, but were you ever a farmer?"

Again I replied that I had been up to about a year ago when I sold the farm and the golf course and shifted to London, because my wife had died in a car crash and I disliked living in a large house. "So now do you mind if I turn out the light and go to asleep?"

"You do that," said the voice, "and I do apologise for nattering away in this manner but I am writing a book and I wanted to find someone like you, so would you mind all that much if I rang again tomorrow morning?"

I said that would be fine and said good night and that was that but I was intrigued with that voice, it was youngish, perfectly poised as to an accent and tomorrow beckoned.

Tomorrow came as it generally does and at about 10.00 hrs the phone rang in my small sitting room and there was that voice again, saying "Good morning and I hope that I have not disturbed you."

To which I replied that she had not and then asked her as to what else did she want to know about her book, and why did I come into the picture?

After a brief moment, she said "Did you say that you actually built a golf course?"

I replied that I did with the help of a friend of mine. "When I sold out we had over 700 members which means that people liked it, why do you ask?" I replied before she could draw breath.

"Well" she said, "it sort of fits into the story that *I am trying to tell*. I know that it is a bit rude, but I gather that you now live in London. Do you think that we might meet somewhere, and then I can throw questions at you?"

"What sort of questions do you want to ask?"

"Well" says this charming voice, "how many acres have you actually run on your own?"

I replied "10,000."

"Good heavens" says this voice, "I can't wait to meet you, so what about a beer and a snack?"

I mentioned a pub that was near to me, so I wouldn't have to get the car out, and that was agreed, 12.00 hrs and then I would see who this female was that was so curious about my past history.

But just as I was about to hang up she said, "I am sorry but I find that I have another date. We will arrange another meeting place."

"OK" I replied "but I shall go there anyway."

So that was that, I had things to do in the house which I got on with and at round about 11.45 I shut my front door and walked to my lunchtime pub.

On the way I noticed a somewhat nice-looking car with a female behind the wheel with, of all things, a pair of binoculars which seemed to be aimed in my direction, but I took no notice. I arrived at my pub, greeted my various friends, accepted a drink from one of them and six of us settled down to pull the world apart as was our wont on most days of the week. After a few beers we ordered our various meals and settled down once again to eat and talk when the door opened and a most ravishing female entered. She parked her almost regal bottom on a stool and ordered a drink and then she did a curious thing, she turned round and looked directly at us six, but I had the feeling that she was actually looking at me. But welcome as was the look, I had never glimpsed the girl before, so I took no notice and went on eating, and in time she went and that was that as far as I was concerned.

A few days after that there was the usual get together of some thirty or more friends. This generally happened on a Saturday and we took it turns to 'throw' out the invites and of course supply most of the drink, although I noticed after a few months of this quite nice get together, that quite a lot of people were bringing along a contribution in the shape of a bottle of whisky or gin and sometimes wine. One nice woman brought along a whole side of smoked salmon and her husband, not to be outdone, handed out a loaf or two plus butter, so I started to do the same, but I bought rum and a bottle of lime, which proved quite popular after a few cautious sniffs of the mixture. But the interesting thing was that this girl who I had last seen parked on a bar stool at the pub I frequented, was generally present and I could not help noticing that she always seemed to be glancing in my direction. We used to take it turns to act as a sort of doorman, firstly to check any gate-crashers because it was obvious that a party was going on by the number of cars parked outside the house concerned, and also the noise that was being emitted by the happy guests, and also to collect any bottles, etc., that were being handed in. Whilst I was bending down to 'park' the last bottle, a hand touched me on the shoulder and there she was, as beautiful as a picture and holding out a small bottle of whisky and asking as to whether that was sufficient. I am not often tongue-tied but I knew firstly by the voice on the phone all those months ago that this was the same girl, although she was dressed differently now as when I saw her in the bar. Without further ado I said something to the effect that although we had 'met' on the phone and other places, I had not a clue as to her name, and asked her what it was?

"Amanda," she said.

"And the surname?" I asked.

"Oh it doesn't matter about surnames. Mine is a funny one and people joke me about it, so just call me Amanda and I shall call you John."

I was about to ask the next obvious question as to how she knew that I was John, but she interrupted my thoughts and asked me as to whether I would kindly lead her in. I was about to say that I was too busy for that but there was nobody at the door and her hand was gently but quite firmly leading me up the short stairway into the house. I had no choice but show her where to hang her coat. I then equally firmly excused myself and left her to her own devices after first signalling to one of the hosts that a new guest had arrived. I then dashed back to the front door just in time to greet the next couple who were joining the throng upstairs. I took their bottle, counted up the tally of guests who had come and found that we were complete, so with my volunteer job over I went and joined the party.

"And then there was the excuse me dance and you and I started from there, is that right?"

"Yes" says Amanda. "are you annoyed at how I manoeuvred you into marrying me?"

"You didn't really," I replied "for if I had met you naturally I would have fallen in love with you anyway without the slightest prompting from you. So forget the beginning of you and I and let us get on with this excellent job that you have found for me. I don't know which of us thought about the shop, but it is going very well and the profits help a lot. The local shopkeepers are not all that fond of us, for more or less with every product we have cut their prices to ribbons. I have the feeling that we ought to create a car park of sorts, for the other day I counted some seventy-two cars parked around our little shop, and I also think that we should enlarge it somewhat for the crush is enormous. I also think that it was a mistake to start a milk round, for most if not all the housewives prefer to come to the shop where they get their milk cheaper and their eggs and all the other things that we cart around in the van. Also I am faintly suspicious of our roundsman. I have the distinct feeling that some of the coins that should come our way, are finding their way into his pocket. I have Syd building rabbit hutches by the dozen, and soon we must decide on what breed to buy and produce. The supermarkets are quite keen on this idea of English rabbits as they are with English venison. I also, with all this potential saleable meat on my mind, wonder as to whether we ought to have our own abattoir for the cost of slaughtering an animal and preparing it for sale to the supermarkets is quite considerable. Now you Amanda, might take on that task. You have a quick active mathematical brain, get it to work on that problem, for don't forget although at the moment we are making money hand over fist, we still have to pay your dad his rent for our combined 10,000 acres, not forgetting repairs to the houses that we own, or Ambrose and his problems which I would like to sort out as soon as possible for he does us very well. The other thing that I would like my rather nice partner to think about, is the question of our woods. I suppose we have about three to 500 acres of woods and some of them need felling and replanting. Another little something for your young brain to think about are logs to the shop and all that! Whilst you are contemplating all this, may I remind you that there is a certain noise coming from above our heads which means that Peter George Teele is after a nipple. Shall I bring him down to you?"

So up I went and it was a delight to wrap our son up in his blanket, with his eyes fixed on me, whilst I muttered nonsense to him, all of which I am sure that he understood. I carefully came downstairs with both of us eyeing each other, and I delivered him to the port nipple to which he adhered with a firm grip.

After that session was over, Amanda insisted that she put him back to bed, after a stroll round the garden showing Peter George each plant *ad nauseam.*

We then strode our trusty Honda motorbike and wandered round the estate to see what had been done, what hadn't and what I would personally do from the ploughing point of view, for I was anxious to get our one and only crawler and its six-furrow plough back into action.

Bringing the possible reader up to date, we had been owners, more or less of 10,000 acres between us. We had increased the milking herd to 100 milking cows, and most of the produce was sold in the shop; some of the milk being converted to cream and after that cheese and the remainder, the pigs ate with great gusto. We had started a new farming idea with deer and they and their offspring were doing well and we had even slaughtered a few. I viewed the advertisements in the local shops selling our products with great interest, made even more interesting by the signals that came through to us that they all wanted more and more venison. Then there were requests for rabbits and yet more rabbits but they all had to be ready for the housewife. It was no use giving the retailer a rabbit complete with fur, head and all, it had to be prepared ready for the oven, or whatever the cook wanted to do with it. Syd by this time had produced some seventeen hutches and runs, and they were all full with does and their offspring, waiting for the time to wean them off mum.

I must admit that although the rabbit idea was paying well, I did find them a bit of a nuisance. Mainly because of the two or three buck rabbits that we had who always seemed to spurn the attractive-looking doe that we would throw at them. But my brain started to work when I thought of the rams with the sheep. Each ram's chest was 'raddled' with a colour and he would 'mark' his prospective wife, when he mounted her with *his* colour. So I adopted the same tactics with the buck rabbits and soon found out that the bucks were having a fine old time, mounting their selective wives as often as they wished. So that solved that problem and soon we would be able to sell a load of offspring to whomsoever wanted them.

Amanda thought that she ought to have a nurse for our son, for I appeared to be doing all the work for the two estates and all she was doing was looking after our son and heir. So we advertised and several of the female sex applied and we chose one who did not make eyes at me as most of them appeared to do, much to Amanda's annoyance.

She, my young wife, I soon found out was jealous of my prowess at most things in the farming world, such as ploughing and all that and then there was the animal side of the business for I was quite used to shoving my complete arm up the backside of a cow to see whether she was with calf or not and Amanda wanted to learn the lot. So I started her off with a small three-furrow tractor in a twenty-acre field and I did one half and she did the other. It soon became apparent that her side of the field was just a trifle different to mine and she wanted to know what she was doing wrong. "Just keep that front wheel of yours turning left all the time, but keep it in the furrow and you will find that your plough will do the work for you." Then I gave her discs to bring her furrows down to sowing size, and finally a large harrow, and there was Amanda's field, all of twenty acres, ready to sow, this time with winter wheat. I showed her how to use our one and only combined sower, with seed in one side, fertiliser in the other and with the harrows trailing behind. Off she set, giving me a wave of pure joy as she set off, for she was very anxious to do her bit, as well if not better than her husband.

And so a year had passed. My father-in-law had got more and more interested in how the whole place worked from the machinery point of view, and was becoming quite proficient in most things, but the silage machinery foxed him somewhat for he could never quite get the trailer into which the chopped silage was blown, in the right spot and a lot of what could have been excellent winter fodder was thrown into some convenient hedge. We had enlarged the shop by half and it was still crammed with housewives, some of whom did the picking of our various crops such as Brussels, carrots, potatoes and various other crops that we tried. And even Amanda used to insist on doing a morning's work out in the fields and here was her Ladyship, daughter of a duke, in company with our villagers, filling buckets with all and sundry which finally ended up in the shop. She was also getting keen on gardening. Our half an acre of garden, some of it lawn and the rest down to veg, looked a lot better than a year ago, and she took a pride in showing me what she had done.

Then came the river and the part which we now owned. Although I had ideas about this stretch of water from the point of view of the future golf course, it seemed pointless not to try and earn some money from it now. So I talked to my partner, Amanda and we agreed that we might as well advertise it and charge each rod a sum per 100 yards and see what happened. Having taken a somewhat guilty afternoon off a while ago and tied a decent-looking fly onto the end of my rod, I was somewhat surprised at the number of good-sized trout plus two youngish salmon that fell for my lure. The advertisement went in the local paper which was published on a Wednesday, and by Friday we were full of keen fly fishermen and here was yet another, not so small, extra to our yearly income.

We staked each stretch of water out with white posts and stuck a label on it, giving the name and when his time was up and if he wanted to renew. I put Dick in charge of the fishing and he got quite keen on the sport. I lent him a rod, and the necessary tackle, showed him how to tie a fly, and most important of all, how to cast without getting the hook into his ear. I felt somewhat mean when I told him that if he landed two fish, then one must be put back, and in fact he could not take more than one fish home to his house per day.

Our young beef were growing well and we thought that another couple of months should see them safely into the market.

The pigs caused a bit of a stir in the local market, because as you know we weighed each litter every Friday, and we had decided before we started the pig business that we would take the whole litter, sow and all to market because they would be the worst growers out of some thirty sows. This we did one market day and everyone was somewhat surprised, for although they had seen heaps of pigs and for that matter sows sold individually, they had never seen a whole family sold, especially as I guaranteed the complete weight of the litter. The selling price confirmed that we must continue in this line, for the percentage per piglet was vast compared with a pig of some four months, whilst this lot were only two months old, but they looked good and it was obviously a family concern in the pig world, so the buyer was more than content.

I almost forgot to mention a very strange little income that crept into our account books, and that was the selling of weaned-off lambs to house-holders who for some reason or other, had no dog but the idea of tethering a lamb on their lawn so as to eat the grass and save them from mowing went down rather well, especially as we could sell the lamb for twice what we would have got in the market, and we used to throw in a bag of suitable meal into the bargain.

Peter came round to see how we were getting on. He arrived about gin time, so we sat and talked and we told him what we were doing and for that matter what we had done with the rabbits, the deer, the pig families, the shop and the sheep. But Peter although he was more than interested as to how we were getting on, possibly owing to the fact that we both sent him our respective rent cheques which always arrived on the due date, wanted to know what ideas, if any, I had come up with regards to this golf course idea that we had talked about all those years before. So I told him my thoughts. I told him that I had already got a rough idea of where the course would be, the par and all that, but what I was wondering about were the buildings, the clubhouse, the pro's shop and a whole lot more. I was not certain as to whether our resources at this moment would stretch that far. The course itself, now that I had heard about the river, was forever in my mind because water, indeed running water, used sensibly was an added asset to a golf course. Not only would it water the greens when necessary, but it would add some very interesting holes on the course.

Peter, bless him came up with the thought that he would be responsible for all the buildings, but we, Amanda and I, would have to be prepared to have an increase in our present yearly rent, and he suggested a figure which presented no great problems for us two from a financial point of view.

So casting aside farming chatter we started on this golf business, for Peter was a keen golfer, and so was I, having had some sixteen years of past experience of not only building a golf course, but running it with just one OAP who worked from 06.00 to 12.00 six days a week for three years. We decided that we wanted six par 3s, six par 4s, and finally six par 5s which came to seventy-two. Personally I thought that this was a bit long, not long for the golfer who played more or less every day, but I was thinking of the green fee player who only wanted a morning off work, legally or otherwise, and a par 70 was about all that he could cope with plus a pint and a sandwich. I informed Amanda and Peter as to my thoughts, generated years ago and how well it worked with London taxi drivers coming down for a morning's golf, starting from their home at 06.00 and getting back to work at about 12.00. We used to get thirty at a time.

"So when do we start?" asked Peter.

"When we get planning permission" I replied.

"Oh I didn't know that we had to get planning permission," says Peter.

"And what is more, when the golf club is built, we want a drinks licence thrown in for good measure," says I.

So we went down to the office, having finished our drinks, and started seriously looking at the maps. I had already decided the plan of campaign as to where the first hole would be and for that matter the tenth, because they should be close together. I had wondered how people were going to get to the place, for I was certain that Peter didn't want hordes of cars passing his house day in and day out. I had found a lane on the map, a long distance from any habitation connected with us, and that is where I planned to have an entrance to the golf course. So first to find an architect, then to get a form from the Council so as to apply for planning permission to build an eighteen hole golf course plus clubhouse, pro's shop and a few other buildings that were necessary. Then the thoughts about the necessary machinery to build the course; where to get the turf for the greens, for I was determined to build this one as I had built the previous one, and that was with excellent turf on all the greens and somewhat different turf for the tees; sand for the bunkers and so on and so forth. But assuming that we did get planning permission, then we wanted before anything else to plan out the course, using the river for at least two holes, and as far as I was concerned, keeping the standard scratch score down to about seventy.

I was thinking in the region of about 160 acres plus a practice ground of about fifteen acres, for if this future golf course was anything like the one I built all those years ago, one had very nice people applying for membership who had never played golf in their lives. Whereas they would be more than welcome as members, they *must* learn how to play first and this was what the practice ground was used for with the able assistance of the pro, who taught them for of course a fee. This practice ground had three holes, a par 3, 4 and a 5 and the would-be member had to be able to do this mini course in an acceptable figure. Then and only then could he or she be admitted to the main course; the idea worked well. From the machinery point of view all I wanted was a JCB, for every future green had to be excavated to a certain depth; cinders thrown in for drainage purposes plus a few other oddments, and then and only then could one start to lay down the precious and somewhat costly turf and no way must a human foot be planted on it for at least a few months. So boards were used, on which the feet of the builders of the green walked, and as they walked they placed a turf gently down till they crossed the future green, then moved the planks and laid down another layer and so on till they reached the other side, and then curved the whole thing as they wanted it to look in six months' time.

Our staff had risen to eleven by now for we were milking around the hundred mark. Most of the products went down to the shop where a pint of milk was a lot cheaper than in the local supermarkets, much to their fury, although on odd occasions if and when they got short, they would come along to us and take what we could spare, which had its amusing moments.

The vegetables, although the most profitable commodity that we produced were a bit of a headache, for we had about fifty acres of potatoes, ten of sprouts and a few more acres of this and that. The labour needed was at times vast, for at times some supermarket would ring up and demand a hundredweight of sprouts, ditto carrots and 5 cwt of spuds, not next week but tomorrow. So I had to gather together a willing lot of helpers from the village who would if it were possible come at a moment's notice and do the necessary work; not all that easy for we needed about twenty people to do the picking. We supplied the bags if possible, otherwise the pickers would pick and come along and have their 'pickings' weighed and be paid by weight. Then the resulting produce would have to be taken down to the various shops and money collected.

To add to all these problems, my young wife one morning whilst we were having a quiet breakfast and struggling with the easy crossword in the *Telegraph*, got up and came round to my side of the table, put her arms around me, and whispered that she had something to tell me. I, who was struggling with some clue or other, somewhat impatiently but gently disentangled myself and asked what it was that she wanted to tell me.

"I'm with child again, a friend for Peter George."

I must admit that before I kissed her and patted her rather nice shape, I wondered how I was going to cope with the lot; all of the 10,000 acres and now possibly the golf course, for Amanda when she got pregnant took things very quietly and left the lot to me, but every evening she wanted to know what I had done that day. This reminded me of Chile in a way, for my first wife and I after the war went out to Chile and there farmed the same acreage, i.e. 10,000 acres, but it was vastly different than dear old England. In Chile we had more that eighty men and their wives on the place, and compared with where we are now with a dozen or so, one wonders what all that lot got up to. We did a lot of logging, for we had some 3,000 acres of virgin timber which we gradually felled, up rooted the old stumps, and planted something young and new. We made the felled trees into rafts and floated them down the vast river by our house, and the rafts landed up at a timber yard some forty miles away. There we milked some fifty cows, got foot and mouth more or less every year, and cured the lot, whereas here we kill anything even faintly connected with the disease. There we ploughed by bullock with a two-furrow plough, here we use a nine-furrow reversible plough with tractor.

The other difference which used to worry me was that the workforce regarded me as something akin to God, and would bow every time they met me and their wives would do an old world curtsey. We used to build them small houses for they came to work and live with us with nothing to their name, bar for hordes of children. For the roofs of these little houses, we used to chop up wooden tiles and lay them down similar to tiles, but when they wanted a fire to cook something they would take or rip off half a dozen tiles so as to start the fire, and of course gradually when the rains came, they got somewhat wet.

And then there were the goats. We had some 2,000 goats, merely because years ago some idiot Frenchman brought in a wild blackberry for his garden and the damn things spread and spread over half if not the whole of Chile. There came a law that you had to keep the blackberry in check and if possible kill it off, and goats *loved* blackberry, so we in company with countless other farmers had goats by the thousand, and shifted them on from one patch to another and they really ate the wretched stuff down to the roots. Then we would put in our vast plough, all of two furrows, pulled by one or two bullocks and hopefully turn the earth over and bury the blackberry roots, get in touch with the local powers that be and claim that we had destroyed some number of hectares and would they pay us the going rate, which they generally did. But I never want to eat kid again as long as I live, for although some people think that they are akin to lamb, to my mind they are not, and are far too rich for my taste.

But back to dear old Sussex with a pregnant wife, a very small son, a charming father-in-law in the shape of the Duke of Sussex and about a dozen staff. The first frosts arrived, and with that of course came the time to pick the Brussels sprouts. We had a lot of sprouts, acres of the dear things, plus carrots; you name it, we seemed to grow it and for some reason or other whatever we grew, they seemed to become giants. So we advertised in the local paper and the women came in droves. At one time I counted some fifty locals all filling up their bags, which were then weighed carefully for they were paid by the bag, and then the bag would be delivered to one of the many supermarkets in the area and of course our shop where we almost gave the things away.

To cap all this activity, Ambrose came along one morning carrying carefully our ration of G&T and asked as to whether he could have a word?

"Of course," said I "what can we do for you?"

"Well Sir," said Ambrose, "this is the time when we generally have our fortnight's holiday and we were wondering as to whether this Saturday would be convenient for us to depart?"

My thoughts raged through my head; a pregnant wife; a very busy time of the year for us; the shop was overflowing with customers and in fact I on rare occasions served behind the counter because of the crush of people. Amanda's deer kept on throwing out their progeny; the rabbits were breeding much too fast, *but* Ambrose and his nice wife did us proud, so I said, "Of course Ambrose. Off you go on Saturday and I trust that the weather will be fine for you both."

So I started to think, and Amanda did some thinking as well, for it was autumn, the first frost had come and gone and no doubt it would appear again, so the sprouts, some twenty acres of them, must start to be picked. So I phoned up my girl friend in the village and asked her thoughts on the subject of sprouts and how many girls would she be able to muster.

"After the sprouts, then maybe the carrots, who knows, must take things calmly" said Amanda with her feet up on the sofa and nursing her already somewhat large tum. "Don't forget the potatoes" says my wife, "a mere ten or more acres."

I suddenly felt that the whole world had descended upon me; all these vegetables; the milk; the cream; the butter; customers from the shop clamouring for this and that; ploughing for the next season and the thought of red clover, for we had none, it had died out and we had to resow. And those damn rabbits, they were breeding faster than we could sell them, but I must admit I had never realised the profit there was to make over a mere rabbit. Then there were Amanda's deer, their offspring were in high demand, and one must not forget the pigs. Their complete litters plus their mum were amazing in what they would bring in in the shape of cash. Finally there was the future golf club bearing down on my somewhat bowed head, but at the moment I could not see my way clear to start on that, it will have to wait a while.

Suddenly, for no particular reason, maybe I was looking at my young very pregnant wife, at the thought of children and from children I went on to the many animals we had, I suddenly realised that I had done nothing about our flock of sheep. Between us we must have had about 500 and that was why the tups, or rams might be better description, were making such a noise, they wanted a wife or more and I had done nothing about it, and what is more neither had the shepherd, I must have a quiet word with him.

Now the reader of this tale may or may not know that when you insert a male sheep into a flock of his future wives, you mark his breast with a colour mark, for want of a better word, so that when he mounts his wife, he leaves a mark on her rump. But as half this flock belonged to my wife and the other half to me, it might be handy to know as to which ewe had been marked by which colour, so that in time they and their progeny could be divided up and if necessary sold. So I asked Amanda as to what colour she wanted, and she wanted a plain red, so I settled on blue. The next day with due ceremony, we both opened the rams' gate and in they flocked, and very soon there were red and blue bottoms all over the place.

Then Peter came on the scene again to report that he had permission from the Council to build a golf course and for that matter a clubhouse to boot and various other small buildings that we had nominated. He asked would I kindly draw up a plan with regards to the clubhouse, so we invited him over for lunch the next day.

So with a large G&T on either side of us, bar for Amanda for here I stuck my fatherly foot in, for she was within a few months of giving birth. I gave her a lemonade, which she was not all that keen on.

"Well Peter, for a start you want a flattish bit of ground about 100-feet square near this small road. In it, firstly you want a decent-sized cellar more or less in the middle, and that wants to be about 12-feet square with a headroom of some 8 feet, above it, directly under the bar with three of four openings onto firstly the mixed lounge, the women only lounge, the nineteenth bar, which can be small and the mixed men's area. Then on the first floor you want a decent-sized dining room with kitchen beside it and going back below stairs, an office is wanted to house the secretary and his staff or maybe two girls, but I suggest that is in a separate building. Then there is the pro's shop and a cottage/house for the people who work the clubhouse. That is about your lot, always bearing in mind that the ladies want a locker room of their own with about three loos and a couple of showers, plus about forty lockers, and the men want the same but a bit bigger, not forgetting that in the main building there should be a billiards room and possibly a bridge room and surrounding the lot a veranda. Also there will have to be a car park for at least a 100 cars, which should be Tarmacked with white lines on the slant. Personally, Peter I should get yourself a good architect, tell him our collective thoughts and let him get on with it, and putting in his own, no doubt, many questions. He will recommend a builder, but personally I should go out and make some enquires as to builders on your own, for architects have their own favourite builders and sometimes these firms are very costly. And we must not forget that we have to send the completed plans to the Council for their approval. From our point of view we have to think about future machinery. We shall want a JCB for starters, for eighteen greens have to be built, and here one goes down to quite a few feet so as to insert cinders, gravel, drainage pipes and finally decent earth topped up with a vast number of very good quality turves. Then there are some sixty to seventy bunkers to construct which is a fairly easy job. Where we have corn growing at the moment, and that area is thought to be included in the future course, then undersowing of the corn has to be done very soon. We can cope with the rough with the gear that we have at the moment, but we shall have to buy a mower for the fairways and maybe the tees, and from the point of the tees, we shall want at least three per hole. Manpower; to my mind, although I can do a lot of this myself, I have the feeling that I shall want at least two extra men for about nine months, which is the time that I have set myself to build the course. You Peter must be the first president, for if I may say so, your title will attract a lot of golfers. When we are a little more forward with our plans, I would suggest that you hold a meeting in the village hall so as to advertise the fact that you are going to build a golf course. So now what about a bit of lunch? Not up to our usual standard for our house staff are on holiday, and your daughter and I have concocted this meal, but you should survive!"

After lunch I insisted that my young wife went to have her afternoon nap, for time was running out for her and the future birth of an addition to the family.

When Peter and I were alone I told him that, although Amanda didn't know it, twins were expected, and swore him to keep that information to himself. I was worried, needlessly as it turned out to be, but I could never keep Amanda still for more than a couple of minutes and she was vast, and I wondered as to whether she knew that she had twins huddled together in that vast stomach.

Peter George, our son of this marriage, was causing some worries for I had neither the time or for that matter the inclination to entertain him from morning to nightfall, so we decided, Amanda and I, that we ought to engage a live-in nanny for we had plenty of space, and she could have her own private suite consisting of a bedroom, sitting room and of course her own loo and a bath. But she would be one of the family, so to speak, as long as we could find the right one.

We advertised all over the place, and females arrived and were seen, most were rejected and we even had a couple of men. We checked all their references and finally came down to a couple, from which we chose Phyliss, mainly because at one time in her career she had been a midwife, which as it turned out helped a lot. Peter George adored her which helped, in fact I had the feeling that

Amanda was just a trifle jealous of the feelings that her son had for this nanny, especially when Peter asked as to whether he could move his bed into Phyliss's bedroom, to which we told him that she wanted a bit of privacy, so that ended that one.

Winter was upon us and my big problem at the moment was to get the sprouts picked and sold, together with acres of carrots, spuds by the ton, plus a lot of other vegetating plants that seemed to have taken root all over the place.

Then came the attempted burglary of our house, which couldn't have come at a worse time for Amanda was on the verge of giving birth and I was overworked and very tired. I had gone to bed at about 21.00 hrs together with Marcus, our somewhat fierce Alsatian/ Great Dane cross, who always slept in our bedroom in a vast basket.

I was woken at about 01.00 hrs by Marcus's nose exploring quite gently my face, and I woke and asked in the most politest manner as to what he was trying to do. At which he growled, a deep far down rumble which swept over my face and forced me awake. He wagged his tale with the deepest apology and trotted to the bedroom door, which either meant that although I had shoved him out into the garden before we went to bed, he now wanted a bit more garden, *or* it was something else that was worrying him. And then I heard it, it was a gentle noise where noise shouldn't be, i.e. downstairs, and it was in the drawing room. I slid out of my bed, took my World War One bayonet from my bedside and without waking wife, crept out into the corridor and proceeded very quietly to the head of the stairs, followed by Marcus who also was well into the act, and he never uttered a sound. On the third step downwards, I saw them; two backs facing me and they were more than interested, according to the moonlight coming through the windows in the drawer in which my sleeping wife kept some of her jewels. I didn't consider what was the best thing to do, I just leapt, with my two somewhat large feet extended but flattened, and aimed each at one back. I was lucky enough to hit both at more the less the same moment; one shot into the fireplace and hit his head and remained silent whilst the other started to struggle to his feet. Here Marcus came into the act, he paused just a trifle at the unconscious figure in the fireplace, but pounced on the other figure that was trying to rise to his feet and held him down with a vice-like grip on what I discovered afterwards was the man's thigh. He screamed, so I manhandled Marcus off the thigh, sat on his back and with a lot of luck found a ball of string within reach and bound his hands very firmly behind his back. I got off him and told him to stay quite still as otherwise I would put the hound on him again. I got to the phone and dialled 999 and suggested that they send an ambulance as well for the first man, as after hitting his head on the fireplace he had remained very still; a *fact that worried me somewhat.*

It seemed within minutes that firstly a sleepy-looking wife appeared and then the police car with sirens sounding, arrived followed by an ambulance. I calmed down Marcus, ushered in the police and then the ambulance men, who after examining the recumbent figure by the fireplace, pronounced him dead. The tied-up figure on the floor was then examined by a constable who first handcuffed him and then removed my somewhat amateurish string tying around his wrists. He told him sternly to stay where he was and then they came to me and said that they wanted all the details of this burglary, and in particular how I had killed the figure still lying more or less in the fireplace.

So I explained exactly what had happened, as to how I had been woken up by the dog who knew that something was happening downstairs, and together we went down and how I had leapt on the backs of the two men who were keenly examining my wife's jewellery. "That one was unconscious for he had been more or less thrown into the fireplace, and then I turned my attention to the other man who was at that time attempting to rise to his feet, so I forced him to lie down, bound his hands, and phoned for you people and an ambulance for good measure."

We had been sitting in my study doing all this talking and Amanda was present, dressed in a somewhat flamboyant dressing gown, with her feet encased in an aged pair of my woollen slippers.

At the end of my midnight chat, the police conferred together and the inspector asked as to whether he could have my word that I would not leave my home, and that they would be back in the morning at 10.00 hrs for a further discussion.

The ambulance men then removed the dead body from the fireplace, and it was then that I saw his face for the first time, for when I had hit him in the back he had dived straight into the fireplace with his face down. I recognised him instantly, it was Ron, a close friend of Michael, the ex-manager who had stolen from my father-in-law. Ron was always hanging around the estate when Michael was working for us. I had spoken to him on a few occasions and one day I caught him gazing suspiciously through a window of my house. He said he was looking for Michael, but I didn't believe him. We had a big argument and I threw him off the estate. So I turned to the inspector and told him that now I had seen his face, I knew him, and told him the whole story. The man on the floor was jerked to his feet and escorted out to the police car, and we were left alone for the remnants of the night!

The next morning after having risen at my usual hour of 06.00, dressed somewhat scantily, viewed the milking and saw that everything was more or less as it should be, I saw that Dick was also viewing the workforce that had turned up, and was making a note as to who was still absent. I had a word with him as to what, out of the various jobs that I had 'thrown' at him a few days ago, he was going to do and departed for a shower and a shave.

The police arrived at about 09.00 and asked me politely if I would come down to the station and make a statement as to what had happened last night, so they could get their facts straight, as of course there would have to be an inquest.

I said that I would be with them at 10.00 and they departed. Amanda and I started to discuss the whole wretched business, and firstly I cursed myself in telling the police that I knew the dead man on the floor. It made the whole thing look just a bit suspicious in that I had known the man that I had killed, and worse still was the fact that we had a row before he finally left. Still the deed was done and it seemed obvious at the time that Ron was as usual more or less broke and needed money badly, possibly because of his drug habits, and our house seemed to be the best bet, although the duke's house was a lot bigger than ours, but he had dogs roaming the gardens.

The police were more than pleasant. I was asked as to whether I would like tea or coffee, and two of them plus the usual microphone settled down to hear my story, starting years ago, from the trip to Dunkirk and rescuing the future duke and also of course my future father-in-law, to the present day. I told them also about my wife's suspicions with regards to Michael, and how in the end I had proved her right in that he had been stealing left right and centre, and in the end how I had sacked him.

"Well that's more than kind of you, Sir John" said the senior policeman. "I don't think that you will have any further troubles with this case, although of course you will have to attend the inquest and may be called to give evidence of this accidental death of a burglar."

So that for the moment was that. I went on with my work, constantly worried as to when Amanda was going to start her pains. A couple of days later the police rang up and said that the inquest was for tomorrow, and would I be present at 10.00 hrs ready to give evidence when needed.

Tomorrow arrived and down I went to the court and when asked gave what evidence I knew about the man who I had accidentally killed. A verdict of misadventure was returned. I must admit that I was more than relieved, for it is not everyday one just happens to kill someone who you knew, albeit for only a week or two and be acquitted, in fact, the bench praised my actions on that somewhat action-filled night.

We then returned, mentally at any rate, to the estate and of course the future golf course. I had arranged a well-publicised meeting, at the village hall, and primed the duke on what he had to say. I got his solicitor to be there as well just in case there were any awkward questions. I sorted out chairs and on the due date waited in some trepidation as to what was going to happen that evening.

But I need not have worried, the place was packed. I think that the people who came were firstly interested in meeting a duke face to face and also, even more important, there was at that time an acute shortage of golf clubs in our particular area, and they wanted membership even before I had started work on the place. I had taken the precaution of drawing up plans for the course, and these were on a board for all to see. The river became a great source of discussion at the meeting, because I had arranged the first hole, albeit a par 3, to cross the water, a somewhat daunting thought when one walks on to the first tee on any course. I envisaged sometime in the future of rigging a net under the water so as to be able to collect the fallen balls. The distance as far as I could judge in those early days, was in the region of 150 yards from tee to green, with some convenient bunkers placed round the green. The meeting went well; the hall was filled to the brim with a lot of people having to stand as we had run out of chairs. The duke gave a fine speech, for after all he was quite used to making speeches here and there. At the end of the meeting, the possible future members were asked to write their names down on the paper that I had left on each chair, together with their address, phone number and if they were a member of a golf club at the moment and its name. The last bit of information was handy because if one was not quite certain about a future member, one could always phone up the secretary of the club concerned and make some discreet enquiries.

After the meeting where at least 300 people put their names down for future membership, came the tricky business of choosing a builder for the future clubhouse because although I was more than happy about the actual building of the course, although I needed some two extra hands for the work, the club building had to be perfection.

So we advertised for builders who had actually built a golf clubhouse, rather than the no-doubt excellent people who built bungalows by the score and several came and looked at our plans. We of course asked them as to which clubhouse they had actually built. Then life became a lot easier for all one had to do was to phone up the secretary of the club concerned and ask them their opinion of their clubhouse and we narrowed the list of about six to a firm two. Neither Peter or I could make up our minds, so we gave the decision over to my very large pregnant wife and left her to choose. She decided on one chap because she found out that his wife was expecting twins at any moment. The two met and Amanda came back having told me which she had chosen and said that she wished that she could have twins. I nearly told her that she *was* going to have twins anyway but thought better of it in the end and kept my big mouth firmly shut.

Peter, bless his kind heart, insisted that we share the cost of building the clubhouse and ended by accepting 5% of the net profits (if any) generated by what this clubhouse would actually make.

So yet another facet was included in this 10,000-acre estate. The clubhouse builders and I, purely by coincidence, started work on the same day; they with their machines for excavating the foundations and me arguing the toss with the first somewhat tricky hole, which crossed the river. I had to make quite certain that the direction of all the tees were directed at the centre of the proposed green, and also that the green itself was not all that close to the river, otherwise all hell would break loose.

I thought that a leeway of round about fifty yards from the edge of the river to the centre of the green would be about right, but luckily I remembered what I did years ago when I built my first golf course. I got three friends of mine, all reasonable golfers, to aim shots from the first tee, although in that case there was no river to contend with, but here of course there was and this is where these mates of mine came in more than handy. Andy played off a 4 handicap, John was in the region of 12, and Steven was on a somewhat dodgy 18, whilst I was in the region of 20 with the wind firmly behind me! So I bought about fifty old balls, plonked them down on the first imaginary tee and having stuck a stick in over the river where I thought the centre of the green might be, told them to start shooting. Simple for Andy, over the water he went with some lofty iron, whilst John with about a three wood also passed well over the water, but the remainder of us amateurs lost at least half a dozen balls into the water. So the distance from the water to the green had to be shifted by at least thirty yards, and the resulting bunkers' positions had to be shifted somewhat.

Whilst I was fiddling about with this new venture Syd came along and suggested that I look at the foundations of the new clubhouse after the builders had left for the day. Dear old Syd had been a builder years ago and knew quite a bit about the trade and the builders were doing us out of at least a couple of feet, for their foundations were nowhere like 100 feet apart as was laid down in the original agreement, so just for the fun of it, I got out my second-hand JCB and dug down to where 100 feet should actually be.

In the middle of all this, my mobile phone started making a noise and there was Phyliss, our new nanny saying that my wife was starting to have her birth pains and what should she do about it? I told her somewhat abruptly that she as an ex-midwife ought to know better than I. So she suggested an ambulance forthwith to which I agreed and told her that I was on my way as quick as a JCB could take me, and asked which hospital my wife would be in? All of this information I wanted on my trusty mobile by the time that I trundled home.

I arrived home, dirty, dusty and more than tired to find that I had just missed my pregnant wife by about ten minutes, and she was livid with me for making her go to a hospital. Although to give her her due, she did agree with me afterwards of the twin birth, about which she knew nothing, that I had been possibly right.

I didn't trouble to change but hopped into our somewhat fast car and raced to the hospital where I was greeted by a somewhat aristocratic doorman, who when asked by me as to where Lady Amanda Teele happened to be, looked at my farm clothes with somewhat obvious distaste for my gumboots were covered with you know what. But in the end after some somewhat terse words from me, he gave the information I needed and eventually found my darling wife, who having given birth to the first twin was now waiting with some puzzlement for the second to emerge from the depths. Which he did and there we had a boy and a girl, the girl senior by about three minutes.

For some reason or other I had a camera in the car and excited as I was when I leapt out at the hospital, I remembered to sling it round my neck. The nurse, kind girl that she was, deposited my brand-new twins, one in either arm, and then standing behind Amanda's bed, she took a picture of the happy foursome. I stayed a while telling her how clever she was at producing two at a time, and she looked me in the eye and said she thought that although she loved me to distraction, she had the strange idea that I knew all along that she was going to produce twins and how glad she was that I hadn't told her!

So with regret I had to say farewell for a while for the future golf course was waiting and nothing would be done unless I got back. So I kissed her fondly and off I went in my smelly boots, back to work to find Peter on the site. I told him the glad news that he had twins as grandchildren and to delve into his family history for some suitable names.

Then back to the problems of not only the first hole, but the building of at least two bridges over this river. Between the four of us we thought that the green was more or less where it ought to be, and then on to the second hole. The second was without doubt a stunning hole. Firstly it was a par 5 and it wound its somewhat tricky way through belts of trees, which only needed a bit of cutting here and there to produce a decent 100-yard fairway. And so it went on through the kindness of my three friends, we did have a slight argument with the twelfth hole because some 150 yards in front of this tee was an enormous hill and I thought with some devilment in my mind that a green perched on the top of this mound might just make the hole of the century, and it did. We had room enough to plant a somewhat smallish tee to attack the thirteenth which of course was very much down hill and made a divine par 3, and was most popular with the future members.

So that was all planned out and I found my two extra men, one of whom became our head green keeper and occupied one of the few remaining spare houses. His name was David, he had a nice wife and she was enchanted with her tied house. She persuaded her husband that handing over £200 for me to invest for them, payable monthly, was an excellent idea. She was also very keen on sheep, and although our flock was improving mainly because I kept a beady eye on Clive who would fall asleep at the slightest provocation, she proved a great help at lambing time and also aided Clive with feet trimming and one or two other things besides, she was Priscilla.

David's assistant we were lucky enough to find in our village. He had been an assistant green keeper on a famous course some years ago and knew his stuff. He was Neil, a likeable man and the two got on well together. Both were somewhat amazed when they found out that I knew as much if not more than either of them with regards to the running and working of a golf course.

I insisted on soil samples being taken all over the place, especially the greens, and in all I suppose we had some eighty-five different bottles all labelled as to where they had come from. Each day I marked out with sticks as to where the next hole would be, marked also the width of each fairway and also for good measure the rough. When I had a spare moment which wasn't often, I dug out a green, ordered the necessary filling and gradually a course started to take shape.

We were somewhat inundated by the people who attended the meeting in the village hall, and although I did not allow anyone on the course to be, I did have a patch which I intended to make into a practice ground. It was about ten acres and several of our would-be future members spent many a happy hour there. They insisted on paying something so as Christmas was looming, I started a staff Christmas box and most of them although not all contributed a pound here and there.

From the golf point of view I had invested in a nice six-bladed mower for the fairways, but had left the greens' mower to a later date, and as we had a fairly large mower for our own garden, I used that instead of spending a lot of money on a Toro or something similar.

So life went on, we were both earning money, not a lot because the wage bill was pretty enormous; there being some fifteen pay packets to make up each week. But the shop was a godsend; it made money hand over fist. Amanda's deer were selling well and she had more than doubled her original herd. The sheep held their own but did not bring in a great deal. The main thing was that the flock had doubled in size and their turn would come. The pigs did well, We used to sell a sow *and* her litter at the local market and give the weight of the litter at a week old and now at the sale, which showed that they had put on a lot of weight. I carefully left out the amount of food that the litter and their mother had consumed since the birth; that of course was the reason for the sale as their weight was not economical to the cost of the food consumed. The corn income on the other hand was considerable and our two tractor drivers' perks in that direction were the envy of their fellow workers. It paid well from our point of view because the tractors and in fact all the machines that the two tractor drivers used were very well looked after, for if they forgot an oil change or something similar then the resulting repair bill came off their pay 'dividends'. I had experimented with about ten acres of wheat which produced a length of straw very suitable for thatching, and although we had to use an old binder to harvest the stuff and go back in time to when one 'stooked' sheaves, the end result was more than encouraging and I all ready had requests for a lot of thatching straw for next year.

Amanda had of course arrived home clutching her twins. Phyliss had her hands full, for Peter George who had been used to having all the attention from Nanny, found that he was now a third and for a while he didn't take kindly to the change, but in time he came to be more than fond of his new brother and sister. Bar for breast feeding which Amanda insisted upon, she was more than eager to get out onto her patch and see what money she could earn on her own. Of course her deer herd was the centre of her attraction and she started looking around for yet another man whose sole responsibility would be her herd which now numbered about 300.

Peter, who came round to see how we were going, responded to my question with regards to names for his new grandchildren with Piers and Dierdre; both of which had been on his ancestral tree of long ago. So that was settled bar for the fact that we found out somewhat late in the day that they were identical twins; both, for instance had a mole on their respective bottoms and sometimes I had to turn each over to see who was who. Amanda, I was glad to see, had had the same problem.

Meanwhile to return to the golf course, nine holes were about completed and this effort had taken some six months of hard work. Christmas was looming, I thought that those who were interested might like to join up at half price and play in the opening round. We were besieged with people who wanted to join and they didn't seem to care less that the greens were as rough as old boots, they just enjoyed playing on what they now considered as their course. The opening-day match produced a lot of mirth, but the winner was presented with a £100 cheque which made his day, and his name went down on the future honours board.

I had to leave the other nine holes to our two green keepers because things in the farming world were getting out of hand. Firstly the 1,000-bird battery was doing fine and the eggs in the shop coped with about half the output but the other half were building up. So I took on the job as a salesman to various multistorey shops who took the remainder, but they had to be delivered so the milk roundsman was persuaded (somewhat forcibly) to cope with that little problem which of course added to his profits.

The other problem with these dear hens was the produce from their rear ends which had nothing to do with eggs. The resulting pile was growing by the day, and looking at it one morning I decided that I must 'borrow' the JCB from the golf course and sort this lot out, for there must have been at least fifty tons of pure chicken manure which needed spreading. Although our two tractor drivers did a good job, this was something extra that they couldn't cope with, so this was something else on my list. We had some rough gorse land on our 'patch' which never did anything bar produce a grouse or two and sometimes a cock pheasant, so I thought that I would use this 'muck' and try and improve it. So I cut the gorse down to ground level and then applied tons of chicken manure and the end result, with a bit of rough grass thrown in for good measure, was more than interesting. The hen 'stuff' more or less killed off the remains of the gorse and a 'ley' of sorts sprung up with no doubt a bit of surprise and there we had a few more acres to play with. We fenced it in, and to the astonishment of our well-heeled neighbours we brought in about fifty goats plus of course a 'billy' or two.

Now why goats of all animals? Well I suppose firstly that I knew something about goats from those years in Chile. After the war we *had* to have goats to keep the blackberry down to legal levels, and we ate kid instead of lamb with great delight.

So on my rounds of my various enormous supermarket customers I mentioned goat as an interesting dish. "Something different," I said with a smile. "Get your customers interested in a leg of goat instead of a leg of lamb, and of course it is cheaper," said I with my tongue firmly wedged in my mouth. Amanda would at times, when she felt that the twins were in safe hands, come with me on these selling trips and afterwards she would say that she would never believe another word that I said!

So the goats came, all fifty of them, and to the annoyance of the billy goats we treated them in exactly the same way as rams and coated their 'bosoms' with suitable colouring so we knew which 'nanny' goat had been 'covered' and by whom, then we waited till the young arrived.

I must admit from the birth point of view they were a damn sight better than ewes. I hardly had any bother with any kid that was born in our lot, whereas the ewes, at that time were a different matter. They at times kept me up all night for dear old Clive would not dream of shoving his arm up the backside of a ewe, so I had to do that job. However he was improving vastly with other matters concerning his flock; weighing each week the lambs from a certain ewe, trimming their feet and docking their tails, so I kept him on.

Amanda had never eaten goat, nor had Ambrose or his wife Helen and they regarded the first joint with some suspicion, but after they had eaten a mouthful here and there, they changed their respective minds and waded in. So did the supermarkets. They took every wether we had to sell and yelled for more; their customers loved it.

Our rabbit population were becoming to my mind just a bit of a nuisance. We started off months or maybe years ago with about half a dozen does and a buck and they bred like proverbial rabbits, and now we had in the region of thirty does and God knows how many bucks. *But* on the other hand, they sold well and money was made, not only from the rabbit meat but also from the skins. We decided to keep them and gave the lot to Priscilla to look after and included them in her weekly wage packets, plus of course a nibble of the profits that *her* rabbits made.

I showed her how to skin a rabbit in more or less a minute, something I had been taught in my youth as a jackeroo in Australia. First kill your rabbit, something that she was not all that keen on, but I gradually taught her the knack, and then a sharp knife down the insides of both hind legs, a join in the middle, then pull the skin right off up to the neck and then dispose of the head. Then get about thirty inches of strongish wire, bend into a bow and insert into the bottom of the rabbit skin and slide it up to the neck, so that the skin is stretched fur side in. Then find a warmish spot, hang it up and it will cure itself to some degree.

We used the hen battery house for this exercise and soon had about fifty well-preserved skins hanging up. I then phoned the nearest furrier to see whether he was interested, and I was astonished at the numbers who turned up, firstly to view what was on offer and then tell me what they were prepared to pay for a skin.

The twins were blooming, and were crawling all over the house, watched with some awe by their brother Peter George. To give George his due, he did try and look after them on the rare occasions that Phyliss was not around.

Their mother Amanda, after some suitable time had somewhat reluctantly given up breast feeding and was itching to get out onto her patch of 5,000 acres and to see what was going on. So our three young were more or less thrown at Phyliss and Amanda bought herself a second-hand Honda motorcycle and after some tuition from her husband, toured the estate. She would come back and tell me ghastly happenings about which I knew nothing, neither did Dick, the foreman.

I remember one day when her father and I were having a quiet midday tipple, Amanda hurled herself at me and said that one of her stags was caught up in a tree and would I go *now* and do something about it.

"Why me?" I asked quietly. "You have staff of your own. Why not go and get one of them to assist this stag of yours?"

"They will be having lunch," says Amanda.

"So will I," I replied "after your father and I have finished our drinks!"

This was our first full-blown argument since we were wed and I must admit that I did give in at the end. I hoisted Amanda onto the rear end of my bike and off we roared, armed with saw and brush cutter. We arrived at the spot only to find that the damned stag had freed itself, so we returned and I had another G&T with my patient father-in-law.

Meanwhile the golf course was taking shape. Our two men worked well together and when I could spare one or both of our farm tractor drivers, they also lent a hand. We had trouble with the fifteenth, for once again I used the river only to find the hole heading straight for one of our woods. There was nothing for it but to cut through the woods with a fairway of only about twenty-five yards. My past training as a lumberjack came in handy, for I found that none of our vast staff had the slightest knowledge as to how to use an axe properly and how to fell a tree where you wanted it to fall. Anyway by the time that we had finished cutting through about 100 yards of thick woodland, we had enough firewood and potential stakes to last us for quite a while.

Then came near disaster, for sleeping the sleep of the just and I may say somewhat weary with my young wife asleep beside me, there came a thunderous knocking at the front door. I stumbled out of bed waking Amanda at the same time who demanded as to why I was scrambling out of the marital couch in such a hurried manner, to which I replied that if she couldn't hear I could. It was the front door knocker and someone, at this hour, looking at my watch which said 03.00, wanted a chat!

I stumbled down the stairs and with my right hand in my pocket which held a somewhat formidable knife, I opened the front door to find my father-in-law's butler holding a bit of paper and asking to come in.

So in he came looking less like a butler because he was wearing pyjamas with a different coloured top to the bottom and the whole lot was covered with a somewhat woebegone-looking dressing gown, and he thrust this paper into my hand and gasped "He's been kidnapped, Sir John. What shall we do?"

The bit of paper merely said 'Mayday Ch 16 PS to JT'. The last bit was easy, that meant Peter Sussex to John Teele, but why the 'Mayday'? Then of course I remembered in my sailing, that the word Mayday meant 'Help' from the sailing or boat point of view, and Channel 16 was the wavelength which you used if you were in trouble.

So turning to this butler I asked him to explain what had happened and he said that he had been wakened by a noise coming from downstairs and he had got out of bed to see three men dragging the duke downstairs in his pyjamas and he yelling *'Help'*. "By the time that I had got myself fully alert, the front door had slammed and the noise of a car being driven away at high speed suggested that I come to you as soon as possible. I went to the duke's bedroom and found it in a shambles, *but* on the floor under a sheet was this message which I think is addressed to you, Sir John."

"Right" I said, "come and sit down and although it is only 03.00 hrs, how about a whisky? I will join you for you have had a fright and this might help," pouring out a very generous measure for this pyjama-clad figure, who thanked me profusely and sank the lot in one gulp.

Amanda by this time had come downstairs, dressed, I was glad to see in something presentable and asked what was going on. So I told her that we thought her father had been kidnapped and no doubt a ransom would be demanded for his safe return. Without wasting another minute I rang police HQ. I explained who I was and also what had happened to my father-in-law and would they send someone over forthwith if not sooner.

And then I sat down with my somewhat early in the day measure of whisky and with Amanda talking earnestly to the butler, whose name I have forgotten for the moment, I thought about boats and why was this 'signal' so obviously pointing seawards. I used to have a Nicholson 38 which with some reluctance I had sold years ago, while Peter had had a fast cruiser which again he had sold, so why was this signal pointing so obviously seawards? Who else had we known who was the slightest bit interested in boats? Then of course it struck me; dear Michael the man that I or for that matter the duke had sacked from his post somewhat forcibly, for we had caught the chap out stealing goods in the shape of livestock from his employer. I knew that he had a boat, whether of course he still owned one, I had no idea.

To give the local police their just due, they arrived in about fifteen minutes. We all sat and first the duke's butler told the inspector what had happened and then explained about the note he had found which he had passed on to me.

I then gave the inspector some of my thoughts. I told him of the obvious enmity between Michael and the duke, and me as well for that matter, *but* the question was where was the boat *if* of course the duke was in fact being held captive on a boat? I indicated the phone and looking through my somewhat aged file, gave him various boat yards to ring so as to enquire whether a Michael Warren owned a boat in their yard.

We went through quite a lot of numbers till we came to Brighton Marina where I used to keep my Nicholson, and there we struck gold for the man at the other end said that they did have a Michael Warren and what was more, the boat concerned had informed the yard that they were about to set forth for the French coast and had they our permission to leave, which was given.

So our inspector got cracking, and I must admit I gave him full marks for what he did, he first phoned his superior at the Yard and asked permission to talk to the Admiralty about this case, as he wanted a fast boat within the next hour and a crew of at least four, all armed. We would meet them at Brighton Marina and lastly their craft must have radar on board, this was because we would be at least an hour behind this suspect craft.

Amanda insisted on coming, so she rushed about discarding nightclothes for very warm day clothes and I did the same. As my car was a lot faster than the inspector's, we used that, somewhat to the inspector's concern for I drove fast and he had no idea that I had been racing in my extreme youth and did know just a little bit about driving fast.

We arrived at Brighton Marina before the dawn broke, and as we arrived there was a roar of marine engines as our MTB arrived at more or less the same moment, so we piled aboard. The skipper, quite a young man with a couple of rings on his sleeve, asked me as to what directions I could give him. To which I replied, "Not a lot but head for France at your best speed and get your armament in working order, as we might need it." So we headed south at full throttle and the radar soon picked up a slight signal dead ahead of us so we got ready for what might occur. I explained the situation as I understood it to the skipper and said that I had no wish to have bullets swishing around the suspect boat as my father-in-law might be on board. "If you can, after giving them a signal pull alongside and let us see what happens, but have your men and their weapons at the ready."

Slowly but surely we overtook this craft and finally drew alongside. With a loud hailer the skipper told the boat to heave to as we were customs, which of course we weren't and required to search their craft.

At this a voice, which I knew at once to belong to Michael, insisted that they had nothing on board of an illegal nature and that they should be allowed to be on their way.

"Sorry" says our skipper "but rules are rules and we have to obey them. So heave to and let us board you and providing that we find nothing of a illicit nature, then of course you can proceed on your course."

At this there was the sound of a shot and a bullet whistled past the helmsman's head and then action took place. We lurched against their starboard side, ropes were flung and armed men leapt aboard. I went with them having pinched a spare .38 Webly which was lying loose, After checking that all chambers were loaded, I was about the third man aboard and there was dear Michael crouched down behind a table taking careful aim at one of our men, so I extended my right hand, cocked the .38 and carefully shot him through the right shoulder and that was about that. There were some three other men aboard, but they gave us no trouble and then I went searching for my father-in-law, and found him trussed up in the 'head' parked on the seat with his mouth gagged. I swiftly untied him, first removing the gag and the language that erupted from a duke of the realm was past believing. In time he calmed down and enquired as to how I had been so swift to get there and rescue him, for I gathered that the asking terms for the ransom note was in the region of £100,000.

Meanwhile the crew of the boat that we had boarded were handcuffed, including Michael who protested loudly at suffering the indignity of wearing handcuffs and were hustled below onto our craft. We then delegated one of our men to take over Michael's craft and we headed for home for us and a jail for our prisoners.

"Do you realise, my dear son-in-law," said the Duke of Sussex, seated more comfortably on a stern seat of our boat, "that this is the second time that you have saved my life? There was Dunkirk and now this episode. I must admit that dear Michael was a bit of an idiot in that he allowed me to visit the loo before I was abducted and thus somebody found the message that I had left written on loo paper. But you see I knew that Michael had a boat and I heard one of the three talking about the tide, so from one thing to another it seemed reasonable that I was going to be abducted by boat, thus the signal which you were clever enough to decipher. How is my daughter with all this?"

"Worried" said I, "but I sent a signal though a few minutes ago saying that all was well and that you might need a hot toddy by the time that we arrived home."

And so life resumed its normal ways. We inserted my protesting father-in-law into bed. I made him drink a very strong hot whisky and malt, and we left for our own home with an embarrassingly grateful wife praising my every move in rescuing her father.

Ambrose had prepared a meal for us, a nice bit of steak and a chip or two plus a sprout, and he was also embarrassing in his praise for what I had done. I almost was rude enough to tell him to shut up but manners decreed that I should listen to his eulogy of praise of what little I had done.

So we departed to bed, made a lot of love, enjoyed by both of us as was our mutual 'wont' and slept the sleep of the very weary; from my point of view anyway because I didn't wake till 08.00 which to my mind was a disgrace, for 06.00 was the time that I usually stepped quietly out of the front door, leaving my sleeping wife in the bridal bed, and then I would depart to the milking parlour and see that all was well. Then I developed the habit of going down to our farm shop, for that opened at 06.00 as well to see what they were short of and made the necessary arrangements.

This farm shop had developed over the years to something more than just a farm shop, for we had four tables so as to seat sixteen people and we served food, always providing that the table was booked beforehand, and the profits were enormous. Why other farmers in the area didn't copy this I never knew, but they didn't which in a way was a blessing, for the profits helped no end to produce a decent balance sheet at the end of the financial year. We had also developed a sort of home-made wine. I always felt a bit guilty selling this stuff for none of us knew the slightest thing about wine growing, bar that quite by accident a friend of mine from Australia sent me some vines and told me to plant them which I did and year after year they produced grapes that we ate with great pleasure, but one year we thought about producing some wine from our somewhat extended vineyard and having cautiously tasted it, we obtained permission and a licence to produce wine. The customers adored it for some reason best known to their good selves.

What an extraordinary conglomerate of an estate that we found ourselves involved in. There were the cows, milking round about 100 per day, and most of their produce was sold from the farm shop. Then there were the sheep, now in the region of 500 and here we had developed not only a meat avenue but we sold the wool, carded and all to various interested bodies, and then there were the lambs, they went like hot cakes to the local butchers. The veal was almost as good, the goats did their best and added to the considerable profits, and the 1,000 hens, they were sometimes an embarrassment as getting rid of all the eggs at one go was a bit of a problem although the shop helped by producing vast omelettes for little price.

The golf course was beginning to advance. We had completed the second nine holes in thirteen months, and more and more applicants were applying for membership. I was starting to get somewhat choosy in who I established as members, for they all had to come before me and my wife and explain as to who they were, what they did, and generally explain themselves. If we were not certain, about a chap or a lady we would make enquires from the secretary of their last known club and depending on what the secretary said, we would either take them on or give some excuse that we were full up with their particular handicap.

Then came another adventure into this farming estate that we both owned, and it was my dear little wife who thought this one up. She woke me up in the middle of the night and I thought that she said b***. I gently remonstrated that firstly she didn't need to wake me up in the first place merely to hear her swearing. She turned on her side light and explained that she had said *bees*. "You know, John," she said, "insects that fly and make honey."

"So what about bees?" I asked in a sleepy voice.

"Well" said Amanda with a smirk on her pretty face, "we haven't got any and they make money. We should start and get Syd to make some hives and then find some bees."

"And *who* is going to look after this new venture and be stung in all the wrong places?" I asked.

"Tell you in the morning," said Amanda who turned out her light, put her arms round me, snuggled up and was asleep in minutes.

We always seemed to end up with far more ideas than usually spring to mind. For instance I thought vaguely with regards to Amanda's bees that we might stretch to say three hives, but we ended up with twenty-three and finally had to banish the colony a long way away from the farm buildings and houses as everyone including me got stung. The move was settled for Amanda got stung three times in one day and one of the 'bites' was on her bottom. Her command was "Shift these bloody bees." Syd who had been put in charge of the hives, poured smoke on all of them one late evening and we loaded the hives onto a trailer or two and departed into the hinterland.

Syd who said that he knew something about bees, having one hive at his home, for some reason best known to him or the bees *never* got stung, a fact that I found just slightly annoying, but Syd was more than satisfied with the 'cut' that he got from producing honey for the shop and other places.

I should have mentioned Michael and his three henchmen, for he got twelve years for kidnap and ransom demands and the other three got ten years each. We had signalled the police from the boat that we would be coming into Brighton Marina and they were waiting for us and our prisoners. Michael's parents did have the decency to write to the duke and apologise for their son's behaviour.

The golf course was thriving. We had in the region of 700-plus members and our best profit year was £52,000 net. We had the usual complaints from members generally about the fifteenth hole. I must admit that the fairway concerned was narrow round about forty yards for about 100 yards, mainly because we had to go through a wood. But otherwise, bar for a burglar at the clubhouse who burst in and removed the considerable takings from the one-armed bandit, and tried the same trick the next week, but he failed for I had somewhat illegally made the 'bandit' live with 240 volts and I have the feeling that he had learnt his lesson. I was warned in a friendly fashion by our local police force that although my way of catching a burglar was quite unique, for the poor chap did not recover consciousness for at least three hours, I was breaking some law or other and would I not repeat the same exercise, to which I replied that would a cattle electric fencer be within the law, to which they answered that it would as far as they knew.

So life went on, the duke was back in his house; he was playing golf once or twice a week. Amanda was at last satisfied with the efforts of Phyliss with her three offspring and as a nanny, I thought also that she was doing a good job.

We now had sixteen helping hands on the estate, seventeen really for one or the other of the two cow hands, Sam or Bill, would lend a helping hand with Amanda's deer whose herd was now growing apace and I wondered when she would think of culling some of the elders. The young bucks gave her a good living for their meat was more than interesting to not only the butchers around us but also the supermarkets, the only snag about the latter was that we had to do our own butchering and deliver joints as requested.

We were at our usual Friday morning meeting, everyone was present bar for my young wife, and just as I was about to ask as to whether any of the sixteen hands present had seen her, my mobile rang and there was a terrified scream at the other end. There was Amanda being gored by the sound of it, by one of her stags, and then there was muffled sounds and I wasted no more time. Turning to Geraldene our office girl I told her to get on to an ambulance, tell them the story and point out that a 'chopper' would be better. "Look up the map reference," I said, "Now move please and fast." Turning to Pierre, I told him to get his tractor hitched up to a trailer, put two bales of straw into the trailer and shift himself to field number eighty-nine. I luckily had brought along my triple 200 rifle because it wanted oiling and there was oil in the workshop, so I grabbed that, plus ammo and fled to my Land Rover which was a few yards away. I put my foot down hard and fled along the track that we had built years ago so as to be able to gain entrance into any of the hundreds of fields that we owned.

It took me all of seven minutes to reach this particular field and there was a ghastly sight with this stag trumpeting loudly, and at his feet a still figure and on his horns were tattered bits of Amanda's clothing. I rammed four slugs into my rifle and waiting for the right moment, shot him through the neck and the head and down he went. I reloaded and ran towards Amanda who was lying still with her eyes shut. To make certain I shot the stag through his head for he had not stopped moving and I wanted no more trouble. Then Pierre arrived with his tractor and trailer, and we cut the strings on the two bales of straw, and were about to lift her into the back of the Land Rover when the 'chopper' arrived. At my signal to the pilot he set the craft down and out came the medics, much to my relief. Stethoscopes were brandished, and after a swift examination she was declared to be in the land of the living but only just. They asked my permission to take her to their hospital forthwith, and of course I agreed, so off they lifted and roared away. I and Pierre turned round and went home. On the way I used my mobile to phone Dick the foreman to explain the situation and I told him to conduct the meeting in my place as I was headed for the hospital. I should have mentioned that we loaded that damned stag into Pierre's trailer and I told him to contact Dick and get the animal skinned and cut into joints and put into the freezer.

After half an hour's very hard driving with the speed limits scattered by the roadside, I reached the hospital and was taken into the 'danger ward' where my darling wife lay still unconscious but breathing, with a nurse by her side and a doctor hovering in the background. I went to the man with the stethoscope hanging round his white gown and asked him what chances had I on seeing my wife living again.

"Oh yes," says this doctor. "she will come round soon, but you have lost your baby."

"What baby?" I asked

"Well I am not certain which one, but your wife was pregnant when I first examined her, but the child was dead due to the stag, as I understand it, goring her."

So that was a bit of news that I knew nothing about, so I drew up a chair beside the bed, groped for her hand and waited. In about half an hour her eyes opened and she looked at me and whispered, "What happened?"

So I told her the bare facts, leaving out the fact that I had shot her assailant with some degree of pleasure and that he now was carved up into saleable joints in the deepfreeze.

After a fortnight which wasn't pleasant for her, she was allowed home with the strict instructions that she must take things easy, and the meanwhile I had been looking after her interests.

She was a very silent girl after she had been brought home, and I could see that she was making up her mind to tell me something. I thought that I might be able to help, for on one quiet evening I asked her as to why she was worried about something and did she want any assistance, and perhaps it might have been about the coming baby. At this her face lit up and she asked as to how I knew about the baby? I confess that I hadn't told her what the doctor at the hospital had told me, so I merely said that I had guessed and she was not to worry. What had been done, was done and best forgotten. "But" said Amanda, "will I ever be able to have another one?"

"We can always have a try" said I, "for I have the idea that we both like trying."

"Yes" said Amanda, "I adore trying, it makes my day or generally my night." She went on and I was horrified to see both her beautiful eyes suddenly fill with tears and she looked at me and wanted to know *if* she couldn't have any more children would I leave her?

"Don't be such an ass" I replied, "you are my life. I adore you, I couldn't live without you so forget such idiot talk, will you and what is more never mention the subject again. We are happily married with or without hordes of children around us, we have three anyway, so I suggest that you depart to bed and I will be up soon. But don't hurry, don't forget you have to take things easy."

So up she went and I got down to the endless business of accounts of all our enterprises. The one that worried me most were the hens. Here we were with 1,000 birds and most days they gave us around about 1,000 eggs, which meant some eighty dozen to get rid of, and although Syd was doing a good job, his real role of mending this and that and building repairs was fading into the distance, as he hadn't the time. The eighty dozen had to be graded in the machine that we had; each egg had to be stamped with the date of lay, packed into countless boxes, some with small eggs and some with large, and then there was the question of feeding this lot, which also took up quite a bit of time. I had organised the question of the manure, for 1,000 birds gave us about 15 cwt of chicken manure every day of the week. This was automatically shovelled into bins at the end of each row of birds, and every morning bar for Sundays, when I generally did that chore, one of the tractor drivers would come along with the muckspreader to take the load away and spread it. So I decided that once more we must find another hand for this job, and I wondered as to whether any of the wives that we had would care for this work. I got Geraldene in the office to send round a suitable letter to each household, giving the particulars of the job, what the wages would be, plus of course a free egg or more.

The other item that worried me was the golf club, because although I was able to spare a little time to the running of the place day by day, and Geraldene helped with the office work, again when she had the time, I lacked a full-time secretary and I decided that I must get my wife's ideas on this point because I was doing at least an eighty-hour week and I wasn't getting any younger. So I shut up my books and departed to bed to be greeted as usual by a more than happy and loving wife. I had the idea that she wanted me as wives sometimes do, but I felt that with her recent injuries this part of married life must be left for a while and that she should see our family doctor about that somewhat interesting part of a marriage. So I made up a tale that I also wanted her but the doctor had said that we must wait awhile to check that she was well enough to continue our 'tumbles' round our vast bed. So we talked about the estate in general, hens in particular and the need for another body, and lastly the golf club. We decided that come what may, the club itself was making a handsome profit but that a secretary was necessary.

So the next day, I put an advertisement in a golf magazine, requesting the services of a golf club secretary who was able to do anything necessary in a golf club. I gave my phone number, said where the club was and waited. I was deluged with calls within days and I arranged appointments of an hour each.

The trouble started when I said that I had in fact built a golf course years ago and ran the whole work on the course on my own with the able assistance of one OAP for three years. So when the first applicant arrived, I had carefully arranged my Torro greens' mower, a tractor with a trailer unattached and for good measure the fairways' mower with all its six blades in the upright position and locked. With Geraldene's able assistance I had also got the office computer in a tangle, just to see whether the person concerned knew anything about this somewhat modern 'art'.

The first few were more than annoyed that they were expected to know the slightest thing about mowing a green or for that matter a tee. "But what happens," I asked "if one of your staff fell ill? You only have two at that." Most of the first half a dozen left in a bit of a temper. But I carried on for about four days and must have seen some forty applicants. Most of them came because of the wage offered, which was a bit above the ordinary run-of-the-mill salary, but then at last came along an ex-farmer, who knew more or less everything about machinery but nothing, or not much about running a modern office, computers and all the rest. His golf was reasonable as well which helped, so asked him whether he had a house nearby because the job did not include a house, and I found that he lived only about five miles away. So we agreed that I would pay him half the salary concerned for three months, and if at the end of that time he passed muster, then he could go on to full wages, and that was how we increased the workforce yet once again.

Our next problem was my very nice father-in-law, the Duke of Sussex, who caught this wretched flu bug and didn't tell anyone. He got worse and worse till finally his butler swept down to our house and told Amanda that we must do something or otherwise he felt that he would die. So up we went and more or less forcibly swept Peter off to hospital, having warned the staff beforehand as to what to expect.

With a bit of luck, what with his age and a spot of pneumonia, he was surviving and Amanda went in to comfort him every day, whilst I tried to join in when I had a spot of time to spare which was not often.

One day for instance, I arose quietly out of the marital bed at my usual hour of about 05.45, to the annoyance of the two cowmen, for their spot was my first visit of the day and milking must be on time, as cows get impatient if kept waiting. Then my mobile phone bleeped and there was Guy bleating away that he had a sow that was farrowing, and there was a piglet left inside which he couldn't get out. Could he have the vet or for that matter ME!

So onto my trusty motorbike and I sped off in the cold of the morning to the land of the pigs. There was Guy with his arm up the rear end of this sow, swearing away. "Come here you little bastard." So I dug into my bag for my rubber elbow-length gloves and waited till Guy had finally given up and then I had a go. I must admit that he was right, this one seemed to scamper around the womb on skates till finally I managed to catch a couple of legs and willy-nilly drew this protesting piglet into the light of the dawn. I held this tiny thing up to what dawn light there was and noticed at once, firstly that it was a male, but much more important or curious was that it had a black spot on its forehead. As at this time we were breeding pure whites, this was interesting to say the least, so I gave instructions to Guy that this piglet we could keep, as I had strange ideas on this little animal and I wanted to see what he bred like.

Then seeing that the dawn had hardly cracked I got on my trusty steed once again and sped off through the dawn to where Amanda's deer were situated. Now I always either carry a rifle or a shotgun with me if I am away from our HQ for any length of time, and I arrived at the deer sanctuary armed with a 12-bore, but after watching what was going on, I wished that I had my .222 with me for there was a lorry parked in their field and two men were ushering in deer through the tail gate. So I stopped, loaded both barrels and opened the throttle wide and roared towards the lorry, firing one barrel as I went and the shot must have rained down on the two figures for they took one look and fled leaving the tail gate open, out of which poured some six of Amanda's fawns, stumbling somewhat as they leapt out. Now all the staff carry a mobile phone on them, it is part of the drill, a trifle costly at times but in this case it worked well for I called my local 'nick' told them the tale and they caught up with the lorry within a mile and arrested the two concerned. On my evidence in court at a later date they each got three years inside.

My next problem to sort out were the hens, 1,000 of the dear things in a vast shed, each in its own cage. When it laid an egg, the egg would roll down the gentle slope ready for Syd, to pick up and register the cage number. He was more or less the temporary hand with this job, for Syd if you remember was supposed to be the man of all trades on the estate. I mean for instance, he built the farm shop, he repaired this and that and he did a lot of work on the golf course buildings, pro's shop and various other quite big jobs, but my insistence of keeping very accurate records of all the activities that went on in this now somewhat vast undertaking was getting Syd down and as I didn't want to lose him we, that is Amanda and I had to think about yet another hand. It may sound simple keeping 1,000 birds in cages but you *had* to check as to what each bird was worth from the egg point of view. You could for instance find that cage number 100 had produced ninety-eight eggs and that cage number 700 had produced only twenty-two eggs *but* they both cost the same to keep from the point of view of labour and food.

We had advertised for someone a few weeks earlier, but hadn't found anyone suitable, so once again we advertised for a 'body'. It didn't really matter if it was a female or a male, and we were lucky in that we got an answer from a village girl who had just finished her agricultural degree at some university or other, who wanted to have a year or more specialising in one of the many facets of farming. She was called Pauline

Then came an episode which I would rather forget, for at about 08.00 when I had finished with cows and most of the estate and Amanda had fooled about with the children, breakfast was about to be served when came a ring on the front door bell. There, according to Ambrose who answered the ring, were two police officers, one a sergeant and the other a constable. I invited them in, and asked them whether they would like tea or coffee, to which they both replied, somewhat stiffly I thought, that they merely wanted to ask me some questions. So I replied that as long as my wife and I could get on with our breakfast, then ask away.

Their first question worried me just a little for they asked as to whether I employed a certain Francoix Pitony to which I said that I did. "And what about his twin?" asks the sergeant.

"Sorry" I said, "but I didn't know that he had a twin." And then I just started to wonder, for there had been odd occurrences over the past few months since I had taken on Francoix that I could not really understand. I would see him, then he would go and the next minute he would appear again, having said that he was going home or something similar, but there he was again as large as life. "Tell me more" I said with a bit of bacon poised between plate and mouth.

"Well" said this sergeant, "one of them according to the French police is wanted on a murder charge, for he is alleged to have killed a French girl some two months ago and they have asked us to see

101

whether this twin has come to England."

"Well" I said having swallowed that bit of bacon and watching Amanda who seemed to be spellbound with the whole episode, "you had better come down to the village or perhaps Francoix may still be with his hens. Let us go and see, but do you mind if I finish my breakfast first? And *do* have a coffee or something to keep us company." To which they both replied somewhat reluctantly that perhaps a coffee might be welcome, so a ring to Ambrose and up comes two coffees. "Sugar, cream, help yourselves," which they both did in a somewhat hesitant way. "Tell me more about these twins," I asked. "I assume that they are identical as otherwise I would have seen the difference."

"I doubt it," says the sergeant.

"Why?" I asked.

"Well" said this somewhat hesitant sergeant, "the difference is in their private parts," and as he said this he lowered his head in the direction of Amanda as if she might not know anything about 'private parts', but eyeing the twins playing on the carpet, he must have revised his opinion because he became just a bit more forthright. "You see Sir, one has been circumcised and the other retains his foreskin."

"Good God" says Amanda, "I much prefer...."

Here I glared at her to say not a word more for I had no foreskin and I had no wish for the information to be published throughout the width of Sussex. "So what are you going to do about this matter? Are you going down to their address in the village and maybe find one twin and demand to take his trousers down?" I must admit that at this moment I had a fit of the giggles and Amanda joined in. Both police officers looked more than uncomfortable. I cannot say I blame them but the whole situation seemed to be out of this world. I had never heard the 'like' as they say in the country. "Tell me sergeant, which one is suspected? I trust *not* the one that I took on, for he is more than competent and very quick at his work." Then I wondered once again, were both of them actually doing the supposed work of one? Here I was paying for the work of one man, whereas there might have been two. And of course when I took this man on and we both agreed on a salary I did *not* ask him to take his pants down so that I could have a peek at his lower regions; not a thing that one does in this part of the country. I hoped that whatever we found, foreskin or otherwise, I would be able to keep a most efficient worker.

When we had been allowed to finish our breakfast, down we went to interview both of them if that was possible. Amanda insisted on coming although I did my best to dissuade her. We stopped outside Francoix's cottage and the police knocked on the door. Francoix opened the door, said good morning to me and looked enquiringly at the policeman as far as I could see, without any sign of worry on his face. I should have mentioned that the sergeant had sent his mate round to the back door with the strict instruction that he should stop anyone trying to exit that way, and by the noise going on, somebody had tried that exit and lo and behold Francoix's twin appeared in an arm lock. To my wife's annoyance both were bundled into the police car to be taken down to the police station to be examined by the police doctor as to who had a foreskin and who had not.

I must admit, looking back on this episode in our quite interesting lives, I had the idea that my young wife imagined that both the twins would 'doff' their trousers and reveal all. She was disappointed, but I was not for the twin that I thought that I had engaged and he confirmed it, was brought back without a stain on his character (or lower regions) whilst his twin was eventually carted off to France.

And then to the golf club. We had established a quarterly meeting for all members who came if they wanted to, and if they wanted to be upstanding and complain about something then I let them have their say. At one such meeting a member got up and complained that the price of our beer was far too high and I ought to do something about it. I thought about this for a moment or so and then replied that we would hire a bus for thirty people and have a pub-crawl. The price of drinks would be on me, *but* at each pub that we stopped only half a pint of beer was allowed and the price noted. At the end of this pub-crawl, if it was found that the cost of the drinks consumed, which in this case came from twelve pubs, was more than what we charged at the club, then my dear members, would pay me for the cost of the evening. On the other hand if we found that the golf club was in fact charging more than those pubs, I would of course reduce our prices forthwith. I asked them if they agreed with my proposal, and to this there was an explosive show of hands. I told them I would sort out the bus and the time, and put it on the board with a name list for thirty members, on which they should put their name and phone number.

The one thing I forgot which caused a bit of a problem, was that having consumed six pints of beer none of the members concerned would be in a fit state to drive home from the club after the pub-crawl. This was sorted out by various kind wives of the members concerned who said that they would drive their husbands to the club, and then after the binge take them home. I in my turn promised to feed the wives concerned with a short supper and a bit of wine.

We were well over-subscribed and instead of thirty members, we found that we had about fifty. As the bus only held thirty, we had to draw lots, but finally the evening of the day concerned drew near and our thirty including me got on the bus, and amongst cheers from the ones left behind, off we went.

I must admit that the evening was quite fun for at each pub that we stopped I ordered thirty half pints of the landlord's cheapest beer which was 'downed' quite quickly, I paid for it, noted the name of the pub, the price for half a pint and on we went.

By the time that we got to the last pub, quite a few of our original thirty were somewhat 'fou the noo' so to speak but I insisted that they 'downed' their ration and back we came to the golf club to be greeted by thirty somewhat shaken wives at the sight of some of their husbands. I must admit that six pints of beer was quite enough for me, and I was a bit more used to drinking than some of them, but we worked out the total spent and I am glad to say that the club won by quite a bit, and everyone was satisfied. I collected my monies including the bus hire and peace at last reigned.

And so life in its not always quiet way continued. Amanda poor girl was torn twixt her 5,000 acres and what lived and grew on it, and the twins and our first son. It seemed to me that I took on more and more of her lot and I wondered as to whether our nice foreman Dick, was actually pulling his weight, so I started to check as to what he actually did and found to my astonishment that all he seemed to do was to follow me around the place. I mean I looked in at the cows at about 06.00 every morning and Dick appeared to do the same thing at about 09.00 — what did he do in between? I would then wander on astride Honda to view the sheep and see whether Clive was about. Then onto pigs and the two tractor drivers, what were they doing? Finally I used to end up by taking a peek at Amanda's deer and then the goats who lived miles away in a somewhat smelly fifty-acre field on the boundary. It was smelly because when we first started this adventure into married life *and* farming, this fifty-acre patch was all gorse and bracken and was a waste of time and money. So we spent quite a bit of time on these acres, firstly cutting down all the gorse and bracken and burning the lot, then ploughing and we then found that there was a good site to get rid of the chicken manure. So every day a ton or so of chicken was spread over what we had ploughed in, we let it rot, and then put the discs in. Slowly but surely we produced a decent weed-free tilth onto which we spread a long ley and when that took we introduced the goats. They did well, in fact although goats' meat was becoming quite popular in the district I found that I had to take a load down to the market now and then so as to keep the numbers down to a reasonable level. Some of our neighbours used to go to market, and one or two came back with one or two of our goats. It was interesting to see how they lived as against with us in the wilds. Here they were allowed into the house and one would find a large goat asleep by the fireside!

Once a month providing that the weather was fine, Amanda and I played golf against Peter and Phillip the golf club secretary. One day in May, a fine morning and the tee was booked for us and off we went. Phillip who really played the game always used to drive the furthest and as the first hole was over the river, he had no problems. Over the water his ball sailed, whereas I used to sometimes do the same as did Peter. Amanda, poor girl's drive quite often ended up with a splash in midstream. It was fun till we came to the seventeenth and Peter who had wandered off into the rough to find his ball failed to appear, so I went to give him a hand and found him face down, unconscious with his bag and clubs spread around him. So I dashed back and told Phillip to run to the club and get an ambulance, and got Amanda to try and comfort her father.

The ambulance arrived and Peter was laid out and off he went to the hospital. We three forgot golf and hurried home and then to the hospital to find several doctors looking grave, for Peter had suffered a bad stroke and it would be touch and go if he recovered. So we waited by his bedside till finally he did at last open his eyes to view his worried-looking daughter and his son-in-law.

He stayed in hospital for a couple of days and was then allowed to come home with strict instruction about no more golf, and that he was to take things easy from then onwards.

Soon after he came home he asked us both to dinner and I was somewhat surprised to find both his solicitor and his accountant as fellow guests. After dinner their presence was explained for Peter had been told quite bluntly that his time was coming to an end and he wanted to tidy things up, thus the addition to the normal family party. Firstly he wanted to know whether we wanted his house, and if we did, would we shift into it? If we preferred to stay where we were, then what ideas did we have with regards to his vast home? This was all rather sudden and Amanda, poor girl, had a sudden moist eye for she and her father were not only father and daughter but really close friends. It affected me as well but Peter was so calm about the whole matter, and in a pause of the conversation he did apologise for possibly being a bit abrupt about the whole matter, but as he explained again, this time a little more gently and slower than before, all he wanted was to leave everything sorted out. He had made out his will and his solicitor and his accountant had a copy, all he wanted now were our ideas about this house with its nine bedrooms, four or five vast reception rooms, bathrooms to each bedroom, a staff flat, and an enormous kitchen plus garages and stables galore. "Well John," says Peter, looking me straight in the eye, "what is your answer?"

So without even asking my wife, I answered that we would like it, for thoughts were racing through my head. It would be too big for us, even with our present three children and our own house could cope with *one* more *if* that event happened, but Peter's house or mansion would make an idea small hotel, which with the help of the inmates of the flat would be an added income, so what had we to lose? The golf club would benefit as well because we could advertise that there was golf included in the curriculum. Admitted there was the upkeep of the place, but Syd could sort that one out, now that he was free of other farming activities.

So the meal went on and conversation flowed around the table. The two professionals occasionally put in a word or two about tax and IHT although I am afraid most of what they said went over my head as I was not trained in those matters.

The pleasant evening ended, the legal types went off to their homes and we finally said good night to Peter and off we went to our own nice house.

All that was on a Monday and on Friday evening the phone went. It was Peter's butler who in a somewhat shaky voice said that he thought that his master was unconscious and would we get a doctor at once and come over?

We arrived more or less as the same time as our doctor who went straight to his patient. We followed and after a while he said that he thought that the duke had had another stroke. He thought that the end was imminent but that he might recover consciousness but he was not all that certain. He expressed his sorrow and regretted that there was nothing more that he could do.

Amanda stayed with her father whilst I went home and collected some bedding for a night or more, for we had both decided that we would stay by his side till he died. Peter opened his eyes at about 01.00 hrs to find his hand firmly grasped by his moist-eyed daughter whilst I was in another chair dozing now and then. He was quite lucid and said that he knew that his end was to be soon and would we stay with him, to which we both replied that of course we would. So the night lingered on with Amanda still holding his hand. There were tears coursing down her cheeks for Peter and she were more like brother and sister than father and daughter, but at about 06.00 Peter's breathing stopped, his body went limp and that was that bar for the fact that Amanda collapsed. I had to carry her to the car, after first telling Peter's butler what had happened and that the undertakers would arrive in due course.

I must admit that I also felt quite lost without Peter's presence by our side, for he and I had become firm friends and he would always lead the conversation on to the fact that I had saved his life twice, and I would reply about round things 'wot bounced'. Amanda on the other hand worried me. She looked such a lost soul, for as I have said, she and her dad were very close, but gradually she became less forlorn looking and even became interested in what I had in mind about Peter's house.

"A small hotel," I replied. At this her face lit up for she did not want the house, in which I had the feeling that she thought the spirit of her father still lived, to be sold to some outsider and the thought that it would still belong to both of us brightened her days.

So I started the long rigmarole of getting a licence to make the mansion into a hotel and then getting yet another 'drinks' licence, for we had one for the golf club, and lastly but not least getting in a sort of hotel surveyor to view the whole set up and let us have his comments.

Firstly we had to make the lounge bigger by knocking down a wall which was reasonably simple, and then one of the reception rooms would have to be made into a small bar. Lastly we would want some more staff, for all that Peter had was a butler and a cook and a nice girl who seemed to do everything in between. Here

I came over a somewhat large stumbling block, for after a meeting of the three of them with the two of us, they thought that they might be able to cope on their own, but could Geraldene assist with the accounts and the bookwork, to which she thought that she could, but could her percentage of the profits be enlarged just a bit? This last bit of news was quite a surprise to the three present staff, for they knew nothing of what went on on the estate where every employee got a cut of the yearly profits. We agreed to cut these three into the profit scheme and we waited for the day when the first guest would arrive.

I think that it was the golf club which attracted a lot of the future hotel guests and also that we had constructed a bowling green. In fact I had made two, one was quite ordinary and the other was quite a newcomer to bowling, for I had included small hills and dales into this one and it made bowling life more than interesting.

It was amazing to me how soon our nine bedrooms were filled up; three weeks more or less. We gave the first couple a rebate on their first three days which pleased them no end, for we charged £100 per head per day, which included breakfast and dinner but *not* lunch. We found that most of our clients went to the golf club for a snack lunch, so that we gained both ways.

The bowling was most popular especially on the 'hilly green'. They had never seen anything like it and I must admit that I was a bit surprised at the success of this particular project for we charged 50p per game which helped no end. The only snag about this somewhat new form of bowling was the mowing, for one had to create slight mounds here and there, but we got over those problems in the end. However we were visited by some irate very senior members of the English Bowling Club who said that we were spoiling the game and that we should stick to the rules, to which I replied by showing them the cash figures of this peculiar exercise and how popular it was becoming.

Our hotel guests made a vast difference in the green fee figures for the golf course because they seemed to want to play more or less every day and at £25 per head per round, the cash flowed in.

We were still plagued with thieves; one would find a dozen empty hen cages, so locks had to be fitted. The rabbits had a habit of disappearing and even a whole hive of bees took a walk during the night, so I hired a firm of detectives for want of a better word, and lent them my 12-bore. They toured the estate on a motorbike every night and the thieving stopped, but it was a costly addition to our debit column.

Having a round of golf with a fellow farmer who also ran sheep, he said that he had bought himself a llama which he introduced to his flock of sheep, and this or he in this case, kept the foxes at bay and lambs were allowed to live without being torn about in the dead of night. So nothing daunted I bought a couple of llamas, so that they might produce an offspring or two *and* protect my flock from all the foxes that roamed our particular area. The end result was amazing, not a lamb was lost and what was more interesting, in a couple of years my so-called flock of llamas had increased to four.

I must say that I took to these somewhat strange creatures, for once they had your scent, then they came bounding along to say 'how do'. The male was just a wee bit suspicious for quite a while but his wife was most put out unless one made a fuss of her and stroked her all over. However later on when she was pregnant and wanted to give birth, I had a hell of a job getting her offspring out into the light of day. In fact at one time I almost despaired and thought that I would have to do my third Caesarean in my career as a farmer.

I can always remember my first for the cow, in this case had started calving at about 09.00 and nothing appeared. So I rang my vet only to find him ill in bed with the current flu bug, so he, after asking me as to whether I minded seeing a bit of blood, to which I replied that blood didn't worry me, started telling me what to do about tea time that day.

"Sharp knife wanted," said he. "Come into the surgery for chloroform and I will lead you through the op. But you *must* have an assistant" said he, whilst coughing his guts up over the phone, "because he or she has to administer the chloroform."

I thought of my present cowman, pleasant man *but* even an ingrowing toenail would put him off, so I detailed one of my then tractor drivers, a stalwart type of 12 stone plus 6 feet to go with it, and showed him what I wanted him to do, i.e. to dip the cloth into the bowl of chloroform and wrap it round the nose of the tethered cow. This he did and slowly but surely my pregnant cow collapsed. I got on with the job with my sharp knife with the telephone more or less strapped to one ear and at the other end was my coughing vet who was most explicit as to where to insert the knife. I did as instructed and blood flowed but after some more instructions, I saw my calf and carefully lifted him out of the mess. At that time there was quite a large-sounding thud by my side and my 12 stone 6 foot employee fell flat onto his back clutching the chloroform rag which fell over *his* face. 'First things first' thought I and flung the rag away towards the nose of my patient and was just able to fit this over her snout and then heave out the quite lively calf. I then answered the queries that were flooding through the phone as to what the hell was going on and did I understand that I had to sew the incision up. All of this I replied to in a somewhat terse voice for I was more than busy, what with a sleeping tractor driver who had fallen in a spot which caused an awkward situation to become somewhat worse. I did a lot of fast sewing, firstly on one foot and with the other, trying to ease the fallen six footer out of the way. In the end all was well. I pummelled the calf and she breathed. I finished my two pearl and one plain, and the mother gave signs that she would like to rise, having removed with a flick of a wrist the chloroformed rag enclosing her mouth and nose. I shoved my foot in to the rear end of my useless tractor driver, and seeing that all was finally finished went home and slightly earlier than usual and had a very large whisky.

I was having less trouble with my llama, and in the end, after turning her future offspring around a bit, I got hold of a couple of feet and started tugging every time she gave a heave. Slowly but surely her 'child' emerged into the light of day. The whole job would have been easier if I had had someone else with me to keep off the attentions of the father of this infant, for he took a most suspicious view as to what was going on at the backside of one of his wives. Every time I had a moment I would swipe his enquiring head away from what I was doing and in the end he did actually deign to lick his child together with its mother.

Peter by this time had been dead and buried for some six months and although Amanda seemed to be able to forget those last awful hours, there were times when I noticed her face fraught with the signs of strain. I wished that I could help and there did come a time when I noticed these telltale signs and I put my arm around her, hugged her and said, "He is there watching you. You haven't lost him, he has been there all the time, I promise you. He asked me to love you and look after you, and all I ask is that you love me as much as I love you."

"Tell me," says Amanda "when did you think that you started to actually love me; not *want* me, just love me?"

So I told her of that party when I eyed her over a glass of champagne and thought that she was the most delightful female that I had ever seen.

"How extraordinary" said Amanda, "for that was when I first glimpsed you and even then I knew I wanted you, not just for the bed but for ever and a day."

So that ended her lapses with regards to her father, but we both often talked about him and what he had done in his life, but it was just reflective talk and it helped.

Meanwhile the hotel as we now called it somewhat grandly, was making a bomb from our point of view. There were a permanent nine bedrooms occupied and a waiting list a mile long, and as for the bar takings, not as much as the golf club bar but per body much more. So we prospered and suddenly we thought that we ought to take a holiday. We had been at this 10,000 estate now for some seven years, had bred three children, had a ginormous workforce *but* on the other hand, our net profit was more than pleasant and we had both worked from morning to night, so a month's holiday was worth thinking about; but where? We didn't want to travel miles so we decided on the coast of Normandy and got in touch with a firm that let French cottages. They sent us photographs of dozens and we chose one which was more or less on its own, but close to a sandy shore and not all that far from the shops.

We had decided that we would go on our own, so we first had to ask our nice nanny Phyliss as to whether she could cope without us but with of course the assistance of Ambrose and his wife Helen. To which she replied that of course she could and then I told Ambrose to look after her. I then tackled Dick the foreman, and here I must admit that I had slight qualms as to whether he could really cope with 10,000 acres, a hotel and a golf club which I had to do every day of the year, helped I am glad to say by my young eager wife who did a great job. Dick said that he could, and after all what were foremen for but to take charge when necessary and see that everything and everybody worked.

So we made plans, packed what we thought was necessary and then down to the port. We drove onto our ship in which we had booked a cabin, found that it was comfortable, opened a bottle of wine and toasted each other for the first holiday that we had had for years, hoping that what we had left behind would be in shipshape condition when we arrived home.

Once I got used to driving on the wrong side of the road the actual journey time was minimal and we arrived after asking the way at various points in my somewhat basic French. Here we were with this quite delightful small house facing us, with its small garden and the sandy shore within slow walking distance. We introduced ourselves to the man in charge who had been waiting for us. He showed us around some three bedrooms, the kitchen, a sitting room, a bath and a loo. We signed the contract for a fortnight and that was that. It was about 11.30 hrs so we wandered around our new temporary home, went down to the beach, looked in the various shops, exchanged some money at the small bank, bought some ready-made food for lunch, investigated the small but nice hotel and booked a table for dinner that night. Then back we came to our temporary home.

Amanda, whilst preparing lunch with a gin and tonic at the ready, stopped for a moment, took a long look round and said very quietly that she wished that we owned a place like this, for she thought that it was perfect. I agreed whilst thinking that in a week's time it was her birthday and she gave me food for thought. 'Let me find out as to whether this place is on the market and if it is, then why not give her this as a birthday present?' We had a healthy bank balance so I decided that tomorrow, without her coming with me, I would make some enquiries.

So after breakfast the next morning I said that I had to go to the bank to exchange some monies and would be back quickly, and then we would go out and explore. To this she agreed and I then got into the car and motored into the village, found out where the local estate agent was and went in. In my halting French I enquired as to whether our temporary home was up for sale, to which the answer was that it was but nobody wanted it as it was separated from all the other houses. I casually asked the price and managed to keep a straight face for the price was about half what one would pay back home for a house of this size. So to the amazement of the agent I said that I would buy it but I wanted the deal done by next week and I wanted the deeds in my possession by the date of Amanda's birthday. Could he do this? He said that he thought that he could, and I added for good measure that I did not want my wife to know anything about it as it was a birthday present to her.

So I returned to our rented home and casually mentioned that I had done our business with the bank and asked what did she want to do between now and lunchtime? To which she replied that she would be happy just being with me, which was nice of her, so I suggested that we stroll into the village. As we had no phone in the house (something that I would rectify as soon as possible after her birthday), I thought that I would like to phone up Dick and see whether everything was running smoothly.

After tussling with the French phone system I at last got onto Dick's house to be answered by his wife, who said that she was sorry but I couldn't speak to Dick as he was in bed with the flu, but everything was going just as I wanted. I said that I would ring up in a few days to see how Dick was and said farewell.

I must admit that this sort of thing worried me. I had great faith in most of our staff but they certainly needed a guiding hand, but here we were and I must keep my fingers crossed that everything would work out alright.

And so the week went by. I called into the estate agent surreptitiously now and then, and the day before her birthday I was at last handed over the deeds and various other documents. I gave them my cheque and went home.

We had met another rather nice English couple and they were in the farming trade, so I invited them round for a drink on the eve of Amanda's birthday. As the evening wore on, I suggested that we all go down to the village pub, where we went each night anyway, and have a foursome. The evening became more than interesting for although I didn't tell them our acreage, I did tell them about our forage into goats, deer and bees, etc. They were more than interested especially when I gave them a rough idea of the profits made in each branch.

The evening passed by and we returned home and went to bed, me being careful to remember to bring up the title deeds of this house so as to present them to her in the light of day the next morning.

I was only just getting used to getting out of the marital bed at about 08.30 instead of 05.30 which was the norm for me every day back on the estate, and after a week had passed I wondered as to whether I could get back to working time? Finally Amanda stirred and I said "Happy birthday, here is a smallish present for you." She sleepily kissed me as she always did and asked what was in this large envelope, to which I replied that if she opened it then she would find out. I then said that I was going to have a pee and would be back in a moment.

I returned and found a puzzled-looking wife looking at the contents of the envelope and exclaiming that someone had made a mistake and had sent her the deeds of the house which we had rented, and shouldn't I send them back to the actual owner of the house who was at the moment staying at a friend's house in the village!

"By all means," said I, "but I thought that you rather liked this place, or that is what you said a week ago! So why not leave the so-called mistake in a secure place, because it must be that the owners of this nice house who we met a week ago have given you a present on your birthday, or although come to think about it, I wonder as to how they *knew* it was your birthday?"

Amanda looked at me from underneath the bedclothes, and said in a firm voice, "Come here and take off all your clothes and get into bed, for I have just realised what this envelope means and what it contains actually means and as I happen to adore you, not just love you, I want your body joined in mine right *now!*"

And so there it was, we made a lot of love and enjoyed ourselves tremendously.

We spent the rest of the week changing this and that in our or Amanda's new house. We installed a phone for a start, we threw out the old cooker which had the habit of declining to cook at odd times, and installed a nice electric cooker with a microwave to keep it company, and we exchanged our beds for new ones.

On the day before we were due to return home, I rang the estate office and spoke to Geraldene and at once I knew for certain that something drastic was wrong.

"Dick died two days ago and we were unable to get hold of you because you had no phone number."

I rang off and phoned Mrs Dick who tearfully answered the phone and said that she was somewhat overwrought, and would we please come home as soon as possible and take charge of things as of yesterday.

So we packed up reluctantly and headed for the ferry and home. We arrived more or less at midnight and so to bed and the usual early start in the morning.

We cremated poor old Dick, and his widow decided that she was going to live with her daughter, which was a blessing because I wanted another foreman and he should have the house concerned.

I advertised in the usual way, *Farmer's Weekly* and all the rest, and as usual I was deluged with replies, but out of the seventy who wrote and said that they were experienced, only four were able to hitch a trailer up to a tractor and back it through a gate. There was just one who understood soil sampling; slight problem with him on the other hand in that he was living with a very nice female who was *not* his wife and did I mind? To which I replied that as long as he didn't create a scandal in the district, who he shared his bed with was nothing to do with me. Of course he did understand that the golf course also came into his orbit, but bearing in mind that the golf course *did* have its own secretary, and whereas he (my new foreman) would have the freedom of the course at certain times, then the job was his. I asked him to begin the next month, which gave time for Dick's widow to frequent the premises.

The name of the new foreman was James and his girlfriend was Jane. I must admit that we started at somewhat cross purposes, for he had the idea that I was just a reasonably rich landowner who knew next to nothing about practical farming. I had to correct this thought in his mind by first demonstrating how to find out whether a cow was in calf or not, by inserting my arm into her backside and finding the uterus. Then there was ploughing, which in my far-flung youth I had won a cup or two, and was reasonably good at this art, so I corrected his faults with a straight face. As to lambing a ewe, this was in his thoughts a phone call to the vet, I changed all of these ideas and he suddenly woke up to the fact that the boss for some reason or other, knew more about his profession than he did.

So after that we got on quite well, bar for the slight problem of his girlfriend, who when she found herself within an arm's-length of me made an obvious pass. I told her to remember as to who she was living with. I told Amanda as to this event, just in case rumours wandered around, but asked her not to start a war, for the girl had taken my refusal to take an interest in her without any outward signs of anger.

Problems don't come once in a while, they have the habit of recurring and this one was a bit of a worry. It was the sheep and although I had or thought I had enough protection in the shape of my llamas, I still found whilst wandering round on my motorcycle which I did every day, dead lambs, and in some case dead ewes torn to shreds. So I tore a strip off the shepherd for not telling me and found that he was just as worried as I was. So together we planned a small plot to catch this animal that was doing this damage.

I lent the shepherd a 12-bore and we both went out after dark in the Land Rover and took up positions on either side of the field where the flock was situated and waited and waited. It was about 03.00 hrs when we heard the sheep stampeding. I turned on the lights of the Land Rover and there was an Alsation chasing the flock in my direction, and when in range I had a clear shot and knocked him flat. It was a lucky shot for the light was more than dim. But what to do? We examined the dead animal who had a collar but no name and address anywhere, so I humped him into the back of the Land Rover having found some sheep's wool on a barbed wire fence, which I inserted into his mouth, just to show what he had been up to and home we both went.

Back to bed and phoned the police the next morning and asked them to come along and take the carcass away, and find out the owner of the dog as I wanted a word with him or her.

The next thing that happened from the dog point of view was that one morning there was a violent hammering on the door. We do have quite a decent bell push, but a clenched fist seemed to be the best way according to this caller. Ambrose went to open the door and a smallish man pushed him aside and rushed into our dining room where we were just finishing breakfast and yelled at me, "Did you shoot my dog?" He was standing just behind Amanda's chair and as I got up he put his two somewhat dirty hands onto the shoulders of my wife, which made me somewhat annoyed to say the least, so I really leapt up and was within 'talking' distance to his jaw within seconds, and the next moment he was on the floor, out to the world.

Ambrose had come in by this time and told me that there was a tearful lady outside the front door wanting to come in, and that he had told her that he would let her know if her presence was desired by the master.

"Phone the police, Ambrose and be prepared to tell them that this man," pointing at the still form on the floor, "was molesting my wife and you were about to come to her rescue but that I had got in first."

"I understand Sir John," said Ambrose and off he went to phone.

The figure at my feet finally stirred but I told him to stay where he was otherwise he might get hurt again. I sent Amanda up to our room to recover, for she was a bit upset with the feel of those hands on her shoulders creeping towards her throat.

And then the bell again, and Ambrose ushered in a sergeant and a constable, so I told the tale, which Ambrose collaborated and the constable helped this man to his feet. He then told his tale about me shooting his dog, to which the sergeant replied that his dog had killed a number of my sheep and that I was merely protecting my property and if he wanted further witnesses, then Sir John's shepherd would no doubt oblige for he too, shot at the dog, and why did he think that his dead dog had sheep's wool in his mouth? At this amount of somewhat damning evidence, the little man asked as to whether he could now depart, to which the sergeant replied that this depended on the owner of the sheep, i.e. Sir John Teele. "He," looking at me, "might wish to bring charges and of course damages, it is up to him."

"An apology would suit the bill, firstly the loss of my sheep and then your filthy hands on my wife's neck, what have you to say?"

The little man looked at the floor, not a glance in my direction and muttered something, which I pretended not to hear. I asked him to repeat what he had just said, and look at me when he was saying it. So there was a pause and I wondered as to whether anything was forthcoming, for if there wasn't then I would certainly press charges, but finally the man raised his somewhat reluctant head, met my angry eyes and said firmly that he was sorry for what had happened and trusted that I would forgive him.

To which I said "On this occasion I will do that but in future mind your manners, don't burst into private houses and under no circumstance lay your hands on a lady's neck. Is that understood?"

He stammered that it was and off he went with Ambrose behind him to the front door to where his tearful wife awaited him. We had no more sheep worrying for quite a while.

No day passed without the two of us having to make a decision about something or other, and the next not so small worry was that four potential guests for the hotel wanted to know whether we had horses to ride, for although they liked their golf they also liked riding.

We had two horses in the stable at the moment looked after by Felix, so I got hold of him and told him that we wanted at least two more quiet horses within the next fortnight. He replied that he knew just the place and could we all go along together this very afternoon and view what they had for sale.

So after lunch we collected Felix and off we went to this friend of his, who no doubt would give him a rake off on what we bought.

There was no doubt about it, the stock that this man had for sale were quiet, well looked after and not all that costly, so we bought three on the understanding that he would deliver them the next day.

Then back to the office. I got Geraldene to write to these people who would like to come and stay with us always providing that we could hire them out a horse to ride when they wanted.

I grabbed Felix again and off we went and bought saddles and bridles, bedded out three extra stalls, got in some extra fodder and that was that, all done and paid for, and what was more, the guests concerned phoned up that very evening and said that they would be delighted to stay for a week or two and when would it be convenient. So I looked at the register, told them the date and that was that.

The next little item to sort out was connected with golf and the times that the hotel guests could play, because we had over 700 members and it was the question as to who had priority as to times and for that matter days as well. So I got hold of Phillip the golf club secretary and for good measure the current captain of the club and told them my problems. I told them that the hotel had certain clauses pertaining to letting rooms, and one of the clauses was that they could play golf on the estate golf course providing that they booked in and that they would pay a reduced green fee, but I wanted a certain day and a certain time laid down for hotel guests to play golf. "What ideas if any have you two on the subject?"

Phillip suggested a Sunday morning between 10.00 hrs and 11.00 hrs, always providing that these hotel guests actually came along and put their names down and paid their green fees, to which, I was glad to hear, the captain of the club agreed. So we sorted out the future booking sheets for this Sunday business, giving the persons concerned ten minutes to tee off and get out of the way of the following couple. It was also agreed that the people concerned should be given some form of identification from the hotel, so that from the pro's shop point of view they knew what to charge.

I then had to go back to the hotel and discussed the whole matter with the hotel staff which numbered three; Garry, who used to be Peter's butler but now was in charge of running the hotel, Mary the cook who again used to be Peter's cook and lastly Shelia who kind of crept in when nobody was looking and who attended to the bed making, the cleaning and a host of other items. None of these three were married to my information but I had the vague idea that Garry had the free use of two beds for the night bar his own, but who was

I to interfere, as long as they did their job and the guests were satisfied and the monies balanced. So I told the three of them about the golf business and that he, Garry should be responsible for issuing out tickets to would-be golfers, confirming that Mr and Mrs Smith were in fact staying at the hotel. Mr and Mrs Smith would read the instructions on the ticket which said that they must go to the pro's shop at the golf club, present the hotel's ticket and put their names down for one of the allotted slots on the starting sheets for the coming Sunday.

Then came James our new foreman with whom I started to get slightly tough, for I had explained a lot of things that we did, or Dick the previous foreman had done before he unfortunately died, and when I asked for information with regards to pig families and who had come out bottom as it was these that we had to sell, he looked quite blank. He apparently had not taken in that all costs pertaining to all the pig families *must* be logged. He had not weighed any of them and the whole thing was in a mess, so I gave him a somewhat strong lecture for the second time and told him quite bluntly that this was the only way of making a profit, but if he felt that he was not up to it, then by all means go and look for another job.

There was a bit of a silence on both sides after my tirade, but he finally came to the decision that I was right and that he was wrong and would I give him time to get things right. To which I replied "I will but don't forget, that we have sheep, we have goats and a host of other items, they all have to be gone into and the information filed. OK?"

We seldom ever argued, Amanda and I, there was an enormous amount of love on both sides, both physical and mental, but one day she said that she was getting short of money and why was my farm account so vast and hers more or less empty? So I asked her what her foreman did from the point of view of telling her which family should be sold, for instance her deer herd. There were some very small fawns always seemingly belonging to one particular hind, what were the weights concerned and then what about her half of the pig population? What were her figures like? For good measure I showed her mine and the profit that I made.

"Will you talk to my foreman?" asked Amanda.

"No I won't" I said "but I am more than willing to be with you when you tell him what a mess he is making of your stock."

And there came our second very small 'bust up'. She thought

that I should do her work for her and I thought that she ought to take charge of her own affairs, but in the end, she saw my point of view, we kissed and everything was back to normal, until of course the meeting with her foreman, a chap that I had seen about but never seemed to be very active.

Then sparks flew and he was told what he should have done for years on end and why hadn't he? He asked various questions and Amanda turned to me for help and I explained to this man what should be done to discover which 'line' of animals were producing the best profit and who were the losers.

In the end he gave in his notice, so then I talked to my foreman, and asked him as to whether for an increase in salary he would take on the job. To which he replied that he would welcome the idea, it would make life simpler, but could we buy him a computer for his farm office which he inherited from poor old Dick. He knew a bit about computers and it would help with the records, for he now had sheep, pigs, poultry, milk, deer, corn, bees and one or two other oddments on his shoulders, but given a prod now and then, he was more than capable, for he had never done our sort of farming before and he was anxious to learn. It would seem, as he explained to me one day, that the farmers he had worked for in the past could not have cared less as to what amount of food they fed their animals; they never kept records and quite often took to market an animal that was the best on the farm from the profit point of view.

I had this possibly stupid idea that we farmers in the area should form a sort of syndicate and have a central shop where all our collective produce was sold. We could of course keep our own shops if we had one, and I learnt later that out of some forty farmers who joined the scheme, I was the only one that owned a shop.

I advertised in the local paper the facts of this scheme, and that we would be holding a meeting in our local hall in a month's time, and if anyone was interested, then come along.

On the date concerned I went down to the hall with the idea that a dozen or so people might turn up and I should organise some chairs. I was astonished to find a queue yards long waiting impatiently to get in, so I grabbed a few willing hands and sorted out chairs for at least 100 farmers.

I then when everyone was seated, including Amanda in the front row, got up and explained what I had in mind, that we would buy/ hire a building large enough to take what stock we wanted to sell, which would of course be live and dead stock including veg and anything that we as farmers produced that could be sold. *If* they were interested, could they elect a chairman to run the 'thing' and then could we have their collective ideas as to whether it would work etc.

I was inundated with people leaping to their feet and asking this and that, to which I replied that they must elect a committee to sort out their questions. I was merely the 'idiot' who had brought the matter up so as to possibly help my fellow farmers make a better living by selling their produce straight to the public rather than to a wholesaler, who would then sell to a retailer who at last would sell the item concerned to the gullible public.

Somebody shouted that I must be the first chairman, to which there were shouts of approval, and then we started on the election of six committee members, which went off quite calmly. I asked those six to stay behind and announced that I would be putting an advert in the local paper as to when the next meeting would be and also to confirm that the whole project was approved by their committee. We had a brief talk, these six farmers who were now elected onto this possibly odd sort of gathering, but we thought that we must do something to allay the suffering of hundreds of farmers who relied upon the government to keep them in the land of the living. I explained what I had done, in the shape of building a farm shop and also of course delivering round about a 1,000 pints of milk per day, plus of course eggs and all the rest down to FYM to my customers. And so we sketched out an advert for what we intended to do with this building and why didn't the public try our fresh wares at a lot less that anywhere else.

We had taken the precaution of getting all the farmers who were at the first meeting to put their names and addresses in a book, and one of the first things that we did was to write a letter to each of them and hundreds more which we found in the telephone directory telling them of the progress that we were making and greatly daring to ask each and every one of them to subscribe whatever they could afford so as to make this scheme work. I also pointed out that we had to find a building suitable for our collective needs, but if and when we made a profit, then subject to the future rules of this venture, they who had subscribed at the start would reap a dividend, always providing that we had enough support.

In the meantime I had to get on my own work on our estate. One of the first problems was Geraldene, our office girl, who was first-rate but found with the records she had to keep and all the staff off the estate who at times needed assistance from the office, that either she wanted an assistant or she wanted some overtime.

"I have files on all the staff employed here," said Geraldene, "and it might be worth your while to have a look at it and also the profit or loss accounts for each of the many ventures we had started all those years ago. Take staff," says Geraldene, "here is a list, and their weekly wages beside each one which of course is transferred into the account book every week. The foreman, James; his wife, Jane; the shepherd, Clive; tractor driver, Pierre; tractor driver, Sam; pigs, Guy; odd-jobman, Syd; your butler, Ambrose; his wife, your cook, Helen; office, me; shop, Monty and Mary; cows, Sam and Bill; head green keeper, David; his wife, Priscilla; assistant green keeper, Neil; poultry, Francioux; golf club secretary, Phillip; hotel staff, Garry, Mary the cook and Shelia; and groom, Felix. That comes to twenty-three, says my efficient office girl, Geraldene, "and here are all the accounts that I keep pertaining to each department. So may I have an assistant, Sir John, for it is all a bit of a load?"

So viewing all these figures, even down to the deposits paid on each tied house and the interest that was paid to the occupant, I agreed forthwith but suggested that she tried out some of the wives of our staff and asked as to whether they were interested in this sort of work and had they had any training. We then agreed upon a wage, and I asked her to keep in touch with whoever she found that would assist her in her work.

Next came Phillip, the quite efficient golf club secretary who was worried about the falling profits in the bar and the catering side of the club. I noted in my mind that he was also worried about *his* percentage of the profits of the golf club as a whole, so I had a chat and I came up with the idea of putting a sum on each member's yearly account which had to be spent either in the bar or the cook house, and we agreed that £50 as a starter might not cause all that amount of a row twixt members and us who ran the place. As we had in the region of 800 members, this £50 would come to some £40,000 if not all spent in their membership year. Of course the vast majority of the members rather liked going to the bar and presenting their 'card', collecting their drinks and paying nothing, but of course the machine that we had in the bar swiftly deducted the sum concerned off the original £50 donation, and I was glad to see that profits did in fact increase both with the bar and the food side of the business.

"The next thing, Phillip is for you to organise a pro-am here. Let me have your ideas with regards to firstly how many entries do you want? How are you going to sort out who of our best members plays with whom from the pro point of view. The 1st prize for the winning pro and his partner (who of course will be one of our members) and what prize would you offer our winning member? Then just to keep you from becoming bone idle, organise a golf ladder, which" anticipating his puzzlement, "goes like this. Firstly you put up a notice giving all the members, and I mean girls as well as the men, that there is a free annual sub to be won and the rules are as follows. Firstly the names of all the members go into a hat and a board is constructed. The board contains some 750 slots and into each slot goes the name of a present-day member. To win his or her free annual sub, he or she has to challenge the name above them, pay that name 50p and also pay 50p to the office and then play a half round of golf with your opponent. If you win then your card goes up one slot and you challenge the next name. The winning name must be at the top of the list on Christmas Day by 12.00 hrs and *that* name gets free golf for a year. Look into this Phillip and let me know if you think of any snags, but it is a money-spinner from both sides, ours and of course the member concerned. Don't forget though that the winner of this competition, although he or she gets a free golf year, will also be presented with some vouchers for the bar. What next is troubling you? Don't forget that anyone can come along and see me in the office at 09.00 any morning bar Sundays, so take your pick."

So from golf back to plain plumb farming to find that once again that the shepherd had the idea that his lambs were being taken by something or somebody, and the man who looked after Amanda's deer also reported that three of his fawns had 'walked' and he had no idea what had happened to them. Whilst we were all thinking about this, the back door of the house rang and there was a rough-looking chap who insisted that he had three fallow deer for sale; all well bred and in good condition and that he only wanted X pounds for each which I must admit was cheap.

"Can I have a look at them first?" at which request he reluctantly agreed and I went down to his truck and examined three very nice well-fed good-looking fawns. I made an excuse that I must go and get my cheque book and whilst in the house, phoned the police and told them that I had found my stolen fawns. I informed them of the circumstances, to which they replied that they would be with me in ten minutes, so I went back to keep my friendly 'rustler' company.

We chatted a bit and then the police arrived and all hell broke loose. My 'rustler' ran at me to get away, but found myself a bit bigger than him and easily held him till the handcuffs were fixed.

I identified my fawns by their earmarks, and I must admit that my thief looked a bit disturbed at finding out how he had been caught. I took my fawns home, calling in on Amanda on the way and she made a great fuss of the three of them. Their various mothers seemed more than pleased to see them but objected to three eager mouths searching for milk.

By this time, having inserted various advertisements in the local papers requesting information from anyone who had a building for sale so as to use for our future combined shop, Geraldene came along one day and said that we now had ten reasonably good offers and maybe I should collect our committee members and go along and have a look. So I asked her to get in touch with each of them, arrange a date and time and I would go round and pick them up.

This we did, and went and saw the buildings which were all large barns belonging to farmers who needed a bit of capital. We decided on the one that we thought best and offered him a price, subject to contract. And also whilst we were at it, we obtained a licence to sell our various wares from all the farms concerned to the general public. The owner of the building haggled a bit but he wanted the cash so a bargain was struck and in a short while the building belonged to the syndicate.

There was a slight problem of finding the necessary cash as I soon found that Amanda and I were more or less the only ones with the necessary boodle, but luckily in our various meetings that we had over the last six months, it was decided that the members concerned would each put in a sum to a named account in the bank, and should the whole idea prove successful then the members concerned would be paid a dividend. So although there was not enough to cover the whole cost of the building, and of course the alterations to the interior, we were able to fund the project with us as the main subscribers.

We managed to find a good firm of carpenters who were reasonable in the costs; discussed the plans for the interior with them, such items as the storeroom a large area for the cold rooms, the length and place for the counter and left them to it.

The committee and I visited them once a week to see how they were getting on, which was just as well for we had forgotten a number of essentials. One being a loo or to be exact two, one for men and one for women, and then the question of lighting and also somewhat daring, we expected in time, always providing that we were doing well, to provide cooked food for our customers, which meant a small cosy dining room. A dining room is not much use without a kitchen, so that was included and by this time funds were getting somewhat low. A cellar was vital, so us Teeles injected a bit more cash and finally the whole thing was finished. We asked our local mayor as to whether he would do us the honour of opening the place which we called, after a lot of discussion Farmers' Own.

I found the mayor, nice chap that he was, somewhat costly for he assumed at the last moment that our invitation to him included of course his committee which consisted of ten stalwart drinkers, and they made it quite plain that the only drink that they ever touched was of course champagne and they cost us some dozen bottles of the stuff. The bar with its brand-new licence went down well and the small dining room was packed. The counter filled with home-produced farm produce went down well and we made, in spite of the mayor, quite a handsome profit.

Then the organising had to start, for Farmer Brown, with a ton of spuds which he wanted to be rid of, argued the toss with Farmer Smith who had a mere cwt. *But* Smith was an investor in this project as well, so we on the committee had to sort the thing out so that both investors were more or less satisfied.

Once again staff had to be found; a girl for the miniature office, although it had to be doubled in size within four months as we became more and more popular. Then firstly we tried to do with just one nice hard-working girl behind the counter, but that didn't work for customers were kept waiting, which they didn't like, so yet another girl had to be found. Then finally, for a while at any rate, we had to have someone to cope with the waiting at table, for although we started with just six tables, that had to expand to a dozen within three months, and we found a nice man who lived nearby and who liked waiting on people. So we had another five on the staff, but it started to make money hand over fist, people would come along and fill their shopping bags, look at their watches and find that they would not have the time to get home and have lunch, so they stayed with us.

We started with some fourteen farmers who invested what they could afford and reaped a small harvest every month from the profit that we made, always of course depending on what they had subscribed in the first place. We were becoming more and more popular in the farming world as the news got about that if you invested something, then you got something back every month, and we were besieged by farmers miles away who thought that this was a winner, till they were told in no mean fashion that what dividend they received depended on how much of their produce they brought into Farmers' Own.

I must admit that although this new scheme was doing well and that farmers were making a lot more money by selling to the housewife, more or less direct, I as chairman of the whole set up was finding life just a bit hectic. For behind all this was our 10,000 acres which needed constant attention and Farmers' Own also needed looking after. Somebody for instance had to go round all the supermarkets and shops and check their prices, for we advertised that we were cheaper than anyone in the district and we had to check that this statement was actually true. The monthly dividends had to be checked, cheques had to be signed, mail sent off and a hundred more items had to be looked at. So at one of our committee meetings, I put it to the members that I wanted assistance. I told them what I had been doing since we opened so could I have some thoughts on the subject. After I had opened the meeting I told my committee that I would abide by their thoughts on the subject and that I would leave them to talk amongst themselves. I would come back in fifteen minutes' time, but before I went I gave them some idea as to the hours that I worked and for good measure reminded them of my age, and then left them to it. I went and had a beer in our new bar and pondered as to what I would do if the committee considered that I should continue as I had been doing, and made it quite plain if that was the case, that I would resign the chair and let them get on with it.

When my time limit was up I went back in and asked them for their verdict. To my surprise, the show of hands voted solidly that I should have a helper. As soon as I could find a suitable person, be it male or female.

So we advertised in the local paper and loads of applicants came along, but when I and some of the committee told them what would be expected of them for at least six days every week, the queues got somewhat slimmer till one day whilst in my farm office I had a knock on the door and who should be standing there but Pierre's wife. Pierre if you remember was one of our tractor drivers, and his wife was Marie. So I invited her in and enquired what I could do for her. She replied that she might be interested in this job as my number two in Farmers' Own. Could I explain what she would have to do if of course she was considered suitable? I liked the look of the girl, and although French, her English was excellent and it had that slight feeling of making the person to whom she was talking, feel that she had been waiting for just this opportunity to make their acquaintance.

I offered her a chair and then ran through what I did with the regards to Farmers' Own from the time that farmers delivered their goods for sale. I gave them a receipt for same, entered that in the daily book, and carted their goods into the storeshed. All this I reminded her had to be done between the hours of 09.00 and 10.00. I then checked the bar takings from the till in the bar, left the daily float, entered the takings in the book concerned and did the same for the dining room till. "One very important item is to make certain as what has been with drawn from the storeroom and enter into the book concerned what the farmer concerned has earned, and enter that also into the book concerned." I said that I could not give her a set number of hours, for some days differed from others, but that the wage for the week, i.e. Monday to Saturday was as follows and if she was interested then she should meet me at Farmers' Own at 09.50 tomorrow and I would show her the ropes.

Tomorrow came and there was young Marie, looking very spruce with a notebook and pencil all ready; a point that I liked for all the many people that I had seen for this job had never thought to bring a notebook, let alone a pencil. I ran through the items that would be hers and the only snag came when 1-cwt bags of spuds had to be carted from one spot to another. For this she asked as to whether she could borrow her husband for a few minutes and that he would make up his time on the estate. That was fair enough *if* it worked but thought that she was the best of the bunch that I had seen so far so agreed to terms there and then and that she could start the following Monday, and that pay day for her would be Saturday.

I gave Marie a month's trial and all seemed to go well. I was relieved of that burden which was really becoming a bit much with 10,000 acres on the side to look after plus a budding golf course, so I told her that she was now one of the permanent staff and that I would come in now and then to see whether she had any troubles which needed ironing out.

I called the committee of Farmers' Own and gave them the good news that all seemed to be functioning but doubtless there were things that we had not thought about. Such as the possible necessity of having an individual bin for each farming member of this brand-new company in which he could place his goods, and on which he would have his name printed for all to see, so if the public preferred Farmer Brown's spuds to Farmer Smith, then Smith would have to pull his socks up! But on that score it was felt by the committee that the farmer concerned would have to provide and pay for his own bin or crate, which seemed fair enough. We wondered on through points till someone got up and declared that they wanted me to be chairman of the company for a period of five years and that I should be paid a salary. I remonstrated a little bit about this idea, not a lot but I felt that I ought to, and a vote was cast and of course I lost. So there I was, a paid chairman for five years.

I found that Marie was excellent, if she found a problem she would come to me in the estate office and explain her worries, so I felt that was one chore off my back. But there were others looming and the main one, anyway for the moment, was our garden. For a start there was a grass tennis court which I mowed every week. There was an area the same size as the tennis court on which we grew our own veg, although most of our so-called 'rough' veg, such as spuds, etc., we pinched off the estate, and then there was another area in which there was a swimming pool and a quite ornate garden. Although Amanda and I used to try and cope with this as well as half a dozen other items such as running the estate for a start, and from her point of view coping with three children, it was becoming slowly but surely too much of an uphill battle.

One day when we had both stretched ourselves to the limit and returned home about tea time, we viewed the garden. The lawn wanted mowing, the tennis court looked like a hay field and as for the so-called ornate garden, that resembled a wilderness and we both uttered the same words. "We want a gardener."

"Can we afford it?" asks Amanda.

"Yes" said I. "What with the golf course, the hotel and the shop, plus the estate itself, oh yes we can afford it all right."

So the next morning I went down to our village and inserted an advert in our local paper requesting the services of a gardener from Monday to Friday.

That very evening, came a knock on our door and there was Pierre our nice French tractor driver, apologising for coming to our house but he understood that we wanted a gardener. For a moment I wondered how the devil he had heard this bit of news but anyway I asked him in, sat him down in my study and asked him as to what he could do about the question of our gardener.

"Well Sir John, it is my brother, who is a gardener in France. His present employer has just died and he will want another job. We have a spare room and I was wondering as to whether you would kindly grant him an interview?"

"Is he married?" I asked. "And how long has he been with his last employer who has just died, and has he a reference?"

"He has not a reference from his last employer," said Pierre "but he has one from his previous one and he is married with one daughter."

"All right" I said. "Ask him over and I will pay something towards his fare. But in the meantime talk to your wife as to whether she can cope with another three bodies in her house."

And so Francois arrived in a couple of days. I liked him at once and his wife was charming, so I took him around our apology of a garden and he agreed politely that we did indeed require the services of a gardener, and he without any asking said that he would work for six and a half days per week till he got the place shipshape and after that with my agreement would work from Monday to Friday for quite a reasonable sum. After consulting my young wife, who also sat in on the interview, we took him on. I paid him a reasonable sum for his travelling costs, agreed a date when he could start and off they went back to France.

We had agreed with Francois that he would start in a fortnight and that I would meet him and his wife at Dover and drive them to their new home. He would let me know the time that the ship docked.

In this fortnight I bought them both a couple of beds and a bit of furniture for his new room in his brother's house. To be on the safe side, I took Marie along with me as I thought that she would know what her brother-in-law would need. We took a chance between us that they slept in separate beds, and bought single pillows and sheets.

A carpet was fitted and I made arrangements for electric plugs to be fitted in the bedroom. After a morning we both surveyed the list that we had made out and thought that they would be more than satisfied with our purchases.

I must admit that at times I felt that I needed an overall manager for this ever increasing load that we had started all those years ago. We had met, Amanda and I, and she steered me up the marriage aisle. I met her father who turned out to be a duke, he had kindly given us half his somewhat vast estate, half to Amanda and half to me, plus all the stock and then we seemed to endlessly increase the size of the place. There was the farm shop, cow numbers increased, sheep flowed in, pigs as well, deer by the score and then poor old Peter, my father-in-law died. There we were with a vast manorial house which we turned into a small hotel suitable for about a dozen guests. The guests wanted to ride, so horses came and somebody had to look after the horses, so a groom appeared. The golf course came into being which needed two groundsmen plus a secretary, a girl for the bar and her husband who was an excellent cook. And then a mere 1,000 hens in batteries who needed quite a bit of attention, not forgetting a brace of tractor drivers together with a man who looked after six beehives plus a lot of other items. The hotel had three permanent staff, the farm shop had two full-time girls, and to add to all that I found myself landed with being president of this Farmers' Own, and holding my agitated hand was my excellent office girl, Geraldene; what I would have done without her I have no idea.

So one evening when we were toying with our usual whisky and soda, I asked Amanda as to how many deer she had and when had she last examined them? To which my young wife looked quite blank, and also and quite rightly somewhat sheepish, and replied that she had not looked at them for at least a month as she left everything to the man who was in charge. "What about numbers?" I asked, somewhat unfairly. "Don't you think it might be an idea to have a muster of *all* your deer? Have an accurate count, have the vet present and generally get organised in *your* department."

To this my somewhat subdued wife agreed and said that she would let me know the time and the date of the muster.

So a bit of dinner and after a while bed. I lay thinking of the fair success that we had made of this venture. The money kept rolling in, the golf course was I suppose the best earner, then came our small hotel, and all the rest of what we had started, like the cows, the sheep, pigs, chickens, Amanda's deer, corn, the shop even down to beehives, and one or two other oddments that brought in a bob or two. I went to sleep over the wage bill per week, for that like the incomings as against the outgoings was somewhat hefty, and on that note I went to sleep, all seventy years of me with my much younger wife, nestling against my thigh.

Such bliss of course could not on any account last, for at 02.00 the phone went by our bedside and the voice announced that he was the senior policeman in our nearest quite large village, and would we check *forthwith* as to whether our deer were where they should be and not wandering over the whole of their village, destroying every garden in their path. He estimated that there were at least 500.

I nudged Amanda somewhat forcibly. She took some waking and kept on muttering that it wasn't light yet. So I gave her the glad news about *her* deer and asked what was she going to do about it and for good measure as to whether she had taken my advice a while ago to insure against this very happening?

Whilst my half-naked wife was considering as to what to do, I got hold of our home mobile phone which was connected to all the houses on the estate and much to their annoyance, woke the lot up. I explained what had happened and asked them to come to my house forthwith dressed suitably for the night air and we would motor into our small town and endeavour to round up some 700 deer and bring them back to where they belonged and just because I felt like it, I mentioned to all the staff concerned as to where the fault lay, i.e. the man who looked after the deer, it was he who should have looked after his fences, gates, etc.

In half an hour some twelve staff had mustered and off we set in two trucks, Amanda driving one and me the other with directions to report to the police station on arrival.

This we did and were told somewhat forcibly as to the situation by the on duty desk sergeant, and off we all set to round up as many as we could find in the darkness. We soon discovered that most of our animals were searching the vegetable gardens around them and were creating mayhem, so much so that most of the owners of the gardens were awake and trying to shoo off the offending deer.

By the time that most if not all were rounded up into the village square, our name was mud with a capital M, for a lot of damage had been done. But as luck would have it, just as we were about to set forth driving the mob home, there came screams from a nearby house and a female voice shouting "Don't touch me, go away."

So shouting at four of my largest staff, we headed swiftly in the direction of the house from where the screams were coming from. We bashed in the front door and were greeted by two men who were raping a lone female. The four of us pounced and dragged off the attackers, bound their hands behind their backs, assisted the raped female into some clothes and down we all went to the police station once again and in so doing, passed our mob of deer going home.

The station sergeant was this time more than friendly, for it appeared that we had captured two wanted men who had been doing this sort of crime for quite a while. The poor female that we had rescued told us not to bother about what damage the deer had done, what we had done to help her more than repaid anything.

The four of us escorted our poor raped female back to her home where she insisted on kissing all four of us and said that she would spread the news of her rescue throughout the whole town. At which pronouncement I said that it wasn't necessary, but she was adamant so we said good night and left in our last remaining vehicle. We caught up with the herd and had a rough count as they went back into their own domain, and reckoned that we were six short.

Back to what remained of the night, crept into bed and were wakened as usual by the tea machine yelling its head off at 06.00.

The usual morning, cows first, I always had the idea that our two cowmen took a gloomy view of me actually having the nerve to check their work, and what was more at times finding faults, as their previous boss or manager never got up in time. I dashed off in the Land Rover to view Amanda's deer and in particular their fences and then back to a nice breakfast and a loving wife, wondering where I had been since 06.00. So I informed her that she ought to go out and inspect her herd and calculate how many were missing and what was she going to do about it?

We had both finished the usual bacon and fried egg, both of which we produced, or to be more exact, I produced for the hen battery and the pigs were on my side of the estate. There was a pause in the usual chatter and Amanda put down her bit of toast and honey and said that we ought to have a chat about the estate, for she felt that I was doing at least three quarters of the necessary work and that she with three children to look after, was not doing her fair share. At this somewhat interesting remark, I also paused in my eating and asked her as to what she had in mind.

"Are you happy and content with the life that you are leading and even more important are you happy with our marriage?"

She had a look on her face that shook me rigid, for I was more than happy and wondered for a ghastly moment as to whether she shared my views. The next few minutes convinced me that she shared my thoughts about our marriage, for she leapt up from her chair, removed the bit of toast that I was about to insert into my mouth and kissed me somewhat strongly on the mouth, and said "Darling I adore you *but,*" and resumed her chair. And then she started with such items as to what I did on the estate and how often I wandered off to her part and corrected things that were going wrong. "Remember my combine," she said "and how you tore a worthwhile strip off my head tractor driver and saved my part of the harvest, and a lot of other things ending up with my deer? And then there was that wretched tractor driver of mine who was using a six-furrow plough with only two points, the rest were missing, and then the goods that you shove into our shop and we share the profits whilst I contribute more or less nothing."

I seldom bark at my very nice wife, but I barked now before the last bit of toast and marmalade and said "Whoa" or words to that effect. "You my girl manage three children. You keep the house in a beautiful state. You cope with my masculine desires, which I must admit are slowing down somewhat but what is left I enjoy and I trust that you do as well, so let it rest, I am more than happy in my work."

I finished my coffee, kissed my wife and departed for the morning's work, but as I got to the door the post arrived and I thought that I had better take a look at it. So I returned to the breakfast table and got out my trusty pocketknife, which had a dual role of trimming sheep's feet and a hundred other uses including self defence because it had a five-inch lockable blade. I had been told by my friendly local copper that it was illegal, but it was an old friend of at least thirty years, so I kept it. I opened the first letter and there was an invitation from a group of local farmers to give a lecture to them on how to make a profit on a farm, because they added that they had heard that I and my wife made quite a handsome profit. I must admit I wondered as to where they had heard this quite correct news, for it was quite true. If one reduced our 10,000 acres down to say, 100 acres the resulting profit was still quite considerable. I took that and the rest of the mail down to the office to the patient Geraldene and sent this group of farmers a letter saying that I would be glad to give them what few words of wisdom I seemed to possess.

Then I started with Geraldene's assistance to map out this so-called speech that I was expected to make, and paused for a while till she, bless her heart, said, "It's all a matter of figures, Sir John."

"What do you mean?" I asked.

"Simple" she said. "I know a lot of farmers and none of them take the trouble to do what you do in weighing every beast you rear, down to even your latest in the shape of rabbits."

She was quite right, for none of the farmers I knew ever weighed a beast every week as we did here. We weighed a calf at birth and continued weighing the poor wee thing till either it went to market because the weight gain was not enough or it became old enough to produce a calf of its own. We did this same exercise with sheep, all the lambs were weighed each week and the same with the pigs, although with the pigs we were inclined to weigh the whole litter and of course every animal on the whole place had its own ear mark. I had some trouble with the staff when I started this all those years ago, for it had never been done before and they were inclined to think that it was a waste of their time and my money. But with the start of giving the staff a percentage of the *net* profit and they saw the cost of feeding stuffs, they started somewhat slowly to come round to my way of thinking. But of course there were slight rows between the staff when their percentages were paid over, for of course they compared notes, for instance the pig man found that his monies were considerably less than say the two cow types. So the pig chap started to think of ways to increase his profits and of course mine, and the whole exercise became more than interesting.

Then in the middle of one dark and cold night at around about 03.00, I was woken from a comfortable warm sleep with my wife comfortably entwined by my side by the front door ringing. It went on ringing till I stumbled downstairs in my dressing gown feeling just somewhat annoyed at who this might be at this time of the day. I opened the door and in fell a child, scantily clothed and frozen to the bone, and what was more he or she was black as my boots. I lifted the child up, carted it up to our bedroom and plonked it down on our bed to be viewed by a newly-awoken wife who at once exclaimed. "Run a hot bath John."

This I did and we undressed the child to find that it was female and plaintive to a degree but got calmer when we immersed it into warm water.

"Phone the police" says my firm young wife, "and explain the circumstances."

This I did and explained the situation and that the child was a girl of about four to five years old, and I was asked as to how I knew it was a girl. "Because Sergeant she is in a bath and there is a difference twixt male and female."

"Did you undress her, Sir?" I was asked.

"No" I replied, getting just a bit tired of all these questions.

"Ah that's all right then as long as your wife undressed the child," said this inquisitive sergeant of police. "We will send someone along to collect her in due course."

"No you won't" said I, "because she will be asleep in bed in five minutes." There was a pause and I was told that someone would call in the morning.

So I went upstairs again and found that the girl was dressed in one of my winter vests that came down below her knees. She viewed my wife with joy and smiled but said little. She viewed me with distaste and not a little fear, which gave me unpleasant thoughts as to *why* she loathed men. Anyway a cup of hot Bovril and milk went down well and she snuggled down, allowed my wife to plant a kiss on her now clean cheek and shut her eyes. My wife sat with her for a few minutes till she dozed off and then we both went back to bed for the remains of the night.

But before our eyes shut we had a somewhat interesting conversation. I started it off by saying that we would be rid of the child in the morning as the police were coming to fetch her.

"I would like to keep her," says Amanda. "We have two sons and a daughter, and I've always wanted another daughter, but we decided a while ago that I should *not* have any more children of my own because if you remember, John, the last son nearly killed me."

I lay back somewhat shaken by these remarks, for we did not have a clue as to where this child came from. She was black, which to me was in her favour, and she had been abused for there were marks on her back and bottom where she had been hit by something. Maybe in the morning she might cease being more or less silent and tell us something of her background. My thoughts wandered on, we would have to legally adopt her always assuming that we were allowed to. So kissing my wife good night I murmured that if it were possible then she would have her wish.

I awoke at my usual hour of about 05.30 and got myself ready to go and talk to the two cowmen, but as soon as I opened our bedroom door there was a noise of pattering tiny feet and our guest of last night shot off from the landing back to her room. When I got there she was huddled down in the bed, covered from head to foot. So without much thought I pulled the sheets off the child and before she could run, I picked her up and took her crying for some reason or other back to our room. I turned back my side of the bed which was still warm, laid the child down and directed her agitated attention as to who was next door to her in the bed and left quietly. Before I closed the door I looked at her, waved my arm to which I think she acknowledged and then she did the nicest thing, she put her tiny small arm round my wife's waist and smiled. Whether that smile was aimed at me I have no idea but from that moment onwards I warmed to Amanda's idea that we attempt to adopt this wee thing as one of our own.

By the time I came back from my morning chores such as the cows, the pigs and the sheep, pausing just for a moment with the rabbits, then onto Amanda's deer, and then telling the tractor drivers what I wanted doing for the day and finally finding my manager wandering about the place looking lost, Amanda had after some persuasion, found out the child's name which was Susan. Dear Susan objected to being dressed in another vest and shirt of mine which had been tucked into an old pair of shorts going back some fifty years.

Finally with Nanny's assistance, calm descended and we were allowed to eat our breakfast and slowly the child's tale came out, or some of it, quite extraordinary. It would appear that her real father had died a year or two ago and that her mother had married again to a *rotten* man, quoting Susan, who beat her and also was inclined to fiddle about with her private parts, again her description. Finally Susan had had enough and she stole some money from her stepfather and toddled along to the railway station in *Liverpool* of all places. More by luck than any judgement she bought a ticket to our station about half a mile from our house, where she was 'decanted' from her seat on to a wet platform with the rain pouring down and about three pence left in her pocket. She was just six years old. So she left the platform in pouring rain desperately trying to find some shelter, and walked and walked, getting wetter and wetter till she saw our front door with a light shining over it, a habit I have had for years, and feeling more than tired and wornout managed to find the bell push and subsided on the mat.

The first and certainly not the last snag with young Susan was that she flatly refused to say where she lived. Whether she feared that she would be sent back home or not I had no idea but the thought stuck in my mind. So rightly or wrongly I told the child that the police were coming to pick her up and to repeat to them what she had said to us, that she didn't *know* where she had lived *but* she would like to come and live with us.

Amanda looked somewhat shocked and Nanny didn't know where to look but this seemed sense to me, and I asked Susan whether she understood. She said she did *but* if she came to live with us, would I beat her? To this I replied I wouldn't touch her.

This seemed to go down well with the child and she suddenly asked as to whether this was a farm on which we lived and Amanda broke in and said that it was. "And have you any animals?" asked Susan .

Then the door bell went and there were the police, a nice sergeant and a female constable. I asked them as to whether they would like a coffee and then they could view the infant at the same time. So head gear was taken off and in they came.

Susan viewing these two flew to Amanda's chair and cried "Don't let them take me away."

The girl constable then thought that she ought to do something so got up and tried to take Susan away from Amanda and got struck in the face with a small fist. So she, poor girl, gave up and came and sat down again. The sergeant said that maybe we ought to have another think on the matter, but firstly he wanted the child's name and address. To which question Susan swiftly exclaimed that she didn't know and repeating herself, said that she wanted to stay on this farm with these farmers.

"But" said the sergeant, "I must have some information, for her parents will want to know where their daughter has got to."

So I took the sergeant aside and told him what I had been told by Susan; the nasty stepfather and the mother who couldn't care less, and that she arrived here by train from somewhere up north, but we were perfectly willing to keep the child as one of our own and bring her up as we had done with our other three children.

"Well Sir John, let us leave the child with you for the moment and I will report the facts to my chief and see what the powers that be think about the matter." Off they went and Susan with the first real smile on her face went back to Amanda and wanted to sit on her lap.

"No" says my wife, "go back to your seat, finish your breakfast and then when Uncle John," says she pointing at me, "has the time, we will take you shopping and get you some clothes."

So a happy little child finished her food and was told that she could get down. An instruction that I doubt she had heard before.

"Take her out John, and show her a cow or two and then when I have finished my chores, we will go shopping for Susan cannot go on forever in an old vest of yours plus shorts."

Susan was just a bit hesitant about taking my hand when we set out to view an animal, but we stopped at the rabbits and that made her day. She was eager to press on to other animals, in fact she was beginning to pull me along which was a bit different to when we started out. We viewed the lambs, the piglets and the calves and then I took her to the office and introduced her to Geraldene who was more than intrigued when I told her the story whilst Susan was fiddling about with an old computer. Then back to the house and off the three of us set to buy some clothes in our nearby town.

It was amusing to a degree to watch this child who had never, as far as we could tell, been in a clothes shop before, and when it came to choosing what she liked for colouring, blue and red were definitely her line of country. We decked her out with underclothes, stockings and all the rest and finally a hat.

"Why do I want a hat?" asked Susan.

"To wear in church," says Amanda firmly.

"Never been to church" says Susan.

"Well you will be starting this Sunday," says Amanda quite firmly.

And so life went on, I must confess that I was worried for Amanda had taken to this child as if she was its real mother, and I dreaded the time when just possibly the police would arrive and whisk the girl away, but it didn't happen. In fact we got a letter from some bigwig saying that if we wanted to legally adopt the child then get on with it, or words to that effect. This we did and we had a celebration with all our children with us who now regarded the fact that willy-nilly they had a sister.

The only snag in the ointment was the fact that I was growing older by the day. Here was I at seventy plus doing the work of a middle-aged man and it could not continue, for Amanda, bless her, was surrounded by young and really left her part of the estate for me to manage and I was feeling the strain. Our so-called manager could not cope, no doubt about that, and I gently gave him the push, to which I have the idea that he was grateful for there was a lot to do, 10,000 acres, a golf course included in those acres, cows, pigs and all the rest.

So now to once again find a new manager who knew something about hotels, for here was my old father-in-law's house which we had turned into a hotel with six bedrooms, and it was always full and raked in a considerable amount of necessary cash. The three staff seemed to be happy in their work and I left them to get on with the job. The only slight snag in that particular business were the stables, for we kept four saddle horses in case the occupants of the hotel wanted either to have a riding lesson or to take a horse out on their own and the chap who was supposed to look after these animals was always drunk and it made life somewhat complicated to say the least. I had to do something drastic about this chap, who went by the name of Terrence. He had a nice wife who did not seem to be able to keep her husband under control.

Then from the new manager's point of view was the golf club, run now by an efficient secretary, who with the aid of some 700 members gave us a net return of some £30,000 per year. But even there they had their problems which needed sorting out. One of the snags was the course itself, built by me some twenty years ago when I had the delightful problem of building a golf course with a river flowing through the middle of it. It was fun planning out holes which had to cross the river from the tee on one side and the green on the other, which seemed to be a delightful par 3 but of course a number of golf balls fell into the river and members through their own fault, not mine, sent their nice new balls straight into the water. So after a time when complaints became thudding in, we rigged up a net on the river side of the green so as to catch the numerous balls that fell short. So when one raised the net there were hundreds of balls nestling in the net and the pro of course claimed the lot. The secretary of the golf club came to me and asked whether I agreed with the idea of the pro being given all these golf balls for free, which he then sold on to golfers for £1.00 each. So I must admit that this must be altered for a number of the lost balls had the name of the member stamped on it, so said that all those marked balls should be kept for the member who had lost them and the pro could have 25% of the remainder of the unmarked ones. I cannot say that the pro liked this idea and called in various frightful senior pros who wanted to argue the toss. So I told them to go away in the nicest possible fashion and added that if the pro didn't like the idea then he must find another club that suited his tastes. We had no further trouble.

But to return to the duties of this future manager. We have dealt with hotel management, golf clubs and then must be added such things like our milking herd which now numbered about a 100 strong. Their aid to our budget amounted to quite a fair profit, for you must remember that quite a lot of the milk went down cartoned up to *our* shop, another lot went into the milk van which we owned and customers' doorsteps were littered with cartons of our milk. Then the calves, A.I. and all that for we had given up the thought of a bull years ago. Quite a big operation one way and another.

Then he should know something about deer which really was Amanda's business, but she had not the time these days for the house at times seemed to be littered with our progeny plus of course the one that we had adopted, the deer herd numbered about 500. I am glad to hear that butchers far and wide liked the idea of venison, and whenever we had an animal to sell, they would come along, get the beast weighed and they would then cart it away, leaving me with a lot of notes which found their way into the bank.

He, this future manager should be able to shear a sheep when necessary and know whether the shepherd was doing his job.

Then came the pigs, and sows seemed to litter up the place for we started with about ten sows all those years ago and now the number was well over the hundred mark. Their progeny was to say the least numerous and I on market days used to take in a trailer load of a whole family, the mother and her litter, and these sold well.

Then the hen battery with 1,000 birds in it, and they needed some expert attention at times. Their droppings which more or less filled one of these nice trailers which with the PTO switched on from the tractor would scatter this quite useful manure far and wide. In fact we tried this exercise out on a twenty-acre field of wheat and compared the end result with another field which merely had the usual fertilizer spread and the hen field won by quite a large margin.

Then came the rabbits which now numbered some fifty does and their progeny took up quite a bit of space. I found that I had to erect an electric fence in order to keep out the various foxes from the rabbit field, which of course was called the *bunny* field.

Then there were the bees, and we now had some twenty-five hives, and I must confess my knowledge about bees was more or less nil. I left the hives to the wife of one of the tractor drivers, and she earned quite a decent wage from the honey that we sold in our shop.

Lastly but certainly not the least were the tractor drivers who with their vast machines, ploughed and finally scattered the seeds of corn over some 500 acres.

It was Amanda who finally pushed me to advertising for this new manager because I would start to stagger into the house for breakfast, as I had started at my usual hour of 06.00 and done my usual two-hour round of everything that we had owned; from the hotel to the golf club, talking to the shepherd, the pigman, the girl who looked after the battery of hens, the brace of tractor drivers and deciding their jobs for the day, and finally the shop which opened at 07.45 and by this time, my seventy-plus years were starting to creak a bit. She, my dear youngish wife noticed this and with her usual efficient self, she started the conversation off with, "Which papers are you going to advertise in?" Then "What are you going to say in the advert?"

So finally after the usual nice breakfast I went off to the estate office with Geraldene busy with the computer and asked her advice as to what to advertise.

"Explain the whole lot, Sir John. What you do and you expect whoever gets the job with a free house thrown in to do the same if not better."

So we fiddled about with the computer and finally came up with something suitable and sent it off to various papers and settled back waiting for a reply.

They came thick and fast, for the salary that I was offering was way above the normal paid to a farm manager, and for days on end I interviewed various well-meaning males but none of them could master all of our various means of income, till finally the phone went one day and a female voice asked "Is that job of a manager still going?"

I replied that it was but, and then I paused, wondering how to phrase it, but finally said "But you are a woman!"

"Quite right, Sir John, I wonder how you knew!" and the remark ended with just the faintest sign of a giggle.

"Well come along and see me. When can you come?"

"Any moment which is convenient" said the voice, "for I am fairly local."

So a time that very morning was fixed up and I must confess I was more than interested for the voice had breeding behind it. It was pleasant and easy to talk to on the phone, but did she really know what this job entailed? I asked her as to what experience she had and her reply was that she was experienced in all the details that she had seen in my advertisement and would 11.00 hrs today suit me, to which I said that it would and did she know where we were situated, to which she replied that she knew the area well and had in fact played golf on my course and had not, and her voice changed showing just a little pride, lost a ball in the water!

Amanda was listening to all this conversation and she exclaimed "No woman could do what you do, and is she married? Or for that matter has she any children?" added Amanda.

I replied that I had not asked her. "Why don't you come along to the meeting at 11.00 hrs and see what you think? In the meantime I am going to see that a tractor is spare plus a six-furrow plough and one or two other oddments."

"Where are you going to have this interview?" asks Amanda.

"In the estate office, because I want Geraldene to be in the act as well."

So I left a note outside our door saying where we would be, primed Geraldene to tape whatever was said and prepared various tell-tale questions, for instance as to whether a certain cow should have 4 lbs of concentrates or less, and all that sort of everyday problem that occurred in my daily chores.

And so Amanda and I went down to the office at about 10.50 hrs and sat and chatted to Geraldene who was most interested in the possibility of having a woman manager, for she had sat in with me on the half dozen or more quite useless applicants that we had both seen over the last few weeks.

At exactly 11.00 hrs the bell went and Geraldene got up and opened the door. She ushered in this latest applicant, enquired her name which she said was Bell, and introduced us two to her. She gave her a chair and I saw Geraldene quietly click the 'on' button for the tape as she sat and listened.

Going back in my mind I confess that I was somewhat surprised at the apparent age of this girl. She looked about twenty-fiveish and my thoughts went to the problem as to how at that presumed age, she had learnt all that I knew and practised.

She started the ball rolling by thanking me to take the time to see her. "What questions have you in mind, Sir John?"

"Well firstly your name is Bell and your Christian name is?"

To which she replied "Mary." Then she paused for just a moment and then to my great interest, said that if I wanted the exact replies, in that she was actually Lady Bell, married to Lord Bell who died some six months ago. Her age was thirty-two and she had no children. She then sat back in her chair looking relieved that she had got rid of what was bound to be asked.

The three of us, Amanda, Geraldene and certainly me looked somewhat astonished at this more than interesting information that came pouring out from Lady Bell.

"But" said Lady Bell before we could utter a word, "if by chance I do get the job, I would prefer to forget the Ladyship and be called just Mrs Mary Bell."

"OK" I replied, "but now let us get down to the real business of this meeting and that is to find out as to whether you are a suitable applicant for this post. For instance where did you learn say ploughing, milking a cow, throwing a calf and a host of other items which we will talk about?"

"On my husband's estate, not as large as yours, Sir John, but I did have 5,000 acres to look after, so I do know quite a bit here and there. And I should add" said Lady Bell, "we owned a pub on the estate so I know a lot about that side of the business as well."

It was a fine day and I wanted to prove that this girl was really knowledgeable, so I had prepared somewhat wickedly a six-furrow plough stuck into the ground with a tractor nearby, but the top link of the tractor was missing, I had taken it away and I wanted to know if she could connect the two and lift the plough out of the ground, quite impossible without the top link. So ended the questions which had proved quite satisfactory, in fact a damn sight better than any of the men that I had interviewed over the last month. I said, "Right let us go outside and see other matters." So we came to this lone plough stuck in the ground and I asked the question "Can you get it out and what is more, plough up to the end of this particular field and return thus making a twelve-furrow return?"

"Oh yes Sir John, always providing that whoever took away the top link remembers where they put it."

I felt myself blushing and even Amanda who knew all about this ploy had problems in stifling a giggle. I was then asked as to what was going to be sown on this particular field as the depth of the plough was important. This almost floored me, who was supposed to be the man asking the questions. "Just six inches" I replied somewhat stiffly, finding the missing top link at the same time. The next ten minutes were really a sight to be seen by one expert looking at another, for this girl knew what she was doing and even pointed out to me that the point on one plough point was a bit past its prime. She ploughed well and her matched return was even better, and when she had finished she remarked that the tractor could well do with an oil change.

We wandered round our domain and I asked Amanda as to whether we should invite the girl to lunch to which Amanda said a definite "Yes." So back we went to the house and had our usual G&T but Mary preferred wine. Whether she did this so as to impress me, I don't know, but wine she had and then we went on to discuss all the parts of our estate that this girl had seen.

Then she came up with a remark that floored me somewhat, for she said "The only thing that you have missed out in showing me around, Sir John, is the hop garden."

"But" said I with a slight pause, "we haven't got a hop garden. But on the other hand I have often thought that there was something missing on the estate and you have hit the nail on the head. What do you know about hops?" I asked.

"Quite a lot Sir John, for we had quite a large acreage of hops, and I was just thinking as you were talking that the field in which you tried to test my knowledge of ploughing would be ideal for it is sheltered with trees and quite a fair acreage to make a start."

At the end of that I looked at Amanda and she gave just the faintest of nods. So I turned to Mary and said "Right the job is yours at the salary indicated, and if you want the free house then so be it. What about the starting date? For the first few days, I shall come with you and show you the ropes and introduce you to what members of the staff we might meet on our round. So congratulations Mary, let's hope that you find the work satisfactory and that you get on with the staff concerned. I have prepared a list of all the staff from the ones in the shop to the milk roundsman, and I will give you a copy when you commence work. So let me know the date and I will expect you at my front door at 05.45 hrs."

Mary then thanked both of us and asked as to whether it would be all right if she started next Monday which happened to be the first of the month. I said that was OK and after farewells to both of us she left in her car, but first saying that she would like to live in the free tied house and would I give her the keys this coming Saturday so that she could get her belongings in, and that she would see me at the time specified next Monday.

Saturday arrived and I had her contract ready for her to sign as I could not pass over the keys without her signature that she agreed to the terms of her contract. She duly signed and that was that, I wished her well and would see her this coming Monday as we agreed.

Then Amanda and I had a talk about this coming event when the whole set up would be passed over to this Mary Bell. What was I going to do if my presence was no longer needed? I must admit that I had not really given this problem much of a thought, for I had been very fully employed for years, running this estate and the thought of doing just nothing appalled me. "So what do you suggest?" I asked my young wife. "For here am I over the seventy mark and you are only just rising above the forties."

"Well" said Amanda, "much as I love having you round the place, I would suggest that you firstly learn something about hops. Then when you are on a 'par' with the knowledge that young Mary seems to have, then I should leave her to it and cast your eyes down to where your boat is moored. Go and 'talk' to her for you have never had the time to even go and see whether her moorings are OK or not."

"Good idea" I said "I will go down after a week with this girl and perhaps venture out which I have not done for years." This idea came every now and then that perhaps as I used to do, I could make some money out of this craft as I had done years ago with the first golf course my then wife and I had built. Members queued up for a weekend on this craft at £100 per day per person and I provided the food and drink. It was still a very welcome income, so why not try again with the present 700 members of the golf club, and for that matter the hotel guests as well; in for a penny in for a pound as

K

the saying goes.

So I rang up the secretary of the golf club and arranged for a notice be put up showing that this craft was available for a weekend, and showing the cost per person. Then I went to the hotel after Geraldene had typed out the same sort of notice and put that up in the lobby and waited to see what happened.

Meanwhile I met Mary at the usual time and showed her what I did every day and instructed her to the same. If she had anything that she wanted to discuss then she could meet me at the estate office at 12.00 every day if necessary. We bought the girl a motorbike for her own use so as to get round the estate, for which she was more than grateful.

Then both the hotel and the golf club demanded my attention, for it would appear that quite a lot of people were more than interested with the thought of a weekend afloat. So I started to go down to the berth, tidy up and get things ready, arrange for a supply of drink and food which merely needed heating up. At the moment I seemed to be cook and bottle-washer plus the pilot of this vessel, and that would never do. I was quite happy being the pilot for I knew the English coast well and a bit of the French coast too, so I started looking round for a man who could insert his body into a minute cabin on this craft and sort out the food side of the weekend.

I have forgotten to mention the pupils that we take in year after year. They pay us a small sum for their keep and for the knowledge that they are supposed to learn in their year with us. At the time of writing this we had three youngsters, two boys and a girl, and they slept in a sort of annexe at the clubhouse. One of the boys came up to me and said that he would be glad to assist on these weekend trips as he was keen on cooking and liked the sea as well. So the next time I went down to Brighton Marina, I took this lad along with me and showed him over the craft and also his somewhat small quarters, and for good measure told him that I would pay him for his time spent on board. This he liked and was looking forward to his first sea outing.

I found that I was overbooked, to which Amanda was pleased about for she and Mary Bell were becoming firm friends and they both seemed to think that at my age I should forget the somewhat hard work of running a 10,000-acre estate. So Mary drew lots and arranged for the first two couples to meet me at the berth concerned at Brighton Marina at 12.00 on the Saturday next.

146

I collected the pupil whose name was Patrick, and together we drove down to Brighton Marina so as to be ready for the first two couples that had been arranged by Mary Bell. I must admit when I first saw them I thought that the trip would be a disaster, for the couple from our hotel were nudging eighty years of age and the other couple from the golf club had hardly reached the twenty stage. I thought at the time of meeting that I must tell Mary to arrange the age-groups in a better manner, but I was wrong they all got on very well. The aged husband had been RNVR during the war and knew quite a bit about boats and was more than eager to steer a given course when necessary. The other two youngsters enjoyed the fun of drinking more or less a bottle of gin between them whilst the old twosome stuck to red wine. We lunched at the moorings and when everything was washed-up and the craft tidy, we cast off bow and stern lines and off we went. As soon as we got out into the Channel the two young wanted to fish, so I slowed up a bit, rigged up two lines and they waited with bated breath for some foolish fish to catch the bait. Luck struck after the first half an hour as we drifted slowly down westward towards the Isle of Wight, for they caught a good-sized cod which they presented to me. I in turn gave it to Patrick who regarded this somewhat large monster with a bit of awe but said that it should last the six of us at least two meals; one hot tonight and the other cold for tomorrow's lunch. We reeled in the lines because I wanted to reach our berth for the night up the Beaulieu River and moor near Bucklers Hard. There were quite a few sea miles in front of us, so I opened up the two giant diesels and after setting a course, invited the old RNVR crew to take the wheel which made his day and off we roared off for Southampton Water. Finally the Beaulieu River came into view as dusk was arriving and then Bucklers Hard with that nice hotel on the port side where we anchored and went ashore in the dinghy, all six of us which was a bit of a squeeze. Our paying guests insisted on buying Patrick and I all the drink that we could consume and in the end I thought that we had better get back on board and have the dinner that Patrick had prepared which was the cod and all the trimmings, and it went down well.

We slept the night rather too well, for we had all drunk a bit much and we ended up with a somewhat large dose of port afterwards. I taught Patrick the proper way to pass round the port decanter which puzzled him somewhat, but the dawn arrived as all dawns do and with all those years of farming behind me I was first up and made a cup of tea for everyone. At about 06.30 I woke them up gently and told them that breakfast would be at 08.00 sharp as we had quite a few miles to cover. I explained the use of the 'heads' which I should have done before as there was a bit of a mess in our small 'loo' yesterday. I also explained how the showers worked and told all and sundry that we were *not* on mains and that they should not waste water.

At about 07.30 the first of our passengers staggered out of their cabin, went to the shower and the head and used it in the proper manner, which showed that what I had told them had sunk in. Then the next two did the same and by the time that they were all dressed, young Patrick had a decent breakfast all ready. We all sat and I told them what was going to happen today, i.e. back down this nice river, into the open sea and back from whence we came. But this time we would head for Rye, weather and all that being kind, as I wanted to show our passengers that nice little town of Rye and the Mermaid Inn for a start, and I knew that I could hire a car for the day. Then after a walk round the place back to Brighton where we would 'decant' our passengers.

All went well; they enjoyed the place and we said farewell at Brighton Marina on the Monday morning and back I and young Patrick drove to our various homes.

I was interested to see how my new manager, Mary had got on in my absence and enquired tactfully at each department as to how things were going. They all mentioned without being asked as to how nice the new lady manager was and how surprised they were at her knowledge in their particular field. So with my wife's blessing and great pleasure, I rang Mary up on her mobile and invited her to lunch with us at 12.30. She said that she would be delighted and how kind we were and how happy she was in her new job, but she wanted to discuss hops prior to lunch if that was OK. I said that I was more than interested, and would she have some figures ready for me; the acreage she wanted, the cost of erecting the actual hop 'garden' and what she thought we could make out of it acre by acre, and even more important, would we need extra staff?

This girl, for I still regarded her in that fashion, she was to me anyway still a youngster, pretty as well, seemed to have a vast knowledge of things that grew which was more than handy to me and the estate, so why not branch out into acres of this and that?

We had a shop which if necessary could be enlarged so as to sell a great range of vegetables, from sprouts, spuds, cabbages and all the rest. When she came and we gave her a drink and sat her down between Amanda and I, she then poured out the hop figures and what she thought we would make out of it each hop year. The result was more than welcome and I patted her on her shoulder so as to show my enthusiasm, only to receive a warning glance from my wife, who no doubt regarded that as quite unnecessary! I then poured out my thoughts as to the question of increasing the vegetable side of the business and the shop from the selling side and how she would gain from the overall profit at the end of the day. I must confess that I was astonished at what this new manager of ours came up with. She implied that many vegetables such as carrots, spuds and all the rest were far more profitable than mere wheat or barley or even oats. We had the acreage so why not start in a small way with a few acres of this and that and also she added, much to my surprise, that my two tractor drivers really had nothing to do in their spare time. So with the meal ended and coffee to hand we decided that we would have a go at this vegetable idea. We sorted out where we would start and off she went, but before she departed, after looking at my wife with a sort of pleading glance, she suggested that I really should leave the whole thing in her capable hands as I was getting old and I should enjoy my boating project. If she wanted to know something then she would come along and talk about it to me at the usual hour cf 12.00 in the estate office, always assuming that I was on dry land.

And so life changed for me somewhat. I must admit that I had problems not leaping out of bed at my old working hour. Instead I lay there listening to my wife's deep breathing till 07.00 hrs came and I could no longer stand the thought of doing nothing, so up I crept, bathed, shaved and took the dogs out before they doused the carpets with you know what. I then laid the breakfast table, woke up sleeping wife at 07.30 and my new day started. I must confess that it took a while to get used to the idea that this new manager of ours was doing her job but I was nasty enough to make discreet enquiries, especially from Geraldene in the office, who was to my slight annoyance quite astonished at the rate that this girl worked and also to the knowledge that she displayed at the varied programmes of her work.

So I, with the possible assistance of a suitable notice in the hotel and also in the golf clubhouse, nursed if that be the right description, various foursomes to become seaworthy each weekend. Not all that easy to choose the right couples. Will they mix or won't they? Did they talk with the same sort of accent? Were they too old? Were they too young? Were they drunks or a bit too keen on drugs? Mary and Geraldene helped me a lot with these somewhat tricky choices. Sometimes we made frightful bloomers, for on one occasion having moored for the night I discovered that the wife who should have been sleeping in the forward cabin was having a gay old time with the male in the aft cabin. They had all changed around which made things a bit tricky at breakfast time. But on the whole it all worked out quite well, although on one weekend we had quite an adventure.

At Brighton Marina I asked my passengers as to where we should go and the majority wanted Fécamp, so after a decent lunch, washed down with a vast amount of liquor, off we set only to have to halt half-way because one of the wives got frightened at not being able to view land. She became somewhat hysterical, so we had to change routes smartly before she threw herself overboard and headed back for the shores of Sussex and Kent. If we were still at sea during the evening, then bridge was played with great force in the middle cabin, although I must admit that I liked to berth with enough light to see where I was heading.

I got used to this changed sort of life after a while, but I found that the time between weekends was somewhat of a bore and started playing golf once again. Having not played for a number of years, I found that my previous handicap of 14 was impossible but was lucky enough to find a number of my age-group who also wanted a nice slow game. We formed a sort of elderly golf society and played eighteen nice slow holes every Wednesday morning; drinks in the bar afterwards and as we paid into a sort of fund for the large sum of a pound, the winner was given 75% of it and the rest was banked for a rainy day.

This was also the time when golf club annual subs were due to be paid and there was great excitement as to who was going to be the top of the 9-hole competition annual game that I started a year or so ago; i.e. each member's name was a board and he or she played the name above, and the member who was at the top of the 700-member list got a free year's golf which in those days was in the region of £1,000. Thus the excitement for 12.00 hrs was fast approaching and I had to present the winner with the suitable members' ticket for the year concerned. I was pleased to see that it was a lady member, a very popular girl who played an excellent game of golf. She had been working her way up the vast list steadily for the last year till today. She was just one from the top and what is more she was playing against a man. I admit that the ladies were granted a slight handicap over the men whenever they met, but very little, so I presented her with her free year's sub documents and then she, dear girl, invited us all into the bar and gave us drinks all round. It must have cost her a fortune as there were at least 200 members present.

Then the usual weekend loomed and the boat was got ready for our four guests; two from the golf club and an oldish couple from the hotel. As usual we met at Brighton Marina at the berth where the boat lay and I was a bit surprised to find that the couple from the hotel were not old at all and what was more, they came with two vast suitcases. I knew the couple from the golf club and greeted them as old friends, so I asked this other pair their name and there was just the slightest of pauses before he replied that they were Mr and Mrs Smith. I asked them as to whether they were happy with their room at the hotel and again there was this pause till the man said that they both found it very nice and their bathroom was pleasant as well. I thought no more about the matter till we cast off. After the usual drink and a snack for lunch we headed for the Thames, with me at the wheel and Patrick washing-up. The pair from the club were sunning themselves on the deck, when as usual I phoned up Geraldene to tell her all was well and then asked who this Smith lot were and when did they arrive at the hotel? I should mention that the phone was in the wheelhouse and I was on my own.

"What Smith lot?" asked Geraldene. The couple who you were supposed to take have just come into the office in a temper, asking why their booking had been cancelled."

"Well" I said, with one hand on the wheel and the other clutching the phone, "they came to the right spot for the boat as did the other two. They replied that their name was Smith and they liked their room at the hotel and they also liked their bathroom, *but....* "

Here Geraldene interrupted and said that they would not have had a bathroom of their own, they would have had to share.

Whilst this was going through my head, there was a scream from the aft end of the boat and also a shout from Patrick. Suddenly the door of the wheelhouse was violently shoved open and the man who I knew as Smith shoved a revolver into my ribs and shouted "Drop the phone and head due south at 180 degrees for France."

I made to replace the phone but was able to mutter "Mayday 180 degrees" before I put the receiver back on the hook.

"Who was Mayday that you were talking to?" asked Smith.

"My wife" I replied with a look of surprise that he didn't know the name of my wife.

"Right" says Smith "keep on 180 degrees and don't try anything silly or you will get this in your guts."

I glanced down at what he was indicating and found myself almost at home, for here was the exact .45 that was issued to me during the war. However unless you cocked the thing it took seconds to fire, but dear Smith had forgotten to cock it, so I took a chance and asked him if he would kindly check my bearing for I didn't want to land him at the wrong spot in France. So for a moment or two he looked at the compass bearing and the revolver dropped somewhat from where it had been pointing, which had been my belly to his thigh. I pounced and he, silly fool, pulled the trigger and shot himself fair and square in the thigh and fell to the floor of the wheelhouse yelling his head off, I removed the gun from his somewhat useless hand, moved cautiously to the door of the cockpit and opened it with due care to find the girlfriend of Smith pointing a somewhat evil-looking knife at the wife of the couple who had come from the golf club. Poor young Patrick was writhing on the floor with this female's foot pinning him in this ignominious position. I can sound somewhat vicious when I want to and my shout of "Drop it" to this female did the trick, for she dropped the knife and did what I told her to do, which was to lie face down on the floor whilst Patrick struggled to his feet. I told him where rope was kept and waited till he had tied this girl up with her hands behind her back and both feet strapped to her hands; a position she disliked for her language was earth shattering. Then having calmed down the wife of the golf couple and peering into their cabin to find the husband tied hand and foot, I got Patrick to release him and told the lad to come to the cockpit with some suitable bandages and some more cords, so as to tie up dear Mr Smith. Wound or no wound, I didn't trust him an inch.

All this took about twenty minutes and meanwhile my dear craft was heading on her own volition towards France at about thirty knots. So I revoked all that and brought her down to a dead stop and took stock of the present position. Firstly I apologised profusely to my two golf club guests and told them that this did *not* happen on the usual weekend trips. I sat them down at the table and poured them out a much needed drink, and told them also for good measure that I had no wish to take any money from them. As soon as we could get rid of our two unwelcome guests their wishes would be implemented.

Suddenly there was a roar of powerful engines. Looking out I saw a nice-looking craft pulling alongside and what was more at least four or maybe five types with machine guns pointing in our immediate direction with a loud voice telling us to receive boarders and to keep our hands up. All of us who were able did in fact raise a hand or two, but speedily told the boarding party that all was well. They had two prisoners, one wounded who needed some attention and the other needed to clean out her mouth for her language at the sight of the law was ripe to a degree. So our two unpleasant types were removed, we gave a drink to the law, thanked them for their assistance and asked them how on earth they had found us?

"A girl called Geraldene phoned us up and said that there was trouble on a craft heading at 180 degrees and would we investigate, to which we did," replied the leader of the group. "Thanks for the drink and we will let you know what might happen to these two after we have opened their vast suitcases."

I heard that particular bit of news a few days later, but in the meantime I asked our two remaining passengers as to where they would like to go to for the rest of the day and for that matter the night as well? They replied that Rye would suit them, so to Rye once again we went. I took them round the town, had an excellent dinner at the Mermaid Inn for which I paid, after all these two old dears had suffered quite a lot and it was the least that I could so as to make amends. I had of course got in touch with Geraldene and thanked her profusely and reminded myself to put a little present in her pay packet at the first opportunity. And then finally back to our nice berth at Brighton Marina to be met by worried wife, for Geraldene had kept Amanda in the picture as to what was happening on the boat to her husband.

The final part of this was of course that I had to attend court and so did the two passengers from the golf club. We heard from the police that both large suitcases were full of drugs and I was very glad to witness that the girl got seven years and the man, when he got out of hospital, got ten years.

I must say I was more than flattered at the fuss my young wife made of me when we finally met after we came ashore. She had brought the two dogs with her for company and they also made a great fuss of their master. The couple who were from the golf club had come by taxi and I felt that the least I could do for them after all the trauma they had gone through was to run them to their home which wasn't all that far away. Then at last to my home and a much needed large Scotch, joined by wife and Mary came along as well and even Geraldene knocked on the front door and we became a happy foursome. I owed a lot to Geraldene, for it was she who saw through my signal on the phone, with a gun pointing at my ribs, and who had saved the day.

So we had a quite happy supper together, and I filled in a few bits that the girls didn't know about, such as the feeling of a gun pointing at you with the finger on the trigger, *but* thank the Lord, not cocked. And when the shot was fired, the feeling of complete relief when my attacker folded to the deck of the cockpit. I must admit, looking back in my mind, I did assist him just a little bit, wounded or otherwise. I felt a bit peeved being held up at gun point on my own craft. Anyway that was that and I trusted that the next foursome on the boat would not have to go through the same agony that the two old dears from the golf club must have gone through. After bidding our two girl guests good night we departed for an early night and I must admit that I slept like a log.

I woke feeling somewhat guilty for the time was nearly 07.00 and I had been used to getting up at 05.00 for years on end. Then I remembered that I was semi-retired. I had a first-rate new manager in the shape of Mary Bell, so 07.00 suited me fine. Carefully getting myself disentangled from my loving wife without waking her up, not an easy task for the last thing that Amanda did every night just as she went to sleep was to throw an arm round my waist, so even if I wanted to spend a penny during the midnight hours, a chore that I found as I grew older was becoming more frequent, it was a bit of a problem at times. But this morning all was well. I shaved and showered and was astride my trusty motorbike by 07.30 and out onto the estate. The first person I met was young Mary also on her bike which we had given her when she first started working for us. So we stopped and exchanged thoughts and the first thing that Mary said was that she wanted to hire or buy some twenty tents.

"Tents?" I asked. "Whatever for?"

"The hop pickers" was the reply. "We shall need at least twenty families, and it is a lot better if we house them here right on the job," said Mary.

I must confess at this stage that although I knew quite a lot about farming in general, I knew next to nothing about hops which Mary had persuaded me to grow when she first arrived. Although I had often looked at the vast acreage of hops that she had planted, the mere thought of picking the 'fruit' or whatever is the right word, never entered my aged head. But it was obvious that the picking time was nigh and something must be done. So I told Mary to do what she thought was best. Then I asked, "How do you find all these people, these twenty families that you were talking about?"

"Oh that's easy," says Mary. "I will go to the nearest Gypsy encampment and pass the news around that we needed some labour. Then there is the problem of sorting the crowd out, for they will come in their hundreds as hop picking is more than popular with them. I always ask as to which farmer they were last with and ring that farmer and ask him whether this family was OK or not. You soon sort out the number we want. This year," continued Mary "we shall have to dry our hops in the same place as we dry our corn, but we really want to build our own oast house with a kiln. It will cost a bit but we might be able to dry other people's hops for them and make a bit more money that way."

"OK Mary get on to at least three builders and get three quotes for this oast of yours so that it will be ready for use next year."

"Right Sir John, I will do that as soon as possible" says my excellent manager.

"Have you any further problems?" I asked.

"Well there is one point that I would like cleared up, and that is to do with the golf club and the course," says Mary. "Am I in charge of that or is the present secretary responsible for the running of the course? I have experienced just a slight feeling that he does not like me interfering in the golf course affairs. The tractors never seem to have an oil change and they are generally filthy and when I mentioned this to him the other day, he almost but not quite told me to mind my own business."

"Right Mary, I will sort that out," I said with the firm determination that the present secretary must be told as to who he should turn to if he had any problems.

155

It so happened that on my weekly game of golf with our newly-formed batch of old types all over the seventy age-group that the secretary did come along and ask me a question about something pertaining to the course. I told him to get in touch with the manager of the estate and that she would give him the answer. That settled that problem quite quickly although I had the feeling that he was not all that keen on the idea of taking orders from a woman.

The hired tents arrived and were erected in a nice quiet spot near the river with trees for shade, and Mary got busy interviewing the loads of applicants who came along with their families in tow wanting to be employed picking our hops. I sat in whilst Mary interviewed a would-be family, and I must say that I was impressed with her ideas on dealing with this sort of problem. She asked first as to who they had worked for last, then a firm almost shout "Keep your kids quiet" which was done very quickly by the mother and so in time the interview was over and this family was ushered out and a new one came in. The same drill was repeated, each family being told that if they did not hear within a week, they must understand that the job was filled.

Then the three of us, Mary, Geraldene and I got down to the task of choosing twenty families out of the forty or so that had come along for the job of picking our hops. We had decided before we started that we would each mark each family out of twenty and compare notes afterwards; the twenty top markers would get the job. This was soon done. There were no arguments between us although I noticed that Mary marked each family lower than either Geraldene or I did. Still it didn't matter and twenty letters were typed out giving the details of the job, the wage per day or per week. So as to keep their area spotless for good measure we supplied litter bins to take care of that problem. The twenty families arrived on a Monday and the work started under the stern supervision of Mary, who told each family what she wanted doing and there were few arguments; a firm girl was our Mary.

So the hop picking started, a work which I knew next to nothing about, so I watched it all with great interest. Mary running around giving instruction here and there and telling one family that if they did not want to do the work her way, then there was the gate and their present half-day's wages would be waiting for them. No more trouble with that lot although the father glared at the backside of Mary every time she passed by. We did have one problem that neither Mary or I had thought about, and that was the question of the Gypsy dogs who ran riot and tangled with our lot at every opportunity. A situation that had to be sorted out at once and although they, the workers did not like our ruling we told them that their hounds *must* be kept on a lead at all times. Then and only then peace reigned.

So hops were picked and dried and then brewers came and examined our quite considerable tonnage. They offered a price and obviously we chose the highest, and after everything was signed and paid for, they swept us clean and that was that. We had made a fair profit even after Mary had her share, and I asked her as to whether we should increase the hop acreage for we had the land, the help was eager and we had made quite a fair profit on the acreage that we had started.

Mary said that she would give the matter some thought but I had to understand that the cost in timber and wire might come to quite a bit. "But if you are willing then let us have a go," said young Mary.

So in time the hop acreage was doubled. We built a suitable oast house supervised again by Mary, and I must say that it fitted in with our countryside very well. Even better still we had letters from other hop growers as to whether we would dry their hops.

There came the day, and it happens to all of us, that I suddenly realised that I was not as young as I had thought. I used to work a ninety-hour week without turning a hair. Admittedly I was asleep by 9 p.m. or thereabouts, but I enjoyed it but one day doing my usual half-day's work, because Mary, bless her took at least 75% of the workload off my shoulders, I felt faint. Here I was on my trusty motorbike, ambling along and all at once everything went black and I awoke some hours later finding myself on a stretcher.

Being carted off by four strong-looking chaps and an anxious wife, plus Mary trotting along by my side. I tried to get up but was gently pushed down again and off we set. There was the ambulance all waiting and I was ushered in. Amanda insisted on coming along as well which was comforting. Then the hospital with doctors all over the place prodding me with this and that till the senior of them came to my side and said, "Sir John, you have had a heart attack or maybe a minor stroke and you must stay with us for a while till you are fit to return home. But" said he with a firm voice, "you are now retired and just remember that as otherwise I will not answer to the consequences."

I was then taken to a nice single room, comfortable bed and Amanda fussing along by my side. There I lay, trying to understand what had happened and she explained that when I failed to turn up for lunch or even the usual midday meeting of the staff, then search parties were sent out. "It was Mary who found you and using her mobile, got hold of me and told me the situation. The rest you know about, the ambulance and the hospital, the doctors and now you must rest and do what they tell you and then you can come home."

I was there in that nice hospital for a week, visited every day by my darling wife and at another time by Mary who kindly kept me up to date as to what was going on in our estate. One day the car came for me and I was told that I could go, but that if I wanted to go on living then *all* work as I had been doing over the years must cease forthwith. "For after all" explained the doctor, "I now know quite a bit about your life and you are more than fortunate in having a number of staff, especially Mary, who dotes on you. So let them be, you do a bit of book work if you want but not more than one hour per day and I shall, with your permission come and see you at least once a month to see as to whether you are behaving yourself."

So home I came to quite a different life to the one that I had led for the past half century. Instead of getting up at 05.00, I was forcibly kept in bed till Amanda got up first at 07.00, and then and only then when she had finished her ablutions was I allowed to show a toe out of the bed. By the time that I had washed, showered and shaved, breakfast was on the table at 08.00.

The first day this happened I ate my breakfast and then went out to get on my motorbike only to be stopped by Amanda who almost shouted "Where do you think you are going?" So I was taken back into the house, told to either open and do my mail or do the crossword, but if I behaved myself I could go down to the estate office at 12.00 for the daily meeting of all the staff.

Mary of course was there giving out orders left, right and centre, telling some what a good job they had done and others that they would have to do that particular task again for the result was ghastly. I was allowed to get up and say how happy I was to be back again and how kind of those who had written get well cards; much appreciated. Then that was that, back home and the usual G&T for both of us. Then lunch and then to cap it all I was told firmly that I must put my feet up for at least an hour and if possible go to sleep.

"But" I said to my firm young wife, "I feel perfectly fit. Why have I got to lie down and go to sleep?"

"That's what he told me" says Amanda, "so be a good chap and do what you are told to do for once in your life."

So this existence went on for some three months. I passed my eightieth birthday and that was a day to remember for the children of my first marriage and their children came along and of course our four, plus Amanda, and Mary and Geraldene. It was quite a party one way and another.

One day I woke at my new retired hour and felt foul, so the doctor was called and off I went once again to the hospital for an X-ray. After that was over the doctor came along and said that he was sorry to tell me but I had developed cancer of the prostate. It was too far advanced to be operated on so I must have an injection every twelve weeks so as to keep the thing from growing.

It was then I suppose that I felt like giving up my life, because I became, according to Amanda, a quite different man from the one she had known all these years. No longer did I take part in animated chat with all and sundry. I found out quite by accident that crowds frightened me, and I became a somewhat silent and probably a very dull individual to have to live with. I had pills by the score and Amanda organised these, five for breakfast and another five for lunch. To cap it all I was not allowed to wear my old farming belt that I had used for at least forty years, I had to wear braces instead. Every twelve weeks a nurse would prod my enlarged belly with a vast needle which maybe did some good, who knows, time will tell.

My life seemed to suddenly change from doing everything more or less on our quite large estate, to doing more or less nothing. There was a debate as to whether each day I could ride my favourite motorcycle. I had the feeling that Mary, bless her heart, sometimes when something went wrong, would withhold that bit of gossip in case it worried my somewhat aged brains. Golf of course, a game I loved, had to go and with it all my clubs and golf gear. These I gave to our family, most of whom now played the game.

Mary came to me one day with a quite personal problem. I was in my study learning, always learning about things to do on my quite up-to-date computer. I sat her down when she asked as to whether I would help her with a problem? I assumed that it was something to do with the estate, but "No" said Mary "it is to do with my personal life and I have a suitor who has been after me for months and says that he wants to marry me. *But* I am not at all sure that firstly I am fond enough of him to get married once again and for that matter leave this place and my job which I adore, and even more important I have the feeling that he is not all that he implies that he is cracked up to be, if you take my meaning. So Sir John, if I arrange a meeting between the four of us, for I would like your wife's views as well, would you talk to this chap, whose name is Bill Summers, and find out what you can about his background and let me have your views? Could you do that for me?"

"Of course I will," I said. "See my wife about when she thinks is a convenient date and we will sort this problem of yours out for you, but" I added "I must admit here and now, he has to be very special this chap, for not only are we fond of you but you manage this place so well, and the thought of a replacement leaves me somewhat cold!"

So a date was fixed and we invited Mary and this Bill Summers to lunch. I always like to see how a person eats his food, it sometimes tells one a lot about his background.

The day arrived and both came to the door. Mary introduced Bill Summers to Amanda and I and the first thing that struck me was he wore earrings and that his razor lacked a blade for his face was scruffy to a degree. Then without any 'by your leave' he dropped my title and called me by my first name and the same with Amanda, and down we sat for a pre-lunch drink of the usual G&T. We talked and I at first called him Mr Summers, but he insisted that he was Bill and nothing more. I asked him what he did for a living and he replied that he had enough money not to have to work.

"You must have rich parents to leave you all the necessary capital," I said, to which he remained silent. As lunch proceeded and I talked to this Bill with earrings, it became quite obvious that he had not the slightest intention of informing me or the others and in particular, Mary, as to anything about his so-called private life, bar that he lived in London in a flat, but as to the address of the flat or its phone number, he somewhat skilfully evaded any answer. So I desisted and thought as to how I was going to find out anything about this chap, but having a somewhat devious mind I thought that after lunch I would somehow or other obtain this chap's fingerprints. This I did by pretending to try and undo a garden tool which just happened to have some tar on it, and asked Bill if he would be so kind as to hold the other end, whilst I twisted the nut concerned with a spanner. This he kindly did and left his thumb and forefingerprint clearly for all to see.

When they both said farewell, I got on to a friend of mine who just happened to be a somewhat high up official in Scotland Yard and also was a member of our golf club and I had played with him a number of times, and asked him as to whether, if I sent these prints up to him, he could look through his records to see whether this Bill Summers had any record which concerned the police.

After two days this golfing police mate of mine got on the phone and the excitement in his voice was more than interesting, for the first question he asked was the address of Bill Summers or whatever name he was now using, for he had a record a yard long and the police wanted to question him with regards to a number of cases. I gave my friend what small details I had obtained which was really nothing, but when I told him that dear Bill was more than interested in my estate manager, he asked me as to whether I would have a small chat with Mary and put her in the picture up to a certain point and inform the Yard as to when Bill was likely to visit us again.

So this I did. I had a word with Mary who sighed with relief for she was certain in her mind that there was something fishy about this chap and gladly agreed to lure Bill down and also inform the Yard as to when he was expected on the estate.

Bill phoned Mary and asked her out to dinner at our local hotel. She told me the details and I phoned the Yard and the stage was set. Bill duly arrived at Mary's house and off they went to the hotel for dinner. In the middle of dinner, the Yard pounced in the dining room which was a bit unpleasant for poor Mary, but the inspector who did the arresting called our Bill Summers quite a different name, in fact it sounded foreign and we did in fact find out later that dear Bill was in fact a Russian engaged in smuggling drugs from Russia to this country. He had been born in Russia, but educated over here and in fact had lived most of his life in this country, thus his apparent English bearing.

Our dear Mary was happy once again. She had been bothered by this man for quite a while and maybe in time he would have got his way with her. Now all that was behind her and she thanked me most profusely, and with a smile to my wife kissed me on the cheek to show her feelings for the man that had saved her from possible ruin, and back she went to manage the estate in a happy frame of mind.

I never thought that I could teach Mary anything about farming but there came a time when noticing the vet's bills were somewhat high, and in particular their visits seemed to be concentrated as to whether a cow was in calf or not. As I used to do this somewhat messy job before I got ill, I thought that I would make some enquiries as to why we didn't do this job ourselves as of yesteryear. So when I had a chance I tackled Mary on the subject and she confessed that she had never learnt how to do this particular job. So it gave me some pleasure to give her a demonstration of firstly stripping off most of one's top garments, tying up the cow concerned and inserting the arm gently up the backside of the animal. Then with the fingers eject the manure, for want of a better word, onto the ground and then exploring still further one found two smallish bits of flesh and if one was bigger than the other, then the cow concerned was in fact in calf.

"Have a go," I said to Mary who regarded my somewhat smelly arm with some distaste. "I will bring you a bucket of warm water, which is something that I had forgot at the start of this exercise." So I washed and watched Mary who somewhat distastefully inserted her female arm up the right spot, ejected the manure and finally found what I had told her. She was pleased with her ability to do what her boss had done and what she should have known herself.

All this exercise made me feel as if I had run miles and I had to lie down for a while. I was told by my good wife not to be silly and remember that I was ill and not fit enough to do that sort of job. "After all," she said, "we have enough money to pay the vet, so why on earth do you have to worry yourself over such trifles!" I suppose she had a point, but it made me feel once again that the end would really be a blessing.

The only so-called active thing left to me was my boat and the endless letters and phone calls that I received from members, wanting a weekend on my boat moored down at Brighton Marina. The charge was still £100 per head for twenty-four hours with free food and drink thrown in for good measure. I would take six bottles of gin and the same with whisky and also red and white wine and the sea would become littered with empty bottles. I knew for certain that some of the couples that came with me merely had one dry sherry each prior to dinner, but when they got onto the boat, then old habits faded and they lashed into the spirits with gay abandon.

After asking my dear wife if she minded me going away for a weekend, I was deluged with comments that I was not really well enough to cope with this sort of thing, but in the end I was finally let off the hook and allowed to go off on my beloved craft with four paying guests. However there was a slight problem that I had not considered, because before I got ill I used to grab one of our male pupils off the estate and he would do the cooking and help in other ways, but I found to my horror that all the male pupils had gone and we were filled up with girl pupils. I asked Amanda what I should do and her reply was to request the help of one of the girl pupils, explaining first that we both had to sleep in the same cabin midships and if they didn't like the idea then I must ask one of the others. This I did and the first two after hearing about their sleeping quarters politely said no, but the third could not care less as to who she slept with, always assuming that the beds were separate. Phyliss came and proved a saint in that she cooked well, looked after the guests and for that matter me as well with a motherly air. When it came to bedtime she asked me politely if I would vacate the cabin concerned whilst she took all her clothes off, had a wash and climbed into her nightdress. She would give me a signal as to when I could safely venture into what was now a double-bedroomed cabin. All of which I did and then without thinking I started to undress and a voice came out of the darkness asking me to divest of my clothing in the bathroom, which I did and came back clothed in my pyjamas, said good night and climbed into my bunk.

We had a very happy weekend. The forward couple were ex-Army, he having retired as a major general and the aft two were Navy, he having retired as a captain Royal Navy. So a lot of the chat midships was connected with war and all that but Phyllis and I got on well together and she amused me by saying that it was the first time that she had slept in the same bedroom with a male. Also if I approved of her work, she would like to repeat the performance for she loved boats and the sea. She asked if we could sometimes make a dash to France, Fécamp if possible where she had an aunt. I said that we would always providing that the weather was kind.

I must say that what with my home life having altered to such an extent, what with my stroke and also I suppose having reached the venerable age of eighty and a bit, I would have been a fool to carry on the way that I did in the past; up before the dawn cracked and around the estate, seeing all the departments working as they ought to be and finally back to breakfast. No those days were over and thanks to our Mary the estate was being well run. The golf club returned a good £40,000 most years, the hotel did almost as well, the corn cheque was a delight and the milk cheque also kept its end up. Then there were the rabbits, the bees, and other odds and ends and we were able to insert the considerable surplus into stocks and shares, helped by an efficient broker. No, life although changed considerably was more than pleasant, the children now all grown up and in various jobs were all happy and grandchildren now abounded.

But I niggled somewhat in that time hung on my hands till Amanda, bless her, who I think at times got a bit fed up with my continual 'bleating' suggested that now was the time to write my memoirs. I was reasonable with a computer and there was Geraldene still in the estate office who was almost an expert in that line. So I went to her and told her this bit of news and asked her as to what make of computer and printer I should buy. She thought about this for a while and then came up with the name of a well-known make of computers, so in I went and bought the necessary gear plus a block of paper. I set it all up in a room that we seldom used and sat back and had a think, where to start?

Before I had really got an inkling as what I was going to say, and for that matter where to start, Mary got on the phone and asked me whether I would care to give a speech to some golf society who had somehow or other heard about our golf club and wanted to know whether we actually made a profit? I said that I would providing that they would provide me with a drink before I started, for although now an old man I was at times a bit nervous at the thought of talking probably a load of nonsense in front of a crowd of people who might know a lot more than I did about the subject on hand, which in this case was golf. So I told Mary to write to them and say that I would but could the venue be reasonably close to my home. So that gave some welcome food for thought for I had about a week to think what I was going to say. I went and saw my excellent golf course secretary/manager and told him that I wanted him there to hold my hand so to speak.

The day arrived and the secretary kindly drove me to this vast hall. To my consternation I found at least 700 or more seats all filled with eager-looking faces, all staring up at the platform where I was to be introduced. The dear chairman waffled on saying what a hard-working chap I was and how I had built a golf course and how well it was doing. I tried glaring at him, willing him to shut up but he continued all this rubbish about me and mine, till I got fed up and took the unprincipled step of getting to my feet before the dear chap had finished. He looked somewhat shocked but I smiled at him and thanked him for all the kind things that he had said and then turned to my vast audience. I firstly assured them that compared to them I was a mere novice, and that I was certain that the net profit that I had made last year of some £45,000 was a mere pittance to what I was certain that the majority of golf clubs made in their respective years. To my surprise there was a vast number of heads shaking 'no' below the rostrum.

I started to explain in somewhat apologetic terms that the figure of £45,000 was made up in the following manner; bar profits, £11,000, and here I paused for there were signs of disbelief in the faces below me, and I explained that I had taken the trouble of going round more or less every pub within my area and noted their prices and then returned and took 5% off all my prices, so members and their friends flocked in, thus the £11,000. Food profit was £12,000 mainly because I bought in bulk from the London market. The one-armed 'gentleman' also made a profit of £12,000, mainly because the stakes, i.e. the jackpot was very high, i.e. £200 and on the weekend I had to have a sort of waiting list for members who wanted to have a 'go' and each one was only allowed ten minutes on the machine. Entrance fees for membership came to about £6,000, and the annual subs came to some £90,000. Then there were the profits from the gun fraternity, for I had a bit over 300 acres and as the golf course only took up about 170 acres, there was quite a bit to spare, so I reared pheasants and charged the 'shooters' a fee which came to about £3,000 plus. Green fees came to round about £40,000, for the course was a popular one. Then with the few acres that I had left I took in grazing cattle which paid about £1,000 per year. Then there was an item which I didn't think many of them had thought about, and that was the mowing of vast lawns owned by private people in my area. They thought that if their lawns looked like my greens then that was money well spent and I did this work on a weekend and gave the green staff a substantial rake off for the time concerned and that resulted in a further £4,000 per year. The snooker table of which I had two gave a reasonable profit of about £1,500 per annum, but the 'ladder' which I will explain, that profit was in excess of £3,500. The 'ladder' was a list of all the names of members of the club, both male and female, and you challenged the name above yours, paid the name concerned £1 and paid me the same, i.e. £1. They played ten holes of golf and the winner's name elbowed itself 'up' the ladder and the name at the top of the list at 12.00 hrs on Christmas Day got a free sub for the coming year, it was *very* popular. The running costs at that time were in the region of £130,000 which included a part-time secretary in the office, a part-time barman and ditto cook, two ground staff and myself, plus of course rates and fuel, etc.

From the point of view of the course, I used to either do the rough once a week or the fairways, depending on the weather and the time of the year, but by and large the two green keepers and myself were sufficient to keep the place in good condition. The only thing that I paid for so to speak was for tineing the greens and the fairways, this was done by a contractor.

I felt by this time that I had done enough, they, the audience must be bored stiff by now. So I thanked them for their kind attention and asked if there were any questions that anyone wanted to ask, which was a stupid thing to do for the questions came thick and fast.

Silly things like 'How do you rear your pheasants and how many per year and how many were shot?' 'How many private lawns did you mow and how much did the green keeper who did the mowing get for his labour on a weekend?' 'Did you do the bar in the evening?' To this question I replied that I did and liked the task, bar for the fact that everyone wanted to give me a drink and I ended up by camouflaging a whisky bottle with coloured water and charged them a little less than the usual tot. And so it went on till I really felt somewhat fatigued and called a halt. I explained that I was getting old and I must look after myself, so good night. I ended up with a lot of applause, most embarrassing. I was driven home by my kind golf club secretary who I invited in for a final drink and he met Amanda going up to bed. She was persuaded to come down and keep us company, so thus ended an interesting day, made even more intriguing in that I found out that without a doubt our golf club on the estate made the best profit for miles around.

Then young Phyllis, one of our remaining girl pupils who had been so good on the boat, got hold of me via Geraldene and said that she had another four keen types who wanted to have a weekend on the boat, always providing the weather was calm and one of the couples were her mother and father and the other couple were farmers and was I interested? To which question I relied that I was and perhaps Phyliss could sort out the date which both couples liked.

This she did and on a nice fine Saturday we all met down at the boat in Brighton Marina. We had a drink or two whilst Phyliss sorted out the lunch and away we went heading for France. We chose Fécamp mainly because I knew the harbour having been there before. We stayed the night and headed back to dear old England the next day, and chose Rye by popular choice. We went ashore to that nice pub the Mermaid, and had lunch and decided to spend the evening in Rye before heading back home the next day. All went well till the next morning when I woke with a nasty pain in my belly. I was faced with quite a bit of a journey back to Brighton and then of course home and a visit to my lady doctor. I made the mooring with some difficulty as by this time the pain was increasing and my somewhat aged stomach wanted attention as soon as possible. I said a hasty farewell to our four guests who were more than sympathetic and back home I hurried, dropping Phyliss off on the way.

Amanda was more than worried and called the riot act that I must remember that I was eighty-four years of age, and boat parties such as the one that I had just been on must cease forthwith.

I called my doctor who took one look at me and my painful belly and ordered an ambulance right away. I was carted off to our local hospital where I was X-rayed and told that I had a severe cancer of the prostate and although they could dose me with pills and hypodermic needles every now and then, they could not promise an early recovery. They were astonished that the cancer had grown all that much without me noticing anything. Back home I came and was promptly put to bed by my stern young wife and was somewhat surprised to find that she had hired a nurse to look after me. Nice girl the nurse, Sally was her name and she was most efficient but I didn't really feel that my condition warranted a nurse living in the house, but I was not allowed to argue.

As time went on I noticed some peculiar changes in my mental outlook. The first being that I suddenly realised that I was terrified of crowds, why I have no idea but I could not do much about it, the feeling was there and I started to wonder at time as to whether this was the end.

I was allowed out of bed after a week and was horrified to find how weak I had become. Simple things like going down the stairs were made only by a careful effort. Getting to the office a mere

100 yards away left me weak and bewildered and Geraldene looked horrified at the sight of me. I asked how things were going and at that point Mary came in and told me everything that had happened since I became ill. "But Sir John," she said, "I really think that you should go home and I will take you there now in the truck." I said that I was sure that I could get home without the use of transport but she was adamant and in a few minutes the Land Rover appeared and I was helped out of my chair. I felt ridiculous having to be hoisted out of a chair by two nice girls, but there it was I really felt weak, so back home I came and was firmly put to bed by Sally the nurse who told me to behave myself. A feeling of great peace came over me as I closed my eyes and went to sleep....

EPILOGUE

Written by Lady Amanda Teele.

The first I heard of this ghastly news was when the nurse, Sally, came charging down the stairs, calling for me. Her first words were graphic to a degree for she just said, "Lady Amanda, I am so sorry to be the one to give you this news but your husband died a few minutes ago, very peacefully and I am certain he suffered nothing. I was at his bedside all the time and was actually holding his hand when it suddenly went limp and after various tests, I thought that you ought to know."

I thanked her and up the stairs we both went into our bedroom and there he was, my darling husband, quite dead and still. I asked Sally if she wouldn't mind leaving me alone with him, then I knelt by his side and talked to him as if he was actually with me. I didn't say anything that needed an answer, but I just told him I loved him and how much I had to thank him for during our years of marriage and how happy I had been. I ended up by saying, "Now don't worry my love, I will look after the estate, so just rest, you have done your bit."

I left our bedroom, no longer 'ours' just mine, and slowly as I descended the stairs the truth suddenly struck me. I had lost the man I adored and there was nothing that I could do about it. Then the tears came with a rush and I sank into a chair unable to do anything but just weep. Slowly but surely, sanity, if one could call it that, came back and I called Mary on the intercom and asked her to come round at once. Mary came and was told the facts and I asked her to tell Geraldene to get in touch with all the family, including the children from his first marriage and of course ours. "Then Mary arrange the funeral. He wanted to be buried *not* cremated, so sort that out for me please."

Slowly, but with a great effort, I recovered and felt the new responsibility resting on my two shoulders. I suppose my first thought was that I must not let him down, he had done so many wonderful things to this estate, let alone saving my father's life in the war. 'So pull yourself together, Amanda and get on with the job.'

I had not realized at that time the things that one had to do when a near relation of yours died a natural death. The police wanted to know the details, the church wanted to know when the service should be, the diggers of the grave had to be told and of course paid, the gravestone had to be ordered and what was more what to put on it. The countless relations who wrote and wanted to know when the service would be held, all had to be told, thank God for Geraldene, she was a saint she organised all those details for me.

Came the day of the funeral and his body, bless him, was in a nice coffin and carried by six workers from the estate which I thought was rather kind of them, and into the church we went. My children and all the seemingly hundreds of relations, they all came and now and then I noticed a tear. Mine arrived when Mary, bless her, gave the address which really was quite fascinating for she had taken the trouble to find out all about my darling husband, from the time that he had been born to the time that he had so peacefully passed away. The silence as her clear tones went on and on through the years and the things that he had achieved was quite fantastic, for there were events that I knew nothing about which she had found.

We all came back to that large barn with its vast oak beams. Tables had been found, again thanks to Mary, food was waiting, drinks were also waiting and people by the score came up to me and introduced themselves. I wondered as to whether I should have brought along a recorder, but I need not have worried for I suddenly noticed Geraldene by my side holding what was obviously a camouflaged microphone. She, bless her, took the trouble to type out afterwards all that the people who had come up to me at that somewhat distressing moment had said.

We had our meal and then all gathered in the graveyard when the coffin was lowered gently into Mother Earth and that really was that, it was the end of an era. I knew I must start to pull my socks up and learn all about the things that darling John had been up to over the past years. The first thing I did after consulting Mary was to call a meeting of all the staff in the old barn in which were all manner of objects that we no longer used but didn't want to throw away. I arranged, or Mary did, for a large barrel of beer plus a vast array of pint tankards to be 'enthroned' on an old table. We arranged the meeting for 11.30 on a Saturday morning, which from the labour point of view was in the employer's time and not the staff's. Geraldene sent off invitations to all the staff and their wives and I must admit I was astonished at the numbers who poured into the barn on that day,. The golf club including wives were twelve for starters, the hotel were also twelve, then the tractor drivers and their wives, the shepherd and his wife, the chap who looked after the vast herd of deer who not only had a wife but three daughters who obviously fancied a beer or two, they looked just about old enough and so on and so forth. When everybody appeared to have a glass in their hands, Mary called for silence. Again I was surprised at her authority for all the chatter ceased forthwith and she turned, after a few well-chosen words, and introduced me. I stood up, took a look round and gathered my few remaining wits and firstly thanked them all for their kindness during the last ghastly fortnight. I then went on to reassure them that the estate would continue as before, and at that remark, I could sense a sigh of relief from all and sundry, and continued to say that I would appreciate a meeting of all working staff every Saturday at 11.30 to discuss the week's work and what was to come. I waffled on for a bit and thought that I had made my thoughts known. I wished them all well and was looking forward to meeting them in the future at their various jobs.

I had long talks with Mary with regards to the future, for I was no longer the young girl who married my beloved husband. I was getting on and I felt that I could not copy exactly the previous example of my husband, such as getting up at the crack of dawn and wandering around 10,000 acres on a motorbike before breakfast. So I left that to Mary who I was sure would cope with everything in her own excellent way, but I asked her if she was happy with things as they were at the moment? Did she want any changes and if so what were they?

"Well," said Mary, "I have no worries about any of the staff, with the exception of our shepherd Clive, who was a doubtful asset and I knew Sir, John felt the same way, but the snag here is that he lives in a tied cottage and if we give him the sack, it might prove tricky to get him out."

So somewhat naughtily we agreed that we would make life somewhat difficult for Clive so that *he* and not us would give us the 'push'. Actually it proved quite easy because firstly Mary would complain about the filthy backsides of various ewes, and then I would do the same. Finally we bought in the Ministry of Ag and Fish, under quite another pretext and in his report he did mention that our flock of sheep let the side down somewhat and what was Clive going to do about it? So one day he handed in his notice after viewing the report. We wished him well and said that his £200 would be repaid as soon as we had the keys to his cottage. So one morning he reported to the office with the keys. We duly went round and inspected the property with him in attendance, for part of the £200 deal was that he should leave the house in good order, which I am glad to say it was.

And so we were 'shepherdless' and I suggested to Mary that she might find a woman shepherd instead of a male and this we advertised. In a week or two after interviewing some twelve would-be candidates, we chose a girl called Sylvia who had an excellent reference from a Scottish landowner.

Sylvia was twenty-nine, and looked more than nice from a male angle and I wondered why she wasn't wed. I found the answer to this quite soon for Sylvia came to me and asked as to whether her boyfriend, Robert could come and live with her as he had done for the last few years. She hadn't mentioned him at the interview in case it spoilt her chances of getting the job, for which she apologised and hoped that I wouldn't mind him being on the estate as they were more than happy together. They couldn't get married for his wife refused to give him a divorce; all somewhat complicated. I told her to send Robert to see me first so that I knew what he looked like and then by all means she could have him with her.

Robert turned up a few days later and I was pleasantly surprised to find him more than pleasant. I asked him what he did for a living, to which he replied that he was a qualified doctor without a practice. The surgery he once owned had burnt down and he was now actively looking for another suitable building and another practice, for his last practice contained his ex-wife and she made it her business to turn would-be patients away from him, thus the need for another building. So I wished him well with his search and hoped that he and Sylvia would be happy.

Thinking about this one day, I thought that we had a vacant sort of barn, for want of a better description, that just might suit Robert as a surgery always providing that he was prepared to do the place up and pay me a smallish sum for the rent of the place. It was suitable from the point of view that it only just bordered the estate, so that would-be patients would not have to enter my property in order to see their doctor. So I called Sylvia in one morning and put this idea to her. She was more than interested and would talk to Robert about it.

In the end after having a look at the place, Robert took it and settled down to create a new practice and patients poured in much to the fury, I expect of his ex-wife. In fact I tried him out myself and liked his manner and became one of his first patients.

But how I missed John. He was such a kind man and looking back on his exploits, such as saving my father's life during the war and countless other happenings, most of them designed for my particular benefit, for ours was a true love match. Although as I understood it later on, his first marriage was the same, but there it is, I must get on, never forget him but continue his marvellous work that he did here on this estate.

And so life, a somewhat lonely one now, continued. I said, lonely because Susan our black adopted daughter who we found on our doorstep years ago, decided that although we had sent her to school here that she must return to the land of her Fathers, or so she imagined and departed with tears rolling down her cheeks to South America. After quite a short space of time we had a letter thanking us for all that we had done for her but she had found at last a man who she adored and they were to be married. So that was that the end of some eighteen years of great enjoyment, for she got on well with her so-called half-brothers and sisters, Peter George our first born and then the twins Piers and Dierdre. They all had fun together and we all missed her black charm.

Peter was now about twenty-four years of age and after his public schooling, he went to university where he studied Agriculture, for he was determined to take his father's place on the estate and now he was a great help to me. The twins, Piers and Dierdre were sometimes a bit of a problem, for although Piers definitely wanted to join in with running the estate, there was the problem of his twin for they were both very fond of each other. So Dierdre decided that she would help Geraldene in the estate office till Geraldene retired which was fairly soon for she must have been at least sixty-five or maybe more. So Dierdre departed on a computer course to come back fully qualified to assist Geraldene, who when she was satisfied that Dierdre could cope with the vast amount of work that went on in the office, she wrote me a charming letter, thanked me for a lovely life that she lived working for us, but felt that the time had come when she must retire and take a rest. So I gave her a quite large cheque and thanked her for all the kindness that she had shown both John and I and there it was, one day she was in her usual spot in the office and the next day she was gone, and there was Dierdre looking more than serene and already thinking of ways she could improve her new way of life.

I was just slightly worried about Peter for he was now working full-time on the estate under Mary, and I had a vague feeling that in time there would be trouble between those two for Peter knew what his father had done for the estate and felt that *he* should now take over Mary's position. But Mary had been a godsend both to John and I, and no way would I be persuaded to ask her to leave. When she wanted to retire, then no doubt she would let me know.

But that problem solved itself, for Mary was due for a holiday and she had been asked by an agricultural university in America to come and give a lecture on British farming with all expenses paid and also, with my permission, to say something about the Teele Estate. So we agreed that she had earned at least a month and off she flew. My eager eldest son took over the running of the estate. About two weeks later I had a letter from Mary saying that she had fallen in love with the professor who ran the university and he had asked her to marry him. She had accepted his offer and would I mind if she gave me her notice and that her sister would come along and clear out her house for her? So I wrote and thanked her for all that she had done for both John and me and wished her well and that was that. My eldest son Peter then took over the running of the estate which had been his dearest wish for years.

I must say that I was quite impressed by Peter, for as soon as he had taken over, his salary agreed, he took the trouble to send to me, the owner of the estate, an exact inventory of all the stock both live and dead that we owned between us as a family. I must say the list astonished me for Peter had taken the trouble to get a valuer in to give us a figure of both live and dead stock for the entire estate. The figure concerned astonished me, for instance we milked every day some 120 cows and their produce went to be sold from the farm shop and also the estate delivery van that went round some twenty-eight miles every day to countless housewives, selling not only the milk cartons but also eggs and vegetables to name but a few. Then there was the sheep flock that had grown over the years and now numbered some 500 ewes and the pig families that now numbered some 100 sows and their various litters, to the deer's and their fawns, the hop quota and the corn and down to the rabbits and the bees, and lastly but certainly not least the farm shop, the hotel, the golf course, I was astonished at the list of what we owned and wished my eldest son all the best with his future.

Ten long years passed by. I was blessed with the continued company of my three children, but every now and then he, my much loved John, would appear in some dream or other and I must admit that being a churchgoer I longed for the day that we would meet again which I was certain that we would.

Peter and his brother got on well together with the running of the estate, whilst Dierdre in the office got more and more interested in stocks and shares for money kept rolling in. It was a waste to keep a vast balance in the bank, so every month or so we had a family gathering to decide which share we should buy or for that matter which we would sell, helped I may add by a most efficient brokerage firm in London.

Peter got himself a very nice girlfriend and I was glad to see that he was old-fashioned enough to want to marry the girl whose name was Prudence, and not just live with her as was the increasing habit these days. So they were wed in our local church and it was a grand day. We appeared to have attracted at least a hundred close friends and relatives, and the party after the service went on for hours with the newlyweds creeping away quietly without much fuss for a honeymoon cruise lasting a fortnight. Whilst they were away, I arranged that Mary's old house, which had been empty for years, should have a spring-clean and I bought all the necessary furniture and had it installed. When they came back I gave it to them as my wedding present. I must say they were thrilled for they had been wondering as to where they were going to live on their return. Dierdre not to be outdone with all this shifting about asked me whether she could create a suite of her own at the hotel, to which I agreed for I had the vague idea that she had a close boyfriend and who knows there might be another marriage within the family!

Then came a nasty shock for I had a letter from Susan our adopted black child, who had left us a few years ago to return to the land of her birth and then married. The letter was ghastly, for her husband had died from Aids and the child that she was expecting had been born dead. As far as she was concerned, this was the end and she thanked us again for all that we had done for her, but she was determined to take steps to return to her husband. That sentence meant suicide without a doubt, so through various agents I found out that she had in fact committed suicide a few days ago, so there was a sad chapter of our lives finished and done with.

So there we were with Peter running the estate, helped in no small way by Piers who dealt with most of the arable side of the business which included the golf course, and Dierdre who managed the office and the somewhat large accounting side of the family.

Affairs and me. I had reached the age of seventy-eight and longed to meet up once again with my beloved John, for I was a great believer in the hereafter and he was I am sure there somewhere waiting to greet me. So I quietly let go my grip on the affairs of the family estate and settled down very quietly to await for the day which I was sure would come soon for I had had one sort of stroke and no doubt there would be another, and of course there was. It happened just a few days after Christmas, where we all enjoyed ourselves, and after saying good night to the last guest, I stumbled up to bed at about 01.00 hrs in the morning. I took off my party clothes, just had time to put on my nightdress and I fell to sleep. I dreamt of my John and there he was, in my vivid dream, sitting on a horse with another horse held by his left hand. He was waving a greeting, and the greeting meant without a lot of thought, "Come along and mount up and I will take you home." The joy that came over me was tremendous. I ran to him and he leant down from his saddle, kissed me and said, "Mount up" which I did and away we went....

Piers picks up the end of this tale. I waited for my mother to come down for breakfast and then went up to find her. I came down the stairs weeping my heart out for we were very close. I rang my brother Peter and sister Dierdre and told them that our beloved mother had died in her sleep. The look on her dead face was something that I will never forget, for it was radiant and it was more than obvious that as she had died she and my father were united. She had seen him and willingly left us and this world to be with the man she adored.

We buried her, still with that radiant smile on her face, next to the man of her life, our father. Hundreds of people were kind enough to come to the funeral and we had a somewhat sad and quiet gathering afterwards. Various kind friends made speeches and that was the end of an era....